THE YOGA OF MAX'S DISCONTENT

THE YOGA OF MAX'S DISCONTENT

Karan Bajaj

RIVERHEAD BOOKS
New York
2016

RIVERHEAD BOOKS
An imprint of Penguin Random House LLC
375 Hudson Street
New York, New York 10014

Library of Congress Cataloging-in-Publication Data

Bajaj, Karan.
The yoga of Max's discontent / Karan Bajaj.
p. cm.
ISBN 978-1-59463-411-6
1. Self-realization—Fiction. I. Title.
PR9499.4.B346Y64 2016 2015024636
823'.92—dc23

International edition ISBN: 978-0-399-57793-2

Printed in the United States of America
1 3 5 7 9 10 8 6 4 2

Book design by Chris Welch

This is a work of fiction. Names, characters, places, and incidents either are the product of the author's imagination or are used fictitiously, and any resemblance to actual persons, living or dead, businesses, companies, events, or locales is entirely coincidental.

For Leela,

So one day you set out to find your own truth.

THE SEEKER

Arise! Awake! Approach the feet of the Master and know THAT. Like the sharp edge of the razor, the sages say, is the path. Narrow it is, and difficult to tread!

—THE KATHA UPANISHAD, 400 BC

1.

I give her a week at most.”

“Don’t say that, Max,” said Sophia.

Max and his sister stepped out of the hospital lobby onto deserted, icy West 59th Street. Sophia looked up at him, shielding her eyes from the snowfall with a gloved hand.

“She’s only forty-nine, for heaven’s sake,” said Sophia. “Everyone else’s parents are alive.”

The wind gusted. Max wrapped his scarf tighter around his neck. They shuffled along in the thick blackness of the night, past the bare trees covered with snow and the closed Starbucks, toward Ninth Avenue. Max tried to find a cab for Sophia to get back to Brooklyn, but none passed. His eyes burned. He’d been up for more than twenty-four hours, since midnight the previous day, when his mother had to be rushed to the hospital once again. The cancer had spread to her lungs, making it difficult for her to breathe.

"Do you want to crash at my place tonight?" said Max, who lived only a few blocks away on 63rd Street and Columbus Avenue.

They turned on Ninth Avenue. Sophia looked up at him, blue eyes brimming with tears, tight brown curls wet at the ends, face creased with years of worry. She looked older than her twenty-five.

Max put his hand on her shoulder. "You'll . . ." He stumbled over something. A man lay slumped against the stairs of the Church of St. Paul the Apostle on Ninth Avenue.

"Watch it, giant," said the man.

"Sorry, sorry," said Max.

The man gripped Max's leg. "Give me change," he said, his red eyes staring out of his pale, unwashed face.

Despite the weathered but thick blanket that covered the man, his unkempt beard was speckled with ice. Max didn't want to see yet another cold, dying body that day. He dug into his coat pocket and gave the man a ten-dollar bill. The man let go of his leg. They had walked only a few yards when they heard him shouting. "Hey, big guy, give me more."

"God bless, God bless," said Max.

Max held Sophia's hand and moved faster. He'd been around junkies all his life and knew how unpredictable they could be.

"Wait, you selfish giant."

Quick footsteps. Max turned around. A shock of white hair rushed toward Max.

"You hit me," said the man, facing him.

The man stood a head shorter than Max's six feet six inches, yet Max's heart clutched. The sidewalk was empty except for a man wearing an orange cloth and frying something in a food cart a block ahead.

The man grasped Sophia's coat. "The city demands compensation, restitution, and retribution, madam. The city demands compensation, restitution, and retribution," he said.

"Don't touch her," said Max.

The man pulled Sophia closer. "The city demands compensation."

"Get away," said Sophia, pulling free from the man's grip.

Max pushed the man back. The man rushed forward and threw a gloved fist packed with ice at him. Max felt the thud against his nose. A warm, hollow sensation pulsed through it. Blood dripped from his face to the ice below. It looked crimson, unreal.

"Get away from him. I'm calling the cops," said Sophia.

The man blew foul air at Max. "The city demands compensation . . ."

A dam burst inside Max. He grabbed the man's neck. The man raised his thin arms weakly. Max let go of his neck and pushed him back with force. The man fell on the ice. Max swooped down next to him and raised his fist to break the man's quivering jaw.

Someone grabbed his hand.

Max swung his other arm back, trying to break free. Again someone caught it. Max pushed his shoulders back. The grip tightened. Max whipped his head around.

A naked man.

Max broke out of his trance. A tall, thin East Indian man with a naked torso held his arms. The bright orange cloth around his waist flapped in the wind. The food-cart guy.

"Yes, okay, sorry," said Max.

The Indian man let go of Max's arms. Max got up from the ice. The homeless man curled up in a ball, whimpering.

"Max, your face," said Sophia, her hair dripping with sweat despite the cold.

Max touched his nose. He was bleeding.

"Should I call 911?" asked Sophia.

He shook his head.

The homeless man picked himself up and limped up the stairs of the church.

"The city, the city . . ." he mumbled.

THE INDIAN MAN had returned to standing behind his food cart, a pan in one hand, a mug of water in the other.

Max went up to him. "Thank you. I could've hurt him badly," he said. "I don't know what came over me."

"Think nothing. Indeed, you are like my child," said the man. He began to cut onions, seemingly unaffected by the cold.

Max stared at him. The wind screamed. No one could possibly live through this freeze without a shirt on his back. Would it be insulting to offer him money? Max took out his wallet. A cab stopped in front of them finally.

"Your face is bleeding, Max," said Sophia. "Should we go back to the hospital?"

Max hesitated, then put his wallet away. He opened the back door of the cab for Sophia. "I'm fine," he said. "Just get home safely."

Sophia got inside the cab. "We never catch a break," she said.

"But we always have each other," Max said, then shut the cab door and rapped twice with his knuckles on the window. She looked up at him and smiled. The cab pulled away.

A cold draft hit the space between Max's eyes. Jesus, what had come over him? Would he have really smashed the homeless guy's face? How quickly he'd regressed to the violence of his teenage years. Max wiped his nose with his scarf and walked toward his apartment.

2.

Max stopped outside the revolving glass doors of his apartment building. Inside, the uniformed doorman was putting flowers in an antique vase on a gold-plated ledge next to the lobby mirror. Behind him, the wall-length painting of a Japanese rice farm glinted in the chandelier's light. A wave of revulsion swept through Max. Just who had he become? A few steps away, his mother lay dying in a hospital bed, a man slept on the steps of a church, and another flipped pitas half naked in the snow. Max turned around before the doorman saw him. He walked along 63rd Street toward Central Park. The freezing wind dried the drops of blood falling from his nose as soon as they hit the air. The homeless man's blow had shaken him awake. He'd finally complete the errand he hadn't gotten to since his mother had been confined to a bed in his apartment three weeks ago.

MAX WALKED ACROSS bright, empty 59th Street and stopped at the Capital One ATM on Park Avenue. He withdrew $2,000 and distributed the bills on his body—in his back pockets, inside his underwear, in his socks, in the sleeve of his shirt, inside his coat pockets—leaving only $40 in his wallet. At 4:00 AM he caught the 6 train on Lexington Avenue to Pelham Bay Park. The preppy drunks in his car got off at the 77th and 86th Street stations, and the fedora-wearing hipsters in Harlem. By the time the train reached the Bronx, the compartment looked much like it had in Max's childhood: a woman high on crack scratching her deathly pale face, leaving thin red lines on it; a homeless man slumped on his seat muttering to himself; and three boys wearing baseball caps and imitation Air Jordans drinking from brown bags and slobbering over pizza slices. The boys stared at him. Max gave them a cool, blank look and glanced away. Lingering longer was intimidation, not meeting eyes was fear—either could leave him bruised and bloody on the subway station and without his $2,000. He'd deserve it too. A white guy in a Boss overcoat in the South Bronx late at night was begging to be messed with. The boys whispered among themselves and laughed. Max got off at the Brook Avenue station. The boys followed him outside the train and up the stairs.

"Where you going, whitey?" they said behind him.

Max didn't turn around. He walked along dark, unlit Brook Avenue with an exaggerated swagger, pumping his chest forward, swinging his arms loosely, chewing the nonexistent gum in his mouth—the pimp roll he had perfected in his childhood.

"You need a hit?" they said.

He turned on East 139th Street. A drunk was rummaging through a trash can in front of a closed pawnshop. Another man in a tattered coat leaned against the glass door of a check-cashing store.

The boys picked up speed behind him. "Whoa, wait, GQ."

Max took a quick left on St. Ann's Avenue. The boys' footsteps died out immediately. Just as Max expected, they wouldn't follow him into gang territory. Two men, one bent over a shining white cane, the other sporting an Afro, stood talking under the streetlight in front of a park next to St. Ann's Episcopal Church. Max's heartbeat returned to normal.

"J," he said.

The Afro turned around, his hands reaching inside his overcoat, likely for his pistol.

"It's Max. Jerome knows me."

The man with the white cane turned. Like Max, he was twenty-nine years old, but he looked twenty years older. Since middle school, when Max and he had studied together at PS 65 Mother Hale Academy on Cypress Avenue, Jerome had been shot by rival drug dealers in both his knees and his right hip and arm. His face was a tangle of knife scars, his hair prematurely gray, and his skin cracked from a lifetime of drug use.

"Da Max," said Jerome, giving Max a high five. His hands were shaking and his voice was hoarser than a year ago when Max had last run into him. "What you in the ghetto for? I thought you'd gone all uppity."

"Not uppity, man, just busy with shit," said Max. "I've come to see Andre."

"Bitch's going to finish school, I hear," he said.

Max nodded. "You should go too."

Jerome laughed. "And your uncle will raise them little 'uns?" he said.

A car blasting Latin music came down the street. Jerome pressed the cane firmly against the ground and pulled a plastic bag with rose-gray powder from his coat. "You want some H, da Max? On the house."

Max shook his head. "Gonna head to Andre's. Some punks were following me, so I turned around."

"Want me to come with?"

"I'm good now," said Max, shaking Jerome's rough, shaking hands.

The car pulled over. The Afro bent over the car window.

"Be safe," said Jerome and hobbled over to the car.

Max turned around and walked beside the fenced park toward 139th Street. Much had changed since his childhood. Then the park had been a barren sandy lot filled with hypodermic needles and blue crack caps. A lone tree had stood in the center of the gravel, its dry branches covered with dolls—some intact, some with missing hands and legs—eerie, makeshift memorials made by parents who couldn't afford any better for children who died of gang shootings and drug overdoses.

I . . . I don't wanna g-get up there.

Sophia's stutter would worsen every time they passed the park on their way from the train station to home. Max would hold her hand and promise her they wouldn't end up as dolls on the tree if she stuck close to him. Now the tree had been replaced with seesaws and slides. The ground was clear of debris, the gravel raked smooth, all signs of progress except for the addicts themselves. Years ago, Jerome's father had dealt crack in front of the park. Now his son, with the same fading ghostly face and hacking cough, was dealing heroin. Maybe Jerome's kids would break the cycle, thought Max without much hope.

A PROSTITUTE IN a tight yellow skirt with haunted eyes and chattering teeth paced outside the brown brick building on 139th Street where Andre, Max's friend since childhood, lived. Max punched the security code on the console and entered the building's cold tunnel-like lobby. A bottle crashed on the floor. Max walked around the broken glass, urine, and other beer bottles next to the doorway and knocked on Andre's apartment door.

No response.

He knocked again and called Andre on his cell phone. The phone buzzed inside the apartment. Andre picked up after four rings.

"Max." His voice was thick with sleep. "Is Ma okay?"

"Yes."

"What's wrong, then?"

"It's just cold outside," said Max.

"What?"

"I'm freezing outside your apartment," said Max and knocked again.

"Shit."

A thump. Wheels rolling on the floor. The door opened. Andre sat in his wheelchair in a white sleeveless shirt and underwear, dreadlocks disheveled, drool slipping down from the corners of his mouth. Max stepped in. The house was heated like a furnace. Ammonia and bleach fumes seeped into Max's skin, making his throat itch. A bottle of E&J, naked lightbulbs, a cardboard box with greasy pizza crusts, broken lighters, razor blades, and a residue of white powder lay on the kitchen counter, the aftermath of a crack binge.

"Jesus fuck, did you call those Bloods motherfuckers over again?" asked Max. "You're gonna get killed, man, you fucking wait and see."

Andre rubbed his eyes. "Quit being a bitch, Ace," he said, his voice still thick with sleep. "Ain't nothin' to it. You work in a bank. I work here. The kids gotta know me to trust me."

Max walked across the floor littered with beer cans and empty glass vials. He poured the E&J into a dirty glass on the kitchen counter and gulped it down. Andre's eyes followed him.

"What happened? Is Sophia okay?" he said.

Max took out the cash from his wallet, socks, shoes, and underwear, tightened it in a roll, and put it on the kitchen counter. "I just came to give you this," he said. "So you can keep digging your grave studying useless-ass criminal behavior at college."

Andre stared at the cash. "At five AM? Motherfucker be crazy?"

"Doesn't your semester start next week?" asked Max. "I won't have time for a bit. Mom is about to go down."

"Naw, hell, Ace," he said, his eyes dropping. "I figured it'd be soon."

Andre rolled his wheelchair up to the counter and poured the last of the E&J into a clean glass for Max. They went from the boxy living room to the even smaller bedroom, Andre's wheelchair knocking down more empty beer cans with its wheels.

Max sat down on the spring bed and downed the yellow-brown liquid in one swig. The window behind the bed was barricaded with thick steel railings to block stray bullets from gang shootings outside the apartment. They looked like prison bars.

"Shit, man, go counsel kids in Manhattan gangs. Enough trouble to put your nose into there," said Max. "Here you're just gonna get banged one day."

"How 'bout we don't talk about me?" said Andre. "You want a smoke?"

Max shook his head.

"I ain't using no more, but fuck it today," said Andre. He wheeled out of the bedroom. Max's head felt heavy from the drink. He leaned against the headboard. His eyes began to shut.

". . . I TELL . . ."

Max opened his eyes. Andre sat opposite him sucking from a plastic Coca-Cola bottle bong with a suction hole at its center. His eyes were glassy, his face vacant.

"Sorry I dozed," said Max. "What?"

Andre burned more weed in the makeshift bowl attached to the hollowed pen-tube wedged in the suction hole. He took a giant suck from the bottle's mouth and inhaled deeply. "Do you know what I tell them young gangbangers about you?" said Andre, enunciating each word slowly. "I don't say shit about you going to Harvard or working on Wall Street. Everyone in the projects knows that. I just tell them about St. Paddy's Day years ago when a bunch of us went to the city. You remember?"

Max blinked away his sleep, trying to focus. Andre never spoke of their childhood. "I guess."

"You don't remember nothin', bitch. It was before all the shit went down," said Andre. He took another drag. "We were twelve then. Or thirteen. You sagged your pants low and rapped and drank in the 6 like all of us. Muscle or Pitbull or someone dared you to ride hangin' outside the train when we got off at Canal. You did it for ten seconds, then fell off and bloodied your nose on the platform. Later that night, we smoked up and you stole a record from Bleecker Bob's. Then, we got back home and crashed. *We* crashed, that is. You came back and studied all night for some stupid math quiz. You recall?"

Max didn't. There were too many such days growing up. "I think, yes," he said.

"That's what I tell these kids. Do what you gotta do to survive in this hell, but go back each night and get your shit together. Piece by piece, build your motherfuckin' empire," he said. He leaned forward on his wheelchair. "You gonna be okay, Ace. On the real. You're always hustlin', always okay. And Ma's suffered enough. She'd want to be at peace herself."

Max throttled the question that came to his lips. Is that what his mother was feeling? Andre would know, though he never talked about the day fifteen years ago when Max and he were caught in the cross fire between the Black Spades gang and some local toughs outside a bodega on Cypress Avenue. One moment, they were sucking ice pops. The next moment, three punks wearing gold chains with pistols in their hands appeared in front of them. There'd been a blaze of yellow light and popping sounds. Max had crashed down on the road, knocking out two front teeth. He was staring at his bloody gum tissue splayed on the ground when Andre fell beside him, his cream shirt colored in red. "Pop, it hurts, Pop," he had shouted. The bullet had pierced his liver, tearing through his spleen, and lodged into his spine, paralyzing him from the waist down. A deep sadness rose up within Max.

"Some world this is, where you're better off dead than alive," said Max.

Andre looked at him with soft, mellowed eyes. "Don't hate, Ace. You always took my shit harder than me," he said. He put the bong down and tossed Max a cushion. "Sleep for a bit?" His arms were thin as spindles and his body was twisted in an effort to avoid pressure sores from sitting in the wheelchair all day. Max's stomach knotted in despair. He forced himself to get up.

"No, man, I gotta be with Mom," he said. "I just wanted to drop off the C's."

"Can I see her today? I'll get a ride into the city."

Max nodded. "She'll like that."

MAX WALKED OUT of the apartment. Instead of going to the subway station, he turned on Alexander Avenue. In the dim light of dawn, 141st Street looked as if it had been bombed by a fighter jet. Overflowing trash cans, a vacant parking lot with heaps of tires, puddles of vomit outside a bar, thugs slumped against closed pawnshops with flashing neon lights. He stopped ahead of Willis Avenue and looked up at a blackened window in the corner-most building of the Mott Haven housing projects cluster. His mother, Sophia, and he had spent most of their lives in an airless one-bedroom apartment on the seventh floor of the building. The brown bricks hadn't seen a single coat of paint in the ten years Max had been gone. With its furrows, cracks, and chipped corners, the building looked like a body ravaged by cancer. Screams ripped intermittently through the quiet morning.

"You best walk away, bitch."

"Maria, open the fuckin' door."

"Whatchu think of yourself?"

Sophia had hated those screams; the gunshots; the kids that called her names—"white bitch," "snow bunny," "nerd"—tore her overcoat and messed up her hair when Max wasn't around; and just about everything else about the projects. Max had swaggered and strutted, rapping, shooting hoops, shoplifting, getting into petty fights—anything it took to fit in. His mother had been different from both of them. She had developed a steely toughness, an indifference to the world crumbling around them. When the gangs started shooting at one another in the alley behind the building, she would clean their apartment vigorously. While Max and Sophia covered their ears and flattened themselves against the wall, she'd scrub the chipped legs of the ragged brown sofa, wipe the cinder-block walls, mop the floors, and move and rearrange the lone table and three chairs in the living room again and again. She'd stop when the shooting stopped and continue with her cooking or sewing as though nothing had happened.

Only when she spoke of Max's and Sophia's futures would her face liven up. "These two will become something," she'd tell her friends in the courtyard every evening before the dealers took over the place for the night. Back home, she'd slowly repeat the names of private schools—Horace Mann, Trinity, Dalton—she'd heard of from people she cleaned houses for in the city. She'd construct tantalizing images of them. Instead of the broken windows and smoky stairwells of PS 65, where they went, these schools had swimming pools and ceramics studios. You didn't have to lay a thick coat of Vaseline on your face each morning to prevent scratches in fights, nor did you hold your stomach for hours in fear that some kid you had a beef with would slash your face with a razor blade if you went into the dark bathroom. She'd been pulled out of school in fifth grade in Greece, but she'd dreamed her kids would go to the best schools in America. And they had. She just wouldn't be around to see them make use of it.

The building stirred to life as the sun rose. Tupac and Nas songs blared from the apartments. A teenager in an ill-fitting jacket and white underwear staggered out the front, an asthma inhaler wedged tightly between his fingers, a dazed look on his face. Was he a crack fiend? Would he also end up dead on the streets as many of Max's friends from childhood had? So what if he did? Max's mother had worked two jobs—cleaning houses in the city in the morning, bagging groceries at the bodega down the street late in the evening—and had been so tired every night that she sometimes fell asleep in her bowl of avgolemono soup. All so they could go to good schools and get out of the projects. Hadn't she realized that illness and death didn't go away when you crossed over to Manhattan on the 6 train? Everything was so fucking pointless. Max went to the front of the building and touched the scratched, bullet-dented metal front door, then turned around and walked back toward the subway station, glad he'd gotten a chance to say some kind of a good-bye to his mother.

3.

Max's mother died the next day, finally free from the kidney cancer that had spread to her uterus, bladder, liver, bones, and lungs over the past three years. A week later, Max and Sophia held her memorial service at the St. Ann's Episcopal Church. They briefly considered holding the service in the St. George–St. Demetrios Greek Orthodox Church in Spanish Harlem, but his mother hadn't identified with the Orthodox faith, just as she hadn't fasted at Lent or sought any Greek family in the United States. "Talking of past is like two birds sitting and knitting sweater. Fool's daydreams. You think only of future," she had said in her halting English whenever Max and Sophia asked her too many questions about her childhood. Not that it mattered. Orthodox or Episcopal, everyone ended in some spot under the earth. At least she had died a natural death. A life not cut short by a shooting or an overdose was a minor blessing in the projects.

On his way back from the Columbus Circle subway station after her memorial service that evening, Max saw the Indian food cart guy from a week before standing on a small stool in front of the open-air cart, still naked from the waist up. He was scraping snow from the cart's tin roof, a look of complete absorption on his face. Max hesitated, then removed his overcoat and walked up to the cart, shivering in his sweater.

The man saw Max and smiled. "From the other night, yes?" he said, getting off the stool.

Max nodded. "I came to give you this." Max handed him the overcoat. "It's very cold here."

The man laughed and his eyes lit up. "Thank you for caring, sir, but I am not in need of a coat."

"Please. Just a small gift from my sister and me. It's not safe to be like that in the winters in New York."

"Indeed, sir, that is very considerate, but I am very fine indeed," he said. "Please believe me when I say I can buy a coat for myself. I have been in America for one whole month, but I have not felt cold here. It is much colder where I come from."

Max put his coat back on and huddled closer to the warm cart. "I didn't know it was that cold in India," he said. "I mean, you are from India, aren't you?"

The man nodded. He pulled a mug of water from the metal tank under the grill surface and washed the grill.

"India is a big country, sir. I am from the mountains, up, very far up in the Himalayas beyond Kashmir, where people rarely visit," he said. He splattered oil on the grill. "Will you have something to eat, sir?"

Eight PM. Max was restarting work the next day after a week off, and he hadn't slept well for several nights. But he felt like talking to someone who didn't know of his mother's death and wouldn't offer unwanted condolences and homilies.

"A falafel gyro," said Max, stooping and moving closer to the cramped, warm cart interior.

"Sit, sit, sir," said the man. He wiped the stool outside the cart with a dry white cloth. "You are tall for my small cart, sir."

Max sat on the stool. "I'm tall for every cart," he said. "And please don't call me sir, I'm Max. Max Pzoras."

He smiled. "Indeed," he said. "My name is Viveka."

VIVEKA TOOK FALAFEL from one of the stainless steel containers on the shelf and put it on the grill. The falafel sizzled. Just inhaling the hot metal smell made Max shiver less. Viveka broke the falafel gently with his tongs, snowflakes falling on his naked back.

Max shook his frozen fingers. "You must feel at least a little cold," he said.

Viveka looked up from the grill. "Oh, me, no, not at all, sir," he said. "If you live in cold weather for long, your body changes. And I am nothing. The Himalayan yogis sit in their caves wearing nothing for months even when the temperature drops to thirty or forty degrees below zero—much, much lower than here."

"But that's just a myth," said Max. "No one has actually seen them."

Viveka put the tongs down. He raised his eyebrows. "Why, I have, sir. Indeed I have. Every day for years and years."

"Up in the Himalayas?" said Max.

Viveka nodded.

"Can anyone see them?" said Max. "Just like that? You hike up the mountains and there they are sitting in the caves?"

"Oh no, no, sir, very much the opposite. Indeed, the yogis do not want contact with people," he said. He began chopping the onions again. "I grew up in the Himalayas, but I did not even see them until the army posted me up on Siachen Glacier, the highest military base in the world, more than twenty thousand feet above sea level. You could get there only on helicopter. There were just some of us in the Indian army station, a few Pakistani soldiers across the border, and the yogis sitting meditating in the caves nearby. It was a miracle how they got there on foot." He shook his head. "Very unusual people, sir. Indeed, I did not even understand the things I saw in those years until much later."

Max didn't fancy hearing about more religious nutters after listening to hymns praising God's infinite mercy and justice at the memorial service that day. But he was vaguely interested in meditation, as were some others in the private equity firm he worked at on Wall Street.

"What are they meditating on?" said Max.

"These are things I do not know very well, sir," said Viveka.

"Why are they at the top of the Himalayas? Why don't they live in a more comfortable place?"

"The silence, the solitude, is necessary for concentration," said Viveka.

"Concentration on what?"

Viveka picked up a bottle of tahini. "They believe—and it is not my belief, sir, so please do not misunderstand me—that the whole world exists in opposites: up and down, cold and hot, darkness and light, night and day, summer and winter, growth and decay. So if there is birth, age, suffering, sorrow, and death, then there must be something that is unborn, un-aging, unailing, sorrowless, and deathless—immortal, as it were. They want to find it. Not just believe in it on faith or scripture, but see it face-to-face."

Max leaned forward on the stool, curiously moved by the words. "And do they find this thing?"

"I do not know, sir, but I've seen things with these very eyes that would make one believe almost anything."

"What things?"

Viveka added the tahini to the falafel. The mixture sizzled. A drop of hot oil splashed on Max's neck. He welcomed the burning sensation, a brief respite from the wind. Viveka mixed red and white sauce into the falafel with a large spoon, scooped it in a pita, and handed it to Max.

Max took a bite. "Very good," he said. "You were talking about the yogis?"

Viveka hesitated. "My daughter's husband grew up here in Queens. He tells me not to speak of such things in this country, sir," he said.

Max put his paper plate down on the top of the beverage cooler. "Please tell me. I want to know."

Viveka splattered more oil on the grill. He fried falafel again, though no new customers were in sight. "I don't know, these yogis were superhuman, like God more than men, sir," he said. "All Indian soldiers selected to go up to the high camps of Siachen had grown up their entire life in the mountains. On top of that, we were put through a year of survival training and a team of psychologists monitored us when we came back. And yet none of us had even a fraction of the yogis' powers. We walked up and down the ice in our five layers of clothes all day to keep warm. But the yogis just sat in the caves, their eyes closed, meditating, and they would come out once in ten, fifteen days, wearing nothing but a loincloth. They walked barefoot in sixty or seventy inches of snow and we used heavy snowshoes with crampons imported from Russia. Yet their feet were quicker, surer than ours. Like machines their bodies were, not human at all."

Viveka turned off the gas. The cart was cold again. Max shifted on the stool and tried not to fidget in the cold.

"Perhaps that's why the animals also never bothered them, sir," said Viveka. "Sometimes a huge Himalayan bear would sit in front of a yogi's cave and we would think of firing above it to scare it away. But then the yogi would come out and the bear, this massive, unpredictable creature, would just slink away from the mouth of the cave and sit quietly on the side. It would return only when the yogi went back inside. Again and again I saw this—first with the bears, then with the snow leopards. It was as if the yogis told them how to behave, strange as this may sound."

Strange, indeed. Not so much the stories but how palatable the idea of living alone at the top of the world figuring out the meaning of life actually sounded.

"What do they . . . ?"

A crowd of young men and women in thick coats and bright scarves came to the cart. Max got up from his stool. The group placed their orders and collected around the cart.

"This cart is the best. I just started coming here," said a young man in a leather jacket with a black fur collar.

"Have you been to Kati Roll in the Village?" asked a bald man.

"Haven't tried it. Thelewala is good, though. But I like carts better," replied the man in the leather jacket.

A brunette piped up. "Moshe's food truck on Forty-Sixth and Sixth is the best."

"Not a chance," said her identical-looking friend. "There is a place where all the cabbies eat in the East Village. Pakistani place. Heaven."

"No way, how did you find it?"

"Just ran into it after Milk & Honey one night."

"Are you a member? Oh my God, their cocktails are so good."

More discussion followed. Authentic Indian and Middle Eastern restaurants, this club and that, what was so good, what was awesome, who was in the know, who wasn't, drinking, eating, and more drinking. Max recalled similar conversations—with a date or colleagues after work—and felt disgusted. Wistfully he thought of the desolate moonlike surface of Kilimanjaro, his only climbing trip outside the country. He had always been pulled to the outdoors ever since the track coach at Trinity—the Upper West Side private school to which Max had won a scholarship—had taken him for a long-distance run in Central Park. Something physical had exploded inside Max that day, as though his lungs were thrusting out all of the worry, stress, and chemical waste that caused asthma in almost every kid in the projects. He had run every day since then, slowly ridding himself of his childhood bronchitis and asthma. Later, he'd run marathons and climbed mountains in the Adirondacks, enjoying the feeling of complete suspension in the present, without memory or past. Now, once again, he felt a strange yearning for those solitary, icecapped peaks, away from civilization with its wants and pains.

The snow began falling again. Max pressed his gloved hands on his wet head and moved closer to the cart. The group found the gyros really awesome so they ordered more, laughing uproariously at their own appetites.

Max shifted in the snow, waiting for them to leave. More people joined them. Their faces blurred with the others. Only the sound of laughter emerged from the snowy mist.

I want to see the unborn, un-aging, un-ailing, sorrowless, and deathless face-to-face.

Max took a deep breath. More than half of the kids from his elementary school had ended up on the streets. One or two different turns and he also would have been sitting on a newspaper on the ice like the homeless man from the other night. He couldn't throw everything away.

Max thanked Viveka and paid him when the others finally left.

"Oh no, no, sir, I cannot take money from you. Indeed, you talk to me like a friend," said Viveka.

"I insist," said Max, putting the five-dollar bill in Viveka's hands. His hands were rough and cold against Max's skin, making Max think of the mountains again. He hesitated. "What happens when the yogis find the unborn, un-aging . . . this thing they are looking for?"

"I don't know, sir," said Viveka. "But I see the faces of those who stop by my cart here. They're like the faces of the soldiers in the army and the people in my village. Their smiles are hollow, their eyes are hungry. The yogis' faces were different."

"Happier?"

"Not exactly, sir, more like . . . silent, complete. Like the mountains around them. Asking no questions, seeking no answers, just certain—as though they knew exactly who they were."

Again Max's heart tugged. He took a deep breath. "Thank you for your time," he said. "I hope to see you again."

"Indeed, sir," said Viveka. "Please do not forget your gloves."

Max picked up his leather gloves from the beverage cooler. "I forgot it was cold for a moment."

"The body adapts anywhere, sir."

4.

A knock.

Max looked up from the clutter of numbers on his computer screen. Outside the windows of his glass-walled office on the forty-eighth floor of the Trump Building opposite the New York Stock Exchange on Wall Street, clouds covered the rising winter sun.

Sarah, his boss and their firm's managing director—a hard-driving woman in her late fifties—stepped into his office.

"How're you doing, Max?"

He stood up. "Good. Thank you."

"No, how are you really doing?" she said, looking up at him. "I know how hard it is to lose a parent."

Max's gaze shifted from the light furrows on her face to her kind eyes. "Really, I'm fine," he said. "Thank you for asking."

She gave him an awkward half hug. "Did you look at the study request? If I don't get the data to Tom by noon, he'll rip me a new one."

"I'm on it."

MAX GROUPED MULTIPLE Excel files together and applied array formula after array formula to make the numbers break and tell him a story. A week ago, the private equity firm he worked for as a vice president had been evaluating the purchase of a midsize snack-food company that made cookies and crackers. Now they were analyzing a fruit-juice corporation. If Max liked what he saw on the company's balance sheet and in its revenue projections, his bosses would decide if they could make a quick profit by buying the company and selling it again in a couple of years. Max compared the company's cost of goods sold to that of its closest publicly traded competitor. His firm could cut $3 million in costs immediately by shifting the apple-juice base to the similar-tasting but far cheaper pear juice. Shortening the juice-box straw by just a tenth of an inch would net another $2 million. Still more could be saved by changing the dark blue embossing on the package to cobalt blue. Yes, it was a great company to buy. With a few easy fixes, you could bleed it dry and reinvest the savings in advertising. Fruit juice made up only six percent of an American kid's fluid intake. If moms replaced just one can of soda or iced tea with the company's juice box, his firm would make a killing.

How did this become my life?

Max's chest tightened. Sweat formed on his temples. He looked up from the numbers. Years ago, the city had put up a medical waste incinerator opposite the children's park in Port Morris to burn amputated limbs, bloody bandages, cancerous tissue, aborted fetuses, and other infectious materials. It was supposed to be constructed on the Upper East Side, but Manhattan residents had protested about the threat of respiratory ailments, so the city had dumped it in the Bronx instead. Children were clearly more disposable there. Each time Max was on a break from school and had walked past the shiny blue metal-top building, he had thought he was on the verge of an insight. He was standing in the middle of two worlds, between the death and destruction in the projects and the hope and life at Trinity and Harvard. He was meant to discover something about the nature of suffering and why it chose those it did. Why hadn't he dug deeper to find that insight?

On the opposite side of the Hudson, a factory emitted a spiral of gray smoke. Sarah stepped out of her office and spoke animatedly to a group of shiny-faced, blue-eyed analysts milling around in the lobby. They laughed with their broad chins and perfectly straight teeth.

After all those years, he was still trying to belong.

While he was in high school, each day from four to six in the morning, he had cleaned the bathrooms of the Harlem Public bar, scraping hardened chewing gum off the urinals, removing T-shirts flushed into toilets, and washing dried vomit from trash cans. At Trinity, he'd rush into the gym showers and scrub himself again and again so his classmates wouldn't smell the Clorox and Pine-Sol on his body. He'd hang with his friends after school, hungrily watching them eat pizza and drink soda at Pizza Pete's, telling them he didn't like the flat taste of cheese, unwilling to admit he couldn't spare a quarter for a slice of pizza every day. Back in the projects, he'd take his shirt out and sling his pants low and play with Pitbull's sawed-off shotgun, not once mentioning calculus, SATs, college applications, and everything else that possessed him. Every day he'd worn a mask. And now once again he was fronting as a suave corporate type with his Borrelli shirt and Ferragamo shoes.

"How's it going?" Sarah popped her head into his office.

Max gave her a thumbs-up.

"Tom's real hot on consolidating the production network," she said. "Can they operate with three plants instead of four? What's the trade-off between transshipment and site costs?"

"I'll dig into it," said Max.

"You haven't gotten to the supply chain yet?"

Max shook his head.

A wave of irritation swept through her face. "If you're not up for it today . . ."

"I'm on it."

Sarah left his office.

MAX OPENED the Excel file. Again, his stomach tightened. Even his kid sister had had the courage to do her own thing. Sophia hadn't fit in with the girl cliques in the projects, so she'd learned to rely on herself. Defying their mother, who'd wanted her to get a well-paying job, she was counseling teen junkies in a

Brooklyn treatment facility. Andre was studying criminal behavior at John Jay to help kids get out of the same gangs that had crippled him. Who had Max become?

So if there is birth, age, suffering, sorrow, and death, then there must be something that is unborn, un-aging, un-ailing, sorrowless, and deathless—immortal, as it were.

He understood now why Viveka's description of yogis on the top of the mountain had struck him. They had stripped their life down to its barest essence to find the same insight about suffering he'd felt close to uncovering years ago. Now that he no longer had his mother's voice in his head prompting him to become someone, nothing stopped him from seeking the same insight. Did the yogis find any answers? After a moment's hesitation, Max switched over from Excel to Chrome and began searching the Internet for information about Himalayan yogis.

HE SKIMMED THROUGH story after story of young Westerners traveling to India to seek spiritual enlightenment. A shadow of doubt arose in him. Was he unraveling after his mother's death, becoming just another privileged white fucker with rich people's problems? Max remembered the strange feeling from last night that he'd heard Viveka's words before, somewhere within the depths of his heart. He tried to dismiss all doubt and tore through the web pages as though scrutinizing a prospective acquisition's noisy balance sheet, deciding whether to invest in the company or not.

A German lawyer's blog caught his attention. She had survived unscathed a car crash that had killed her husband and three children. Her quest for life's answers led her to India. It seemed you didn't even have to throw a stone to find a spiritual teacher in India. Just bending to pick up one would make you collide into one guru or another, all of whom eventually demanded money, gifts, and sometimes even sex. Disappointed, she had given up on her search for a teacher and had begun studying ancient Eastern doctrines in solitude when she ran into a South American man high up in a guesthouse in the Himalayas. The man's teachings gave her journey the focus it lacked before. Her calm, unblinking account was a welcome departure from the breathless, wide-eyed "Dude, I found some enlightenment in India" stories he'd come across. Max searched for more information about the South American.

Slowly a picture emerged from the handful of blogs that mentioned this man. Once a successful doctor in Brazil, he had left everything behind to become a yogi in the Himalayas. Some said he was twenty-five. Others said that he looked twenty-five but was actually more than a hundred years old. That he had penetrated the mysteries of consciousness and the material body and had reversed the process of aging. The Brazilian taught a method of yoga and meditation that allowed one to go deep within the recesses of one's own mind to reach a perfect condition beyond good and evil, birth and death—the end of suffering, as it were. Max's heart stirred. Again the words sounded strangely familiar, as if he'd heard them before. But when? He barely knew anything about yoga and meditation. The rational part of him still didn't know what to make of this mystical mumbo-jumbo. And yet he felt compelled to find out exactly where the Brazilian yogi lived.

An Australian blogger had last seen him in a cave high up in the Garhwal Himalayas. Max emailed him, the German lawyer, and the other bloggers who had mentioned the Brazilian, asking to call or meet them to discuss the doctor and their own journeys. He didn't know where they would meet. They were German, Israeli, Slovenian, Indian, from everywhere, and they seemed like seekers, never still, always on the move. They could be anywhere. Well, so could he.

A shadow appeared on his laptop.

Max looked up, startled.

"Are you done?" said Sarah.

Max shook his head.

She frowned. "Can I see where you are?"

Max pulled up the Excel file. He turned the screen toward her and walked her through his half-baked analysis.

Sarah's face dropped. "This isn't enough. We need more for Tom."

Max saw the concern rise in her pale face. His pulse quickened. She hadn't watched over her shoulder all her life in fear that a stray bullet would paralyze her, nor had she worried each day that the junkies sleeping under the dark stairwell of her apartment building would rape her little sister. His questions could never be hers. He couldn't live her life anymore.

"You're usually . . . can we please get the fuck on it now?" she said. "We have to get it together by noon."

Max shook his head. "I can't. I have to leave," he said.

5.

Time waste. You must not have come now," said the man sitting next to Max on the floor of the train's open doorway.

Max smiled. This was the hundredth time he'd heard that in the last day—on the flight from London to New Delhi, in the rickshaw ride from the Delhi airport to the train station, on the railway platform, and now on the five-hour train journey to Haridwar, the foothills of the Himalayas in Northern India. This was his first time in India, and he had traveled outside the United States only once before to Kilimanjaro in East Africa, but enough images of India had seeped into popular culture so that nothing was completely unexpected. Stray dogs and cows blended with the riot of motorists on the roads, so he hardly noticed them after the initial surprise. The constant honking of car horns wasn't any more overwhelming than the sound of ambulance sirens in Manhattan. And with its shiny new highways and faceless skyscrapers, New Delhi appeared far wealthier than the South Bronx, with its burned-out, abandoned buildings. Even the street hustlers gently whispering of bargains for marijuana and prostitutes were like Boy Scouts in comparison to the pimps and crack fiends back home. There were unexpected sights—a man riding a motorcycle with a sixty-foot ladder tied behind him; a marriage procession in the middle of a highway; colorful billboards of film actors with big-barreled machine guns in their hands and fake blood gushing from head wounds, yet not a hair out of place—but thus far the only true surprise was the unabashed curiosity of the Indian people. He tried to relax and enjoy the barrage of questions thrown his way and not to take offense at people's swift judgment of his travel plans.

"Very wrong decision. You must come back in May," said the man.

The train stuttered in the thick evening fog. A bearded man with a bucket in his hand appeared from the white mist outside. He rushed toward the moving train and thrust one naked foot in the space between Max and his companion.

"What . . ." said Max, jerking back.

The bearded man grabbed the train's door and pulled himself inside the train, his bucket flying behind him. Salted peanuts rained on Max's head. A peanut vendor. He flashed Max an apologetic smile and began advertising his wares inside the train.

Max's companion in the doorway of the vestibule didn't seem to notice the interruption. "Are you listening, bhai?" he said. "Himalayas closed in winters."

Max turned to him. "How can the mountains be closed? They're always there, right?" he said.

"No, no," said the man, shaking his professorial face so hard that Max worried his glasses would fall off the train. "What I mean is, roads are all blocked. Big storms. Forget getting to Uttarkashi even, definitely not farther up."

If that were the case, coming to the Himalayas in December had indeed been a waste of time. From the train station in Haridwar, Max intended to go up to Uttarkashi, a seven-hour journey by road, then take a bus to Gangotri, the origin of the river Ganges, another six hours north, followed by a ten-mile trek up the mountains to Bhojbasa near the Ganges's source glacier, where a lone guesthouse served holy men living in the Himalayan caves. The Brazilian doctor had last been seen in a cave near the guesthouse.

Max hadn't accounted for the roads being blocked, but he had planned well for the trek to the guesthouse. Within a week of quitting his job, he had said good-bye to Sophia, taken care of his apartment and finances, gotten an Indian visa, and flown to New Delhi via London so he could reach the Himalayas before the winter peaked in early January. In his backpack, he had his best cold-weather hiking gear: woolen base layers, insulated down pants, two thick sweaters, one synthetic jacket, one hard-shell jacket with a hood, two pairs of gloves and hats, four pairs of woolen socks, and multiple hand and toe warmers, enough to survive in temperatures much lower than the minus-ten degrees expected in the Upper Himalayas. And somehow he didn't feel cold here in Northern India despite the temperature gauge on his compass hovering just above zero in the train's open doorway.

Of course this had less to do with his resilience and more to do with the heat generated by a few hundred people packed in a train compartment meant for fifty. On a mission to strip his life of the softness and comfort he'd been spoiled by back home, Max had chosen the cheapest compartment in the train. He'd been lucky to get a spot by the doorway. People were sitting hunched on suitcases, lying on luggage racks, even squatting atop the washbasin outside the bathroom—anywhere they could find an inch of space. The return journey wouldn't be pleasant if the roads indeed were closed.

Max's companion must have sensed he was throwing a wet blanket over his travel plans. "If God wants, you will find a way."

"Amen," said Max.

"Christian?" asked the man.

Max smiled. You'd have to know someone for months before you dared ask that question back home. "I grew up as one," he said. "Now I don't know who I am. Perhaps that's why I came to India."

"Good, good," said the man. "If you want to find *bahut kuch kar sakte ho* here . . . *idhar* . . . you must . . ."

Max seized the moment. "Can you teach me some Hindi? I have a guidebook, but I don't think I have the pronunciations right."

The man's face lit up. "You must know Hindi in India. Absolutely must. No problem, I can teach you important words quick."

And just like that, while the train started and stopped in the thick winter fog, Max got an impromptu lesson in Hindi pronunciation. Outside the train, India beyond the gleaming metropolis revealed itself. Half-naked kids huddling around small fires, people entering tiny mud huts with gaping holes, deformed beggars shivering on dirt roads, starving, thin cows languishing next to the train tracks—suffering everywhere in the land that promised salvation from it.

"DHANYAVAD. I can't thank you enough," said Max as the train reached Haridwar station six hours after its expected arrival time.

"No problem. Train took so much time. You have become Tulsidas," said the man. "You know Tulsidas? World-famous Hindi poet?"

Max laughed. His heart warmed. They shook hands.

"Be careful to go up in Himalayas. Winter weather very, very dangerous," said the man.

Max nodded, touched by his kindness. He had planned to make his way up to Uttarkashi that day, but it felt foolhardy to be driven up the icy roads now that it was past ten and pitch-black outside. He said good-bye to the man and took a bus from the train station to Rishikesh, the neighboring town that served as the springboard for journeys into the Upper Himalayas. Once there, he ignored the solicitations for rooms and transport and entered the first shabby hotel he saw. He negotiated the room rate down to Rs 300, six dollars a night. A 400 percent discount from the owner's initial quote of Rs 1500, he ran numbers in his head from habit as he walked up the slippery concrete stairs to the room on the second floor.

THE HIGH OF negotiating a bargain with his newly acquired Hindi skills vanished on entering the room. Even six dollars was too high a price for the damp-smelling room. A lone bulb dangled from the chipped ceiling. The narrow bed would have been small for a man half his size, and next to it was a four-foot-tall cupboard, every inch of it covered in dust. Exhausted, Max changed into his warm underwear and lay down, spread-eagled, on the pink bedsheet. He covered himself with thick blankets and stared blankly at the two brown geckos playing with each other on the faded wall in front of him. He switched off the light.

God, what had he done?

His parents had grown up in wooden shacks outside a farm in Corfu, the children of day laborers. If his uncle, a waiter in a Philadelphia diner, hadn't pulled them into the United States, Max would've grown up a peasant in Greece. How casually he had walked out on everything his parents had moved to a new country for. His mother had doggedly dragged Sophia and him to Manhattan on Sundays so they could see from the outside educated, well-bred people living in doorman buildings and eating in candlelit restaurants and aspire to a better life.

Max's throat tightened. He saw his mother, yellow shirt, green ribbon in her brown hair, her face turning red with humiliation whenever their welfare caseworker showed up to inspect their refrigerator and closets to make sure they were broke. Now he would be on welfare too. A wave of panic surged in him. Unlike his colleagues at work, he didn't have a daddy who played golf with fellow hedge-fund titans in a country club. No one stood between him and destitution. Jesus, he was fucked. He had to take the next flight back.

So if there is birth, age, suffering, sorrow, and death, then there must be something that is unborn, un-aging, un-ailing, sorrowless, and deathless—immortal, as it were.

Max forced himself to think of the naked, shivering children on the roadside. Viveka's serene, sure face had promised answers. He would find them.

Max closed his eyes again, trying to empty his mind of thoughts.

A SCREAM.

Max jumped from the bed, banging his knee against the cupboard. He cried out in pain.

Another scream.

Max looked around wildly.

Loud, toneless music filled the night.

Max's breathing returned to normal. Someone was tuning a large radio on the other side of the paper-thin wall behind his head. Two AM. He had slept only a couple of hours. The radio screamed again. Max went back to bed. He removed the pillowcase and rolled it up in a ball, stuffing it tight against his right ear while sleeping on his left side. The radio made a squeaky, gravelly sound now. Max turned to his right side, the pillowcase bunched up under his left ear. Then again.

He couldn't get back to sleep.

What was wrong with him? He had slept easily through gunshots all his life. This was nothing. Max threw the cloth away and continued tossing and turning, the sound crawling up his spine, not getting a wink despite being awake for more than forty hours. Eventually the sound ceased, or perhaps his mind stopped focusing on it. He buried his face in the damp bed.

Don't go so soon after Mom, please.

Max opened his eyes. Sophia had pleaded with him to stay a

little longer in New York. He hadn't even pretended to think about it. Instead, he had resented her for being too busy counseling addicts in Brooklyn to visit their mother in the hospital. His kid sister. For years, he had sat next to Sophia's crib, driving away the rats that darted out of the peeling walls when his mother went to work. Why had he been so cruel to her?

Stop.

Max got up from the bed. Sleep was impossible. Three AM. Dawn was still far away, but he had to get on with his journey. Max went down the stairs, out into the cold Himalayan air, his heavy backpack straining his tired shoulders.

HE WALKED THROUGH the dark, empty streets of Rishikesh, unsure where he was going, just wanting to stop the restless chatter in his mind. Each street looked the same in the darkness. Shuttered mom-and-pop stores, cobbled roads littered with fruit pulp and rotten food remains, stray dogs shivering on the pavements, and the air heavy with the smell of cow dung. Following the light of a lone streetlamp, he turned into an alley. The air felt colder, fresher. Max tracked the sound of running water. The river Ganges shimmered in the light of the funeral pyres burning on its banks. He walked toward the river past the blackened, charred human bodies cremated on the pyres. Kneeling down, he splashed cold water on his face, ready for a fresh start.

Someone touched his back.

Max whipped around.

A stark naked yogi, his entire body covered in a thin layer of white ash, black eyes blazing, stood in front of him. "Come, foreigner, I will show you God."

Max skipped a breath.

The yogi stretched out a closed fist. "You came from Europe to find guru," he said in a thick accent. "I am your guru."

He uncrossed his long fingers to reveal a black slimy mass. The smell of burning flesh filled the air.

"Take your guru's first offering," he said, holding Max's wrist with his other hand.

There was a touch of white in the black. Jesus, a tooth. Black flesh. *Burned human remains.*

Max pulled his hand away and walked past the yogi.

"Wait. You have to give your guru a donation," the yogi called behind him.

Max moved faster up the street, retracing his steps to the bus stand next to the hotel.

Three bearded yogis, white paint on their faces and fierce red marks between their eyes, sat on a street corner warming their hands over a fire.

Max's heart clutched. What had he gotten himself into? *Relax.* He was in the foothills of the Himalayas, the home of the holy Ganges. The area near the river had to be filled with men of God. Max breathed slowly. The yogis weren't naked or covered in ash. Yellow robes and bright marigold garlands covered their lean bodies.

"Do you want guru?" one of them called out and took a large drag from the bong in his hand.

Max shook his head.

"Take us to Europe with you," said another, pulling his long gray hair in a knot. "Cheap gurus outsourced from India."

The others laughed so much they started coughing.

Max would have to get used to this mocking. Nothing separated him from the throngs of Western hippies searching for themselves in the Himalayas. His Harvard degree, his Wall Street experience wouldn't give him a leg up this ladder. Nothing would—except his will.

MAX WALKED QUICKLY back to the bus station next to the hostel. He knocked on the glass window of the dusty booth at the station entrance. A woman trussed up in blankets sprang up from the floor. Her hair was disheveled from sleep. She raised her eyebrows.

"Uttarkashi bus?" asked Max without much hope.

"Five AM." She shivered in her thin khaki uniform. "Last bus this season."

Max's heart lifted. A sign. Pointing to what, he didn't know, but at that moment he'd take anything.

6.

Max entered the cold bus, his eyes swollen and heavy. It was four in the morning, but six or seven people were already inside the bus, their heads resting on the metal bar of the seats in front of them. Max looked around for a seat. Most were broken, with steel columns jutting out of their back frames. He found one with a thin cushion and settled into it. Freezing, he huddled against his backpack and fell into a deep, dreamless sleep.

The engine's roar shook him awake. Broad daylight. They were negotiating a steep uphill curve. The outside tires of the bus were an inch away from the thousand-foot valley below, and the dirt road was crumbling around them. It seemed wiser to keep his eyes shut, so he fell asleep again.

Max's head banged against the ceiling. The bus groaned to a

halt. Two large boulders lay in their narrow path. He rubbed his head and stepped out to join the four men pushing the boulders aside.

"Did they just fall?" he asked in English.

A man nodded. "One minute back."

Max looked at the giant rocks and weathered trees on the mountains above. No barrier separated them from the road. If the boulders had slipped just seconds later, they would have pushed the bus into the valley below. Every moment on the road was an exercise in surrender.

Max helped the men roll the boulders off the road. Back on the bus, the fifteen or so locals making the journey with Max greeted him with excitement. Two boys, seven or eight years old, wearing imitation Gap sweatshirts gave him high fives. A woman with a rough, cheerful face joked about someone of his height in the tiny seat. Another woman wearing a red sweater over a bright yellow sari offered him apples. A kind-faced man in a hip-length coat with a mandarin collar gave him water. The questions started again. No foreigner ever came in winters. Why was he here? Where was his wife? Did he want a guru? Why was he so tall? The engine roared to life again, filling the bus with an oily smell. The locals left him alone and busied themselves in praying for safety. They folded their hands and closed their eyes every time the bus navigated a treacherous turn. Max stared at the calm, silent face of the driver and slept again, dreaming of burning black bodies with shiny white bones.

The boys woke him up a few hours later. They pointed excitedly to a sign reading *Danger! Accident Zone* in bold black letters.

"Death point, death point, death point, death point," they sang.

The woman who had offered him apples pointed to a curve ahead where the previous month a bus had overturned. Soon Max found out why. When they went around the curve, the outside front wheel of the bus flew out, hanging suspended in air for a few seconds. Max's heart stopped. They were heading straight down the valley, into the swirling, angry Ganges far below.

The driver rotated the wheel furiously.

Max hugged his knees tight, preparing to barrel out of the tiny window.

The bus landed on solid ground again.

Everyone clapped spontaneously. Max's heart pounded. The air filled with audible sighs of relief. Only the kids looked disappointed.

"Why doesn't the government make the road bigger?" Max asked when the bus moved at a steady pace again.

"No government here. God takes care of roads in the Himalayas," said a woman.

THEY REACHED UTTARKASHI twelve hours after they had left Rishikesh, a mere five hours later than expected, despite the rough roads. Max congratulated the driver on his skill. He wanted a photograph with Max, and Max gladly obliged.

"Any bus to Gangotri?"

The driver shook his head. "No, no, never this season. Never."

A stocky Indian man wearing a small ponytail and earrings who had been sitting quietly in the front of the bus came up to him. "I can drop you to Bhatwari village in my jeep if you'd like. It's twenty miles ahead on the way to Gangotri," he said.

Max shook his hands. "That'll be great," he said. "Thank you."

Max helped the man carry one of his two suitcases back to his jeep in a parking lot next to the bus stand. They put the suitcases and Max's backpack in the back of the weathered jeep, and Max joined the man in the front.

THE ROAD BECAME narrower past the Uttarkashi bus stand. They crossed a low-lying cement bridge inches above the river. The riverbank was lined with debris: bricks, concrete, truck tires, engine parts, and tree branches.

"A cloudburst here five months ago," said the man. "Seven days of nonstop rain. People, houses, trucks, all taken by the river. Some people haven't even been found yet."

The roaring, angry river below them was so close Max could touch it. Any moment now, the river could rise and drown them as it had drowned hundreds of others. Or the weak bridge could break. How fragile this body, this life was. The jeep lurched. Max held on tight, feeling a renewed sense of purpose. They crossed the bridge.

A twenty-foot-tall iron statue of an Indian god with long matted hair, sculpted muscles, and a trident in his hand stood incongruously on the riverside.

"Pilot Baba's ashram," said the man, pointing to a cluster of white houses scattered next to the statue. "If you want, you can stay here until the winter ends."

"Is he a guru?"

"Everyone is a guru in India," said the man witheringly. "Pilot Baba was just a regular pilot in the Indian Air Force. His helicopter crashed here and he had some sort of spiritual realization—

perhaps that there is more money to be made in this racket than in flying planes. So he became a guru."

Max laughed. "How did he find disciples?"

"No shortage of foreigners touring exotic India," he said. "Pilot Baba teaches that man loses his ego during orgasm, so there is plenty of sex here. Westerners love it. Spiritual McDonald's."

As if on cue, a dreadlocked white guy in just a T-shirt and shorts emerged from one of the houses. He shut his eyes and spread his arms out melodramatically in the frigid air. Max's face went hot with embarrassment. Was there really no difference between him and these eighteen-year-old hippies? He strengthened his resolve to keep pushing forward until he found a real guru.

"Do you want to get off here?" asked the man, slowing down his jeep.

"I'll pass," said Max. "There is a man farther up in Bhojbasa I want to visit."

"The roads are closed beyond Bhatwari," said the man.

"I'll take my chances," said Max.

They took a steep turn and the statue and houses disappeared from view.

Max's companion raised his index finger. "One percent maximum," he said. "Only one percent of these yogis at most are genuine, and most of them live way on the top of the mountains where you are going. Out here and below in Rishikesh, searching for God has become a joke."

Max nodded. "A man with human flesh in his hands offered to be my guru this morning," he said.

"Covered in ash? Near a cremation pyre?"

"Yes, exactly," Max said.

"An Aghori baba. They eat animal carcasses and human remains to show their love for even the most repulsive of God's creations," said the man. "They look scary but are pretty harmless."

"And the men with painted faces and red marks?"

"Lord Shiva's devotees," said the man. "If I smoked as much hashish as them, even I'd see God everywhere."

So many teachers, so many belief systems, yet none inspired confidence. Why wasn't the path to the most fundamental of human quests clearer?

"What do you believe in?" said Max.

The man adjusted his ponytail. "My father was a priest in a temple here," he said. "I believed in Lord Krishna, his god, until my father got buried in a landslide while conducting a *puja*, a worship ceremony for the Lord. After that I left the Himalayas to work in Delhi. Now I come back only to visit my crazy family. Man is far more reliable than God. He rewards you with a paycheck instead of a landslide when you work for him."

THE JEEP'S FLOOR shook with a loud clunk. Max held on to his seat tightly. The man changed gears nonchalantly and the jeep resumed its smooth motion. They took a turn into a flat valley. In the distance, a colossal tower of ice arose high above the mist, glittering in the fading light of the evening sun. Max inhaled sharply at his first full view of the mountains ahead.

"Is that where Gangotri is?" he asked.

The man laughed. "Yes, Gangotri is at the bottom of that mountain," he said. "That's why all roads are closed beyond here."

The road ahead was covered in snow, as were the withered

trees on either side. The Ganges whispering below them suddenly fell silent, throttled by the heavy chunks of ice floating in its waters. Did the yogis hike up from this point? If they could figure out a way, couldn't Max? He ran marathons in less than three hours; he hiked steep mountains; his diet was predominantly salads and fruits; he'd never been fitter, healthier, more prepared.

"There must be a way, perhaps on foot," said Max.

The man shook his head. "Not until March or April." He took a turn and stopped ahead of a cluster of huts. "Bhatwari village," he said, pointing to the huts. "Ask around there. Someone will know when the road opens again. Perhaps you can even stay in the village for a few months. Who knows, you may become a guru yourself. This place does that to people."

Max shook hands. "Thank you for the ride," he said. He took his backpack from the jeep and came back to the driver's window. "Can I pay you?"

The man folded his hands and lowered his head in a mock bow. "No, no, great guruji. Just bless my family so they are absolved of my sins."

Max laughed. "Please, let me. I know how hard it was to get here."

The man waved his hands. "I was coming this way anyway. My family lives in Pilot Baba's ashram. I told you they are crazy."

He turned around and left.

MAX TRUDGED THROUGH the packed ice to the village, the chill cutting through his bones despite his heavy coat.

A group of men and women huddled around a fire in front of

a small open-air roadside restaurant. Next to it, a bare hut sold cigarettes and biscuits. Opposite it, there were more wooden houses with tin roofs. The village ended there.

Max knocked at the door of a house with a peeling sign reading *Bright Hotel*.

The tall, lean proprietor's eyes widened at his request for accommodation. He showed Max a dark, musty room that had obviously not seen visitors in months. There was no water or electricity in the freezing room, but the owner made up for it with thick piles of blankets and two buckets of hot water. Max's mood lifted. He had a bucket shower, snuggled into the blankets, and slept a little less restlessly now that he could at least see his destination one week after leaving New York City.

7.

Early the next morning, Max walked to the open-air restaurant with his backpack. He sat on a long wooden bench in front of the cooking area, huddled close to the warm stove, and watched the cook make Indian bread. The sun rose between the white, angular peaks of the mountains. Ruddy faces appeared on the streets outside, greeting one another, smiling in their thick, colorful clothes. The air filled with the fragrance of bread and milky tea. Max's spirits lifted. The lone taxi owner in the village had refused to drive him farther up, but at least Max had made it to the Himalayas.

"Where are you from?"

Max turned around. Two Indian boys in their early twenties,

all cheerful, impish grins and messy hair, sat on the table next to him.

"New York," said Max.

"Awesome," said the taller, more confident-looking one in perfect English. "I'm Omkara. I'm going to Cincinnati in three months."

"Cincinnati is a dump. It's nothing like New York," said the other boy, short and squat with a half-Oriental, half-Indian face. "I'm Shiva, by the way."

"I'm Max," he said. "You are going to study? University of Cincinnati?"

Omkara nodded. "Fucking yeah. To study chemistry. I'm breaking bad. The shit I cook up in Cinci is going to be the bomb," he said. He paused. "You've seen *Breaking Bad,* the TV show, right?"

Max shook his head.

"Dude, what kind of American are you? Everyone has seen *Breaking Bad,*" said Omkara. "You are tall, by the way, freaky tall. What brings you here? No foreigner comes here in winter. The Himalayas let no Yankees in in December."

Omkara asked the cook to make him an aloo paratha, an Indian bread stuffed with potatoes. "And make one for Uncle Sam also," he said. He turned to Max. "The parathas here are the bomb."

"Are you guys from the area?" said Max.

Shiva nodded. "My village is close to here."

"We go to engineering college in Rishikesh but drove up last night to take a break," said Omkara. "Two months left for graduation, yet they persist in teaching bullshit, pretending like they are some great American university or something."

Max stared at their black motorcycle jackets and thick biker gloves.

"You came up that road from Rishikesh on motorcycles? Not a chance," he said.

The boys laughed. "We ride motorcycles better than we walk. That's all we've done for four years in college. Up, down, up, down. Otherwise living in Rishikesh is more boring than watching you drink tea," said Omkara.

"As boring as Cincinnati," said Shiva.

"But how can you drive up that road at night? There isn't a single streetlight," said Max.

"We've done it a million times. It's better. Roads are empty then. There are so many jerks driving in India that your chances are much better against the night than against another idiot driver," said Omkara.

The parathas arrived. Max tore the hot bread into pieces and wolfed it down, the spicy potatoes warming him up.

"You eat like an Indian," said Omkara.

Max laughed.

Omkara removed his black gloves and kept them on the table. A crazy idea struck Max.

"Can you ride up to Gangotri?" he said.

Omkara looked up. "Of course. We can go anywhere," he said.

"Like right now?"

They nodded.

"But why would anyone go up there now?" said Omkara. "You can't even get a cup of tea there. And the view is the same. Here, there, everywhere, just mountains and snow, what's there to see? It's not like we have girlfriends to show pretty scenery to."

"Can you drive me up there now?" said Max impulsively.

Omkara stopped eating. He looked at Shiva, then turned to Max.

"I knew you were crazy when I saw you smiling by the stove," said Omkara.

"Why do you want to go up?" said Shiva. "There is no one there now."

Omkara answered on Max's behalf. "That's why, dude, that's why. Americans love their space and me time and all that mindfulness stuff. You are a tribal. You won't understand," he said. "Let's go, dude, we are up for it. Fucking yeah. What else will we do all day here?"

Shiva shrugged. "You can ride behind me so you have more space."

Fucking yeah. This was really happening. He was going to Gangotri, and later he'd hike up to Bhojbasa where the Brazilian doctor lived. A shiver of anticipation went up Max's spine.

"YOU HAVE TO get rid of more than half of that crap, though," said Omkara, pointing to Max's backpack after they finished eating. "Else you'll both topple over in the first valley."

Max hesitated. Every item in the bag was necessary. Knowing he would be hiking, he had scrutinized everything he had put in.

Omkara walked over and picked up the backpack. "What's in it, Uncle Sam? You can't need this stuff in a hundred years," he said.

The three of them went through his backpack. Out went the yoga manual and the biography of Buddha he had picked up in the London airport, the diary, the pens, two hiking pants, three T-shirts, sandals, shorts, swimming trunks, thin socks, malaria pills, a small lock—everything that didn't serve the purpose of keeping the body warm in the cold.

"There, that's a decent backpack," said Omkara.

It was half its original size.

Omkara picked up Max's swimming trunks from the discard pile. He danced around, circling them in the air.

"I'm going swimming in the Himalayas, bitch," he sang. "I'm divin', I'm pimpin' in the snow, bitch."

Max shifted in his chair and tried to smile.

Omkara put the trunks down. "Did you think you'd swim with the yogis in the frozen Ganges?" he said.

"Are the yogis still up there?" asked Max, half interested, half wanting to change the subject.

"They are much higher up than Gangotri, but don't disturb them if you go near their caves," said Shiva.

"Why?"

"Yogis are very powerful," said Shiva. "If you disturb their meditation just for taking a picture or out of curiosity, they may curse you. And a yogi's curse lasts for seven generations in a family."

"Don't listen to his superstitious bullshit. I told you, he is a tribal," said Omkara. "Go give the rest of your stuff to someone to keep safe before we head out."

"I don't need it anymore." Max looked at the books and clothes. He felt lighter and freer. He asked the cook to take anything he wanted and give the rest away.

Omkara came over to Max and high-fived him. "You are

crazy, dude, mad. That's why we like you," he said. "We are crazy too. *Paagals.* All of us."

Max followed them to a shed behind the hotel. His pulse quickened on seeing the weathered black motorcycles with their low seats and wide engines. Royal Enfield Bullet. He'd never heard of the brand. Not that he knew anything about motorcycles except that they were the least safe way to get anywhere even on shiny American highways, let alone the nearly nonexistent road ahead.

"Don't worry. We'll be fine," said Shiva, perhaps sensing his nervousness. He gave Max a knee and hip protector, an open-faced helmet, black glasses, and a balaclava to keep his head warm.

"See this stuff?" said Omkara, pressing his boots against the large spikes in Shiva's motorcycle tire. "Antislip studs made in Norway. We bought them in a black market in Delhi. Fancy, eh? India shining."

They mounted the motorcycles and roared away past the hotel, up the thin, icy asphalt road, toward one of the highest villages in the Himalayas. Max held Shiva tight, shutting his eyes, then daring himself to open them as Shiva skidded and turned, pulled the choke and pushed the throttle, dodging boulders and pinecones strewn across the potholed concrete road. All around them was a deep, silent ocean of white—pine trees blanketed with snow on one side, the frozen Ganges on the other, wispy fog on the valleys beyond, and a thick cover of clouds covering the early morning sun above. Sweat poured down the back of Shiva's neck under the helmet despite the cold breeze. Steering the motorcycle through the slipping, gravely ice was hard work, especially with Max's two-hundred-and-ten-pound frame behind him.

. . .

THEY STOPPED an hour into the ride in the middle of a silent valley. Bright purple flowers grew unexpectedly amid the snow-covered trees. They parked their motorcycles on a dry patch next to the cliffs. Shiva and Max sat down on a boulder on the road-side while Omkara screwed a spike into his motorcycle tire with a small drill.

"So why are you really going up to Gangotri?" asked Shiva, pouring Max a cup of hot tea from the thermos he kept inside his jacket.

His voice was a shout in the miles of silence around them.

Max took a sip of the spicy milk tea. A pleasant burning sensation seeped down his throat. "I'm going to hike up to Bhojbasa to meet a yogi," he said.

"Why?" asked Shiva.

Max told him about his unexpected meeting with Viveka and his subsequent quest to find the Brazilian doctor. As Max spoke, the uneasiness he had felt since coming to India slipped away. Somewhere deep down, he knew he'd been right in coming here. He'd been living a shadow of a life. The dots were connecting themselves. If he kept pushing forward, he would penetrate the mystery of pain, suffering, and death.

"It sounds awesome," said Omkara, who seemed to have heard every word Max had said despite looking completely absorbed with the motorcycle tire.

"What does?" said Max.

Omkara walked over to them. "Your life in New York," he said. He sat down next to Shiva on the boulder. "How did your father die?"

Max was learning not to be surprised when people asked him deeply personal questions casually in India.

"He worked in a garment factory in the Bronx. His lungs collapsed," said Max. He paused, thinking of the one time he had accompanied his father to the hot, dark warehouse in Kingsbridge where he worked. The windows were painted black, the doors shut tight. His father, taller than anyone around, was moving boxes, sweating and coughing, yet joking with short, dark men stooped over machine stations. "I was five years old so I don't remember much. My mother said he was a good man. He didn't drink much and was good with numbers."

"You did well to go to Harvard," said Shiva. "Your mother must have been proud."

Max's eyes watered suddenly. His mother had made Sophia and him practice their English in front of the mirror every night so they didn't pick up her heavy accent. She herself had learned to speak English fluently over the years but had never learned to write in it. Each month at Harvard, he'd receive an envelope with a smudged ten-dollar bill from her. He had never refused her money even though his tuition was covered by financial aid and his expenses by his busing and dishwashing job at the dining hall. She had wanted to keep feeling useful to him. Max took a giant sip of tea from the thermos cup to stop his voice from cracking.

"I still don't get it though. What are you really looking for?" asked Shiva.

Max hesitated. "Spiritual enlightenment, I guess."

"What does that mean?"

"I don't know. I've just started reading books like *The Yoga Sutras of Patanjali*," said Max. "It says there is just one energy in the universe. Everything and everyone are just forms of it. When you get enlightened, you see that oneness everywhere, in everything. You realize that a human body—any body, for that matter—is just a temporary vessel for the energy to express itself so the body's birth or death is inconsequential."

"But what's the point of knowing all this?" said Shiva.

"Have you seen anyone die?" said Max.

"My grandfather," said Shiva.

"Did you see him take his last breath?"

Shiva shook his head.

"When I was five, the kids in my building locked a girl up in a car one night. I saw her blue face pressing against the car's window the next day," said Max. "A couple of days later, my father died in front of me. I've never forgotten either one. It's strange to see someone die. One moment they are breathing and moving, and the next moment their bodies are heavy and solid, like stone. Their spirit is gone. It feels random, not like any kind of master plan. So the idea that you can reach some kind of a psychological whole with a permanent energy even if your body withers away gives more meaning to life, though I'm not sure I buy it quite yet."

Max rubbed his cold, stiff neck and put his balaclava back on.

"You are on the right track," said Shiva unexpectedly.

Omkara walked over to his motorcycle. "You are a fool to come here chasing these yogis," he said. "They are all frauds."

"Don't say that. Are you crazy? Take that back or you will be cursed, fucker," said Shiva.

Omkara kicked his motorcycle to a start and mounted it. Roaring forward, he raised his middle finger. He swerved dangerously. For one heart-stopping moment, Max thought he'd careen off the cliff, but Omkara put his hand down and balanced himself easily. The yogis' curses didn't seem to have hit their target. Omkara raised his middle finger again.

"This is what I think of your yogis," he shouted, zooming ahead.

Max and Shiva got up from the boulder and walked over to their motorcycle.

"Ignore him. He's a city boy from Delhi. He hasn't seen any real yogis," said Shiva.

They followed Omkara, quickly catching up with him. The road turned steeper. The motorcycle decelerated and swerved, then steadied again under Shiva's able driving. Soon the asphalt ended and a gravelly dirt road began. For the next hour, Max concentrated on moving his body in sync with Shiva's as he leaned right and left, forward and back, using the weight of his body to help navigate the hairpin turns.

AN HOUR AND A HALF later they stopped outside a small closed roadside restaurant halfway to Gangotri. The restaurant's tin roof had caved in from the thick deposits of ice on it, and its door was blocked by a six-foot-tall block of snow. No one seemed to have entered it for months. They spread a tarpaulin from Omkara's motorcycle saddlebag on the restaurant steps.

"How do the yogis get up to Gangotri in winter?" asked Max.

"They just walk through the mountains," said Shiva.

Max stared at the blank white mountains surrounding him. He'd never be able to find his way to the guesthouse without a trail.

Shiva seemed to read his thoughts. "Don't worry," he said.

"The trek from Gangotri to Bhojbasa is a joke. We call it a 'ladies' hike' in these parts. It's an easy, well-marked path. A tall, fit guy like you could be up and down in five or six hours, even quicker now that there is no one around."

"Have you been up there?" asked Max.

Shiva nodded. "I didn't stop at the guesthouse, though. I went farther up, where my uncle was meditating in a cave. Serious yogis live much higher up than Bhojbasa. You can't get there on marked trails. Many curious people come here—this researcher from Glasgow University, that writer from Milan—the lower Himalayas are a total tourist trap. Yogis don't want to be found so easily," he said. "And higher up in the mountains, the locals respect that. Even if people want a yogi's blessings, they'll just touch the outside of the cave or the yogi's footsteps in the snow and go. All this watching and taking pictures and gushing over exotic India is done only by foreigners and people from the plains."

Omkara noisily opened a packet of cookies. "All over the world people are striving for progress," he said. "Only in India can you live naked in the mountains like a caveman and have idiots ask for your blessings."

"They aren't cavemen," said Shiva. "They've just realized sooner than all of us that man's soul cries for the infinite in a finite world. That's why nothing ever satisfies us."

Omkara got up from the steps. "My soul cries for an end to your infinite stupidity," he said. He walked over to where the motorcycles were parked and took out a plastic container from Shiva's motorcycle's saddlebag. He began refueling his motorcycle from the container.

"He really needs to watch his mouth," said Shiva. He turned to Max. "You can never talk about yogis like that."

"I won't," said Max.

"I'm serious."

"I said I won't."

"Ever."

"Jesus. Never," said Max.

"Good. One of the yogis in the cave next to my uncle's had kept his right arm raised for twelve years, not even bending it down while sleeping. Every moment of the day and night for twelve years, can you imagine that? My uncle told me that such practices—raising the arm and standing on one leg—train the yogi to treat his body with contempt so he can concentrate undistracted on the divine soul within," said Shiva. "I'll never forget how the yogi smiled when he saw me. His right arm was thin like the dead branch of a tree, just bone and loose skin on top, but his skin glowed like a lamp. It was freaky. A man like that, who doesn't eat, who doesn't sleep, who deliberately withers his arm away to bone, what can he not do? You can't joke about things like this. Everyone in the mountains knows that."

Omkara came back from the motorcycle and joined them at the steps. "What is the height of foolishness?" he said.

"You," said Shiva.

"Nice try, but not good enough. There is an even taller answer," said Omkara. "Give up? It's a seven-foot American on top of the tall Himalayas listening to taller stories from a village hick."

Shiva burst out laughing. Max smiled awkwardly.

"Should we get going?" said Omkara. "Else you may convince Max to strip naked right now and run into a cave."

They walked toward the motorcycles.

"Is your uncle still up there?" asked Max as he put on his balaclava.

Shiva shook his head. "He lasted just two months. It's tough in the caves. The brutal cold, not speaking a word, scorpions inside, bears outside—one can go crazy up there," he said. "Try it. See how you feel. Maybe you'll handle it better."

The solitude sounded nice, thought Max, as he put on his helmet and mounted the motorcycle. With apartments stacked on top of each other and rows of buildings packed close together in the projects, Max felt he could live for a lifetime without seeing a soul.

THE DIRT ROAD turned steeper and the air thinner. Max huddled in his coat, glad for the warmth of the backpack behind him. They approached an iron suspension bridge hanging impossibly in the middle of the mountain. It had no sides. Loose gravel, small rocks, and chunks of frozen ice were scattered over its hundred-meter length. The bridge bounced up and down as though made of elastic when they crossed it. Max closed his eyes to avoid looking at the holes that revealed the frozen Ganges hundreds of feet below. Omkara raised two fingers of his left hand when he came off the bridge. Shiva slowed and dug into the motorcycle handles. A sheet of black ice covered the dirt road ahead. Max tried not to move a muscle. Shiva didn't touch the motorcycle's brake for the entire length of the slippery patch. The motorcycle wobbled and wove back and forth but eventually crossed without skidding.

They took a sharp turn at the end of a patch and climbed up a valley. The wind gusted. For the next hour, they hugged the side of the cliff. The angry wind had blown away the snow on the mountain patch, carving thick grooves and crevices in the stone.

Max held tight. When they reached the top of the valley, the wind calmed again. They stopped for another break.

DESPITE THE FRIGID AIR, Omkara and Shiva were soaked in sweat from steering the motorcycles.

"I can't thank you enough for the ride, guys," said Max, suddenly overwhelmed with gratitude.

"Don't turn all American on us, dude. Friends don't send friends thank-you cards in India," said Omkara.

They filled their water bottles from a small stream trickling down the mountain and stood by the side of the road. Max took a sip. The icy cold water struck his gums and teeth with a crushing force. He coughed and took smaller sips.

"Speaking of Americans, do I have to worry about racism in the United States?" said Omkara.

"No, no," said Max, his teeth still chattering. He paused. Who was he kidding? Hispanic and black kids got high, dropped out of school, shot and killed each other in the projects every day and no one cared, while one isolated school shooting in a white suburb triggered national debate on gun laws. "Yes, but for you it won't be."

"Definitely in Cincinnati," said Shiva.

"How do you know so much about Cincinnati?" said Max.

"He doesn't know jack," said Omkara. He sat down on his motorcycle. "He just doesn't want me to leave India because the rest of our gang is staying here. But if I don't go to America, I will be working in a call center like the rest of these coolies. 'Thank you for calling from Texas, Mary, we will arrange for your carpet cleaning.' 'Of course, John from podunk Iowa town, we will fix your toilet immediately.' 'Yes, Michael, I burned four years of my life and my parents' money studying chemical engineering when I should have read American bathroom plumbing manuals instead.' Like hell I want that. That's why I've been telling him to come with me instead of trying to get me to stay."

"No, no, I know the Midwest," said Shiva. "My uncle lives in Toledo in Ohio. Everyone there keeps asking him if he is Catholic. And if he says he isn't, they look at him as if he is a cannibal or something. Very creepy."

"Your uncles are everywhere from Cincinnati to China and they don't like it anywhere," said Omkara.

Shiva laughed. "All mountain people are like that. No matter where you go, the mountains call you back."

Max's heart clutched. His breathing slowed. *The mountains call you back.* All his life, he had felt the deep inexorable pull of the mountains. It had never made any sense. He had grown up on flat land and hadn't even seen a mountain until he was eighteen. Yet he had known immediately he'd come to the Himalayas when Viveka had started talking about them. The mountains had called him back. He stared at the white expanse shimmering in the faint glow of the midmorning sun. *Back where?*

"I don't care about religion. I'll become a Seventh-fucking-day Adventist or a Jehovah creep if it helps me pick up girls," said Omkara. "I have this dream that I enter a bar in Cincinnati and start chatting with this girl from Poland or Finland or somewhere cold and well, you know the rest. Possible, or will they reject me because I'm a slumdog?" He stared at Max. "You okay, dude? You look pale."

"Yes, yes," said Max. He sat down on Shiva's motorcycle opposite Omkara and took a large sip of the water. The explosion of cold in his mouth brought him back. "Definitely possible. You just need solid game," he said.

"What game?" said Omkara. "You've got to sit with me in the last stretch."

And for the next hour, Max sat behind Omkara on his motorcycle and laughed and chatted over the roar of the motorcycle engine as if he were in a college dorm instead of slipping, sliding, and holding on for dear life on an icy road in the mighty Himalayas.

FINALLY, FIVE HOURS after they had started, they dropped Max off in front of a snow-covered milestone, the starting point of the trail up to Bhojbasa.

"That was brilliant, dude. The best ride we've ever had," said Omkara. "I love the game. I'm going to try it in Bhatwari itself."

"With my aunts?" said Shiva.

"Fucking yeah. With your aunts. I'm going to use the foreigner-in-a-foreign-land game, what say, Max?" said Omkara. He put on a heavy affected accent. "Oh, really, Aunt Nirmala, how charming. In New Delhi, we don't drink milk straight from the cows like you do in your sweet little Bhatwari village. Oh, meeting you is so educational. Your culture is so different from ours." He removed his dark glasses and winked at Max. "They will lap me up. I'll be in their laps. Oh, yeah, in their laps, in their laps, in their laps," he sang.

Max laughed.

"You are disgusting, man," said Shiva. He turned to Max. "You sure you can manage? Want one of us to come with you?"

Max shook his head. "I'm a solid hiker. I'll be okay."

"It's an easy trail. Just keep going northwest for four hours or so and you'll reach Bhojbasa. Fourteen kilometers max. Steep but wide. You'll feel the path under your feet soon. There won't be anyone on the trail, of course, but there is a guesthouse in Bhojbasa that's open all year. If anyone knows about this Brazilian dude, the guy who runs it would."

Max nodded. He had read about the guesthouse online. He planned to sleep there for a few nights until he could track down the Brazilian doctor. No one knew the doctor's real name, but he went by the immodest name of Ishvara, Sanskrit for a supreme being, and he seemed to be well known among the yogis meditating in the caves near the guesthouse.

Omkara dismounted from his motorcycle. "Take this cell phone, dude," he said, pulling a smartphone out of the jacket. "It doesn't work here, but maybe it works up there. These things are strange sometimes. If you get stuck, call Shiva's number. It's stored under his name."

Surprise tears welled up in Max's eyes. If he learned nothing else in India, he'd learn how to open his heart more. "Seriously, I'm okay," he said. "You got me here in great time. It is barely noon. I should be there well before sunset."

Omkara hesitated, then put his phone back. Shiva asked him if he wanted to borrow his thick motorcycle gloves for the hike.

"And how will you go down?" said Max.

Shiva patted the back of his motorcycle. "Without a giant huddled behind me, I don't need to grip the handles so hard."

Max laughed. "I'm good. I have enough gloves for three people," he said.

They shook hands.

"Look us up when you come down," said Omkara. "It's the

only engineering college in Rishikesh and everyone knows us there. We run the place."

Max waved good-bye, wanting to store their kind faces in his memory.

"Be crazy, be safe, Mad Max."

8.

Max's stiffness vanished as soon as he began hiking. He was glad he had kept running through the haze of work and hospital visits over the last three years. His lungs seemed to adapt well to the fourteen-thousand-foot elevation and he breathed easily in the thin air. There was no sign of a man-made trail, but it was hard to get lost. On one side of the thick blanket of snow was a cliff with shriveled trees and large boulders; on the other, a steep fall to the frozen Ganges. There was nowhere to go but straight up. He walked along the packed snow, slipping into a comfortable rhythm, looking ahead, not below, keeping his neck and back straight and his shoulders loose, just as his track coach at Trinity had taught him years ago.

About a mile in, he came across two uprooted trees on his

path. Max scrambled over them, using the snow-covered branches for support. Just a few steps farther, he ran into a boulder, then a few more, followed by more uprooted trees, all seemingly the effects of a recent snowstorm. He looked up. Not a wisp of cloud covered the afternoon sun. The sunlight reached him well before the valley below, keeping him comfortably warm. Luck was shining bright on him that day. Max crawled over the rocks and trees, keeping a close eye on the frozen river hundreds of feet below. One false step and he'd hurtle headfirst into it. But destiny was on his side today. If he hadn't left the hotel in Rishikesh, he wouldn't have caught the morning bus to Uttarkashi and, later, got a ride right up to the trailhead. He'd be in the Bhojbasa guesthouse by four, if not sooner. If his lucky streak continued, maybe he'd even be pointed to the doctor's cave that evening. Max wouldn't bother him much. If he could just get a push in the right direction, he'd figure the rest out himself, working methodically, just as spiritual seekers had done for centuries. And no matter how much time it took, he wouldn't leave the Himalayas until he got a glimpse of the perfect state that lay beyond birth, suffering, and death.

The air got colder and the wind blew harder as Max made his way up. He stopped every few minutes and pulled another layer of clothing from his backpack until he wore almost everything he carried. Two hours passed. He must be halfway there, but there was no way to know for sure. Everything below him, above him, around him was blanketed by snow. He wolfed down the bread and potatoes he'd packed that morning and forced himself to hydrate, adding two packs of electrolytes to his water for good measure. A light snowfall began. Almost immediately, a thick cloud enveloped the sun. Only two-thirty, but it felt like late evening.

He could feel the air get thinner. His throat itched and he coughed deeply. Any moment now, he would be there. Both Shiva and the articles he'd read had said it would take three to four hours for a reasonably fit person, and Max hadn't missed a beat in the three hours he had hiked. Yet there was no sign of the guesthouse or of anything human—just snow, rocks, and bare trees. His heart fluttered a little. Come on, he knew the way of the mountains well, didn't he? Everything was hidden from view until it wasn't. The guesthouse was just around the corner. A turn here, a climb there, and he'd be facing it.

The snowfall increased. Small blue hailstones, sharp as bullets, struck his face. Max put his hands over his eyes and took shelter under a rock jutting out from the cliff. The sky turned darker. He switched on his head lamp in proximity mode to save battery life and wore the last of his layers, his hard-shell jacket and hand warmers. If it got any colder, he could be in trouble. But he wouldn't panic yet. He'd be at the warm guesthouse soon. The rock above him trembled. Max walked out into the snowfall with his hands on his cheeks.

Four PM. By now he should have been there. He checked his compass for the hundredth time. Yes, he was still steering northwest. Had he missed a turn when the sun disappeared? Should he retrace his steps? He kept moving forward. The hail rained on his face, scraping his cheeks like a razor blade. The wind screamed. His knee began to hurt. The lingering running injury was back. Max's heart beat fast. If he got lost, he could wander forever. No one in New York knew he was in the

Himalayas, and Omkara and Shiva didn't know if he was coming back in twelve hours or twelve years. Max breathed deeply. He couldn't think like a loser. He was a survivor, a marathoner, a mountain climber; any moment now he'd find his way.

He climbed higher. The hail stung the inside of his lips. A strong gale knocked him to his knees. He tried to get up. No, the wind was too strong. Flattening himself against the cliff, he picked himself up slowly. The ice seeped in through his mittens. Worried about frostbite, he let go of the rock. Immediately, he lost his balance and fell on the packed snow again. *Relax.* He got up more slowly this time, more focused, touching the jagged edges of the cliffs lightly with his hands and moved forward inch by inch.

Six hours of continuous walking. He couldn't have been walking in the right direction; otherwise he would have reached Bhojbasa two times over at this speed. The compass read fifteen degrees below zero. He'd been in colder temperatures before, but the wind was so strong here that he was shivering despite his layers. He had no more clothes to put on. Electric shocks like sharp pains went up and down his knee. If he kept walking higher, he'd . . .

Everything blacked out for a moment. He blinked rapidly. The black heaviness in his forehead subsided. Quickly, he pulled out his coat and gobbled down three chocolate bars for energy. Panting, he sat down on the ice and devoured yet another piece of the Indian bread he had packed in the morning. The sky darkened even further, yet there was no sign of a moon or a twinkling star. The thick blanket of clouds had obscured everything.

I am lost.

A knot formed in his stomach. Max had to admit to himself that his search was over. He didn't have a clue where he was. Not a soul in the world knew his whereabouts. If he was to survive this night, he had to get back to Gangotri quickly, force his way into an empty hut, and keep warm. Max put his head lamp in full power mode, turned around, and headed southeast, back to the trailhead, with a burst of manic energy, determinedly ignoring the pain in his knee.

HE STOPPED TWO HOURS into his descent. A forty-foot-long bluish-white glacier with dangerous-looking black rock jutting from it lay in his path. Stunned, he stared at the slanting block of ice. Where had this bastard come from? He looked at the ridges in the bare cliff above. It must have slipped down in the last hour. Or had he taken another false turn? He looked around. Nothing was familiar. Should he go back up? Up where—to certain freezing death? No, the ice must still be fresh. He could cross the glacier.

Max approached the glacier gingerly. He took one tentative step. His foot slid immediately. He threw himself to his side and grasped the crumbling ice for balance, stopping his fall. Slowly he crouched back. If he'd taken another step on the glacier, he would have hurtled down the mountain into the frozen river below. God, this was serious. He could die. He took a few steps back from the glacier. Jesus H. Christ. What would he do now? He was suspended in the middle of nowhere. Going up was foolish; going down was suicide. God, he was fucked.

Focus. Focus. Focus. All he needed was a little traction. If he found a dry tree branch, he could wrap it around his shoe. Max walked a few hundred meters back up the mountain. Nothing. The bare trees were covered with snow, snow, and more snow.

But if his tough, weathered Merrell hiking boots were skidding, even a dry branch wouldn't work. He walked back to the glacier. How did the yogis live in the caves?

Like machines, their bodies were. They walked barefoot in snow while we used shoes imported from Russia.

Max's heart raced He didn't even dare to consider Viveka's suggestion. No, it wasn't just stupid, it was dangerous. But it was the only way out. He stood there in indecision. The hail started pelting him again.

Shaking his head, Max removed his hiking boots and three layers of socks and toe warmers and put them in his empty backpack. He breathed deeply and began crossing the forty-foot glacier, taking small, light steps with his bare feet, reasoning that the less force he exerted, the less the reaction he'd get from the ice. *One step at a time. Don't look at the river. Next step. One more.*

Last step. He walked off the glacier onto the path. Christ, he had done it, he had. But he couldn't feel his toes anymore. Immediately he grabbed the matches from his backpack. One by one, he struck the matches against the box, but they were too wet. Desperate, he struck them faster, two at a time. How long did he have before frostbite damaged his toes? Finally he managed to get one to ignite. He looked for his diary in the upper zippered pocket of his backpack. With a cry, he remembered that Omkara had cast it aside that morning. He rummaged in his backpack for something, anything to light. Nothing. His passport.

Max pulled it from inside his shirt and tore off its unused pages. He put the dying match to a page. To his relief, a page caught fire. He added more pages to it and thrust his wet, cold feet on top of the burning paper quickly. His toes burned . . . and thawed. Wincing, he put all his layers of toe warmers and socks back on, wiggling his toes furiously and dancing on the ice until their movement returned to normal. He started walking down at a furious pace. He had walked barely a hundred meters when he saw another glacier in his path.

Max burst out laughing. He was done. He had neither dry matches nor more paper. He couldn't pull the stunt with his naked feet again. Warm tears rolled down his cheeks. He put his head in his hands and sat down on the ice. He was about to be buried alive in the snow. Was he going to die here? Now? Hadn't he been safe and warm in New York just a week ago? What a slow, pointless death.

Keisha, I was so wrong, I'm sorry.

Max's high school girlfriend's bright, animated face rippled through the blurry whiteness. His heart rose up his throat, choking him. He had ruined her life. Was she even alive? Right now he wanted just one more chance to find her or at least come clean to her family about everything that had happened between them so they wouldn't blame her. Max put snow on his face to stop the tears. *Get a fucking grip.* He'd freeze to death like this. He couldn't think of her now.

Max looked in his backpack for something dry to wipe off the snow. Finding nothing, he threw the backpack aside. He removed his shoes, took off one of three layers of socks from his feet, and wiped his face dry with the moist socks. He stared at the socks. Maybe, just maybe, the extra friction could help.

Max put his shoes back on and pulled a woolen sock over each shoe, tearing them at the ends so they passed over the entire sole.

Standing up and leaning to one side, he walked slowly across the forty feet of glacier, catching the packed snow for support after every few steps. His heart thudded out of his chest. Again, he willed himself not to look down.

He reached the other end of the glacier safely and stepped on land again. Science was far more reliable than God. He removed another layer of sock from his feet so he had only one sock left on each foot and jammed the socks on top of the shoes for the journey ahead.

MAX CHECKED HIS WATCH. Nine PM. Pitch-dark. His head lamp was flickering. Where was he? He should have reached Gangotri by now. Or at least the abandoned ranger office he had seen two miles into the journey. All he saw was snow and rock, snow and rock, snow and rock—and the icy river below. And soon he would slip and fall headfirst into it. He was hobbling like a ninety-nine-year-old man because of his knee pain and could no longer walk straight. No guide was going to come out of a tent with Bengay and a hot flask of tea for him, as had happened on Kilimanjaro when his knee had started hurting on the way down from the summit. He tied his towel around his knee. Gingerly he put one foot down and took one tentative step, then another, slowing making his way down, the pain shooting from his knee to his head like a bolt.

Not a sign of anything. He was completely lost, a mere speck in the infinite ocean of ice. He didn't have a chance of running into the narrow trailhead in Gangotri. Should he just make camp here until the morning? What camp? He had nothing but a backpack. Without motion, he'd freeze to death. He moved faster. A sudden wave of nausea surged through him. Warm bile rushed to his mouth. He emptied his stomach and lay down spent in the cold snow. The ice seeped through his overcoat, sweaters, and shirts. He didn't care. He wanted to die.

Enough.

He pushed himself up and took a large sip of the water. He took out the aluminum foil with his food from his backpack and smelled the food. The potatoes inside the bread had gone bad. But it was freezing here. If he died now, even his body wouldn't rot. How could the boiled potatoes rot then? Maybe the potatoes weren't bad. Altitude can make you smell stuff, see stuff, think stuff that doesn't exist, right? Say it, say it, he was going mad. No. He threw the bread away into the blackness surrounding him. He was now officially without food. His head lamp was almost out of juice, lighting the path ahead with just a faint, narrow beam.

Max inched down through the blinding pain in his knee. Shouldn't he see a flicker of light somewhere? Gangotri, Harsil, Dharali, some town from a distance? What had he been thinking? How had he entered the most formidable mountain range in the world so unprepared? He couldn't even walk properly on flat land with his old knee injury. Why had he been so arrogant, so foolish? The snow fell faster. He covered his face to stop icicles from forming. Somewhere behind him he heard a soft, thudding sound.

The Brazilian was here to save him.

Ecstatic, he turned around.

A pair of gleaming eyes. A furry face. A deer. No, a snow leopard. Something.

Max ran forward, away from the eyes, falling, picking himself up again, odd flashes of Sophia, an old priest, and a brown woman passing through his head. He stopped when he couldn't run any longer and looked around. The eyes had disappeared.

Max sat down with his compass, shivering, heart bursting out of his chest, surprised he hadn't steered off course during his mad frenzied run down. He wished he had. Maybe he'd see something other than the darkness and snow then. Perhaps the destiny he'd been so sure of would steer him better than the compass. It was well past midnight. He had been walking in circles for more than twelve hours. He was out of food and battery power, and his knee was throbbing. Max got up again. Should he head up toward the guesthouse that he had missed before or down toward Gangotri? His life depended on the decision.

Max looked up at the starless, cloudy night. Tears rolled down his face. *Help me, please.* But there was nothing out there. Just the consequence of his own choices, and he had made the wrong one in coming here. Now he was all alone, one man inching toward his end in an empty, heartless cosmos. He started walking down but his knee buckled under. He knelt down on the ice, then stood up and turned around, walking up instead.

Breathless and freezing, he stumbled up without a thought, just looking at his compass and the ice and snow in front of him. There was no trail, no path anywhere. His head pounded. He was about to die. That he was certain of. Again and again Keisha's tearful face flashed across the cloudy haze in front of his eyes. He'd abandoned her for his ambitions, to chase the life he thought he wanted. Look where that freedom had gotten him. He'd resented his mother for being needy, for pleading with him to get a good job, to get married quickly and have kids, for feeling anxious when he didn't visit or call home enough. Now, he was free from her, from everyone. Tears blurred his vision, making it impossible for him to see the compass or where he was going.

Max lost all track of direction. The compass needle wobbled. His head was bursting. He put his hand on his forehead, half expecting to find a gaping hole. Just skin. Dry and cold. And dead. But he couldn't die. He hadn't even said good-bye to Andre before he left. He hated good-byes and didn't really think he'd been gone for very long. How wrong he was. The head lamp died, plunging everything into blackness.

Just ahead out of the darkness, a tree stump peeked out of the snow. Max sat down in the snow and slumped against the stump, trying to keep his eyes open. The wind screamed around him. *Sophie, I don't think I'm gonna make it.* His jacket's hood blew off. Icicles rained onto his cap, but he felt no pain in his skull. Nothing anywhere. He loosened his coat. It wasn't cold. It wasn't anything. The mountains had won. They could take him now. Max's eyes closed.

SUDDEN IMAGES. An old white priest dying on a bed. People with tears in their eyes surrounding him. A window looking out to snow-covered mountains. An olive-skinned woman with a cloth covering her head praying in a cornfield. A man kissing an amulet. More men and women, faces melting into one another, lips muttering, eyes watering, hands folded.

I've been searching for Him for so many lives.

Max opened his eyes. He felt strangely calm. His head was

clear. The snow fell gently around him. The wind didn't scream in his ears. A yellow light appeared a few hundred meters in front of him. He got up and limped toward it.

"Help," he shouted, inching closer and closer, when his ankle twisted. He fell. He tried to get up again but couldn't muster the strength.

9.

Max lay on a hard surface, wrapped inside a blanket. A small wooden fire burned beside him. The sun streamed through the closed windows in front of him. He clenched and opened his fingers. They were stiff but functioning. He wiggled his toes. Working. He touched his ears with his hands. Freezing but intact. He'd live. He opened his eyes. Immediately, he sat up and looked around. The kind old woman who had helped him the previous night was sitting on a chair by his side in a white sari.

"Bhojbasa guesthouse?" he said, struggling to speak with his swollen lips and chattering teeth.

The tiny Indian woman nodded. She was nearly bald and her face was shriveled and wrinkled with large splotches of red.

"Tea?" she said in thickly accented English.

Max nodded. His head hurt. The woman got up from the chair and limped to the other side of the large room. She was so tiny, so frail. How had she helped him up? He looked at the snowy mountains outside the windows, shivering. Everything felt surreal, dreamlike.

THE WOMAN CAME BACK with a glass of hot tea.

Max raised his stiff arm to take it. He thanked her for saving his life.

"Okay," said the woman. "Yesterday night is fine. Otherwise storms bad this season."

A fine night. But of course. Thirty below zero wind chill and bullet-like hailstones were routine for these parts. He wouldn't last a night in a cave. If he couldn't do a simple "ladies' hike," if he fainted after eating a heavy breakfast and packed lunch and countless nutrition bars and water with electrolyte powders, how would he live farther north of the guesthouse? He'd be dead in a day. What a rash, egotistical bastard he was. An eighty-year-old woman a fraction of his size had to save his life.

"I make food," said the woman and disappeared.

Max moved closer to the fire. Every muscle in his body ached. The sun was bright, yet he was chilled to the bone despite being wrapped in three layers of blankets. And he was in a hut with a fireplace and a tin roof. Just which cave was he planning to live in? What a cliché he was. An ignorant, arrogant American. He thought he was a mountaineer because he had climbed a few minor mountains with professional guides. He had pondered some shallow questions between vanilla lattes and had started thinking he was a yogi. How callously, how selfishly he had left

Sophia so soon after their mother's death. He needed to take the next flight back to New York and get his shit together. No stupid questions, no privileged pontifications on the meaning of life—just live the life he and everyone else expected him to.

THE OLD WOMAN returned with a plate of rice and lentils. Max devoured the food. Blood pulsed through his veins. He looked up with moist eyes at the woman.

"You saved my life yesterday. I will forever be grateful," he said.

The woman shrugged. "You not far. How you hear of this place?" she said.

"A guidebook mentioned it," said Max.

She shook her head. "No, that is guesthouse on Gomukh trail. This is Old Bhojbasa. Many kilometers off trail. No proper path. No one knows this," she said.

"I lost my way," said Max.

The woman nodded and left the room again.

Max wished she would smile a little so he didn't feel so unwelcome. She must think he was a royal ass—and she wasn't wrong. He stood up. His knee, which last night had felt like it would come out of its socket, didn't hurt quite so much. He limped to the window. They were on the edge of the world. Beyond the cluster of bare pine trees in front of the hut lay the formidable Himalayan ranges. He could make out the contours of caves in the icy cliffs. People lived inside them. What a mockery he had made of their will, their determination.

"A yogi going down tomorrow. Then not for many more days."

Max turned around. The woman had accurately concluded that Max would be too chicken to go down on his own.

"I'm Max," he said.

The woman didn't introduce herself. "He leaves early in morning to Gangotri. From there, jeep goes to Rishikesh. Weather clear for three days. It not last long, so we get supplies now," she said.

So his journey was over before it had started. The Ganges, thin, blue, and frozen, glimmered in the sunlight many feet below. A deer rambled in the snow outside the window. Somewhere a bird called. The same unsettling feeling gripped Max. Who were those people in his dream by the tree the night before? He could have sworn he'd known the old white priest dying on his bed, the brown woman looking at the sky, and the man kissing the amulet. Not just known them. He had felt they were alive within him. Their hearts and minds were his own; only their faces were different. It was as if he'd seen glimpses of a past life. But he didn't even believe in reincarnation. So how had he known them so well? He thought of the words of the Buddha he had read in the book he had picked up in London. The man had been unrelenting in his quest for answers.

Though my skin, my nerves, and my bones shall waste away and my lifeblood go dry, I will not leave this seat until I have attained the highest wisdom, the supreme enlightenment.

Max just didn't have that fire.

"Thank you. I will leave tomorrow," he said.

"I tell him," the old lady replied.

"Does the yogi live nearby?" asked Max.

The woman nodded.

Max hesitated. "Have you ever met a middle-aged Brazilian

man in these parts? He looks much younger than his years. I think he goes by the name of Ishvara. They say he was a doctor in the past. Now he's a yogi."

The woman's expression didn't change. "Many men come here," she said. "Some yogis, some serious seeking, some just curious."

She didn't have to say where Max belonged in that hierarchy.

"You not waste people's time if only curious," she said.

"Yes, of course," he said.

She left.

Maybe she knew him, maybe she didn't. Searching for one man in India was like looking for the tip of an icicle in an avalanche. But it didn't matter anymore. Max's search was no longer urgent. He wasn't prepared to meet men like that.

Max spent the rest of the freezing day inside resting, beating himself up over his foolishness, and puzzling over the images from the night before.

A BAREFOOT YOGI in thin ocher robes and shiny black shoulder-length hair came for him the next morning. He remained silent through the four-hour hike back to Gangotri, and Max didn't feel the urge to pepper him with questions. Max tried to find out where he'd gone astray on his trek up. But they went back down a different way—or perhaps it was the same. The mountains remained as impenetrable on the way down as they'd been on his way up.

10.

Max reached Rishikesh the following morning, battered and sheepish but relieved to be alive and walking on his own two legs. He checked the flight times from Delhi to London in an Internet café next to the bus stand. The last direct flight left at midnight. It was barely noon. If he started on the five-hour journey back to Delhi now, he would reach the airport with plenty of time to spare. He checked his email.

Jennifer, a girl he had dated for six months a couple of years ago, was in Key West and was remembering a trip they had taken there for a college friend's wedding. Max had only hazy recollections of the trip. How sharp his image of Keisha had been during the trek. He hadn't seen her in eleven years, since she had dropped out of high school and run away from home the same year he went to Harvard. A middle school classmate who was a trucker told Max when he bumped into him at a block party on 141st Street during Max's Christmas break from college that he had seen her trading sex for drugs at a truck stop on Interstate 90 near Chicago. Max had left for Chicago immediately to track her down but hadn't found any trace of her. Two years later, Pitbull's cousin had mentioned casually that he'd met a South Bronx girl called Keisha in rehab in Iowa City. On another break from college, Max had visited that rehab and fifteen other sober living homes in the area but drawn a blank. Had Keisha ever contacted her family again? He'd never been able to find out. One summer he had gone to confess everything to her father but they had moved out of their home on Cauldwell Avenue. Was she safe? Alive? He'd been so cruel to her. Max's heart sank like it always did when he thought of her oval eyes and dark braided hair. He forced his attention back to his email.

> **You're right, Maxi . . . I didn't come to the hospital enough, nor did I help you with Mom's bills. I've been thinking a lot . . .The truth is, I pulled away from her even before her cancer. She was getting so needy—all that talk about settling down and marriage and grandkids and having dinner every Sunday as a family!! I don't know what to say . . . I'm sorry. But you've always handled stuff, so I just assumed you'd take care of her. I wish we had talked more . . . I miss you.**

So Sophia had felt the same way. After all those years dreaming of a better future for them, his mother had suddenly become insecure and clingy when they both moved out of the projects. Had her loneliness contributed to her cancer? His stomach tightened. You loved your kids with all your heart. Then they left you and never looked back. The familiar sense of futility began to rise in Max.

More emails. Rachel was having a baby. Save the date for Mike's bachelor party in Cancún. Anne's wedding was now confirmed for California in her dream venue. Barack Obama wanted another donation to create history. Habitat for Humanity thanked him for his contribution to their record-breaking holiday fund raiser. Max was flipping listlessly through the life that awaited him back in New York when he froze at a blogger's response to his email about the Brazilian doctor.

> **Although it has been a while, I may be able to help. Please let me know your question and I will try my best.**
>
> **Anand**

In the email footer, a different name and an address,

> **Marcus Kersnik,**
> **A-18, Kirti Nagar,**
> **Dehradun-248001**

"No," said Max firmly.

"What?" said the Internet café owner.

Max looked up from the computer. "Nothing," he said. He paused. "Where is Dehradun?"

"Two hours away from here by road."

No way. What were the odds of him being so close in a country this large? Then again, like Shiva had said, once the Himalayas took hold of you, they never let go.

"On the way to Delhi?"

"Opposite way," said the man.

No, he couldn't start this search again. For God's sake, he had come close to dying. If he went back home now, he could still pick up the pieces of the life he had tossed away.

Max checked the last of his email. A note from Andre.

> **thank u 4 ur apartment Ace but i aint moving in until we talk. i feel u. After all d shit went down, i also hated for years. call me. or come back.**

At least he had received Max's lease in the mail, not always a guarantee in the South Bronx. Max had paid rent for the nine months left on his Manhattan apartment lease and added Andre to it, enough time for him to graduate from college and find a job in the city.

Max logged out of his email and walked out of the Internet café, thinking of Andre's years of drifting after the shooting. Immediately after learning to handle his wheelchair, Andre had dropped out of middle school and started dealing T's and blues despite rarely having touched drugs before the accident. Kids in wheelchairs got off with light sentences, so the 93 Bloods, the gang he hustled for, quickly graduated him to heroin and cocaine. He dealt for four years, even getting arrested a few times, driving his mother, a mild-mannered grocery store cashier, insane. And then one day, the year Max went to Harvard, he had snapped out of it and got his GED. Was Max also acting irrationally because of his mother's death?

• • •

A SHORT, THICKLY mustached jeep driver at the taxi stand agreed readily to drive him to New Delhi, five hours away. Max sat next to him in the passenger seat and stole one last glance at the icy Himalayas, glittering in the bright afternoon sun like a diamond. He was going from silence, back to civilization.

They stopped for tea at a riverside restaurant an hour into the journey. A Hindu priest in saffron robes shooed away stray dogs that had collected around a burning pyre on the riverbank.

"Mother Ganga. Very holy river. People cremate body here and put ashes in river," said the cabdriver.

Max nodded. More people spilled onto the riverbank. A pregnant lady washed her clothes. A couple sprinkled water on each other. An old man took tentative steps into the river, shivering and shaking as he dipped his prayer beads into the water.

Birth, marriage, old age, death—the whole cycle played out before his eyes.

They finished their tea. "Should we go, sir?"

Max nodded. A dog grabbed a dry human bone that had fallen out of the pyre and scampered away.

They drove off. The Ganges and the mountains receded in the distance.

As the last of the Himalayas vanished from view, Max said, "Can you stop for a minute?"

The driver braked on the side of the busy road. People packed in buses, cars, and trucks passed them, all going in frenzy from one place to another.

Their smiles are hollow, their eyes are hungry. The yogis' faces were different.

Max massaged his temples, thinking of Viveka's words. Andre was wrong. Max felt no anger, no particular grief about his mother's death. All he felt was a detached, objective curiosity. What lay beyond this charade of life and death? He couldn't go back to his empty, dissatisfied life just yet. Not until he gave it his all to see if a different life was possible.

"We have to turn around," said Max. "Can you take me to Dehradun instead?"

"Anywhere you want, sir."

II.

Max knocked at the door of a wooden house on a small crowded street in Dehradun.

A tall, thin middle-aged white man wearing a baseball cap opened the door.

"Anand?" said Max.

"Yes," he said in a soft, barely audible voice.

"I'm Max. I emailed you about the doctor. Ishvara, the Brazilian doctor?"

The man's eyes widened. "Oh, yes." He stared at Max.

"Can I come in?" said Max.

"Yes, of course. I should have asked," he said, his pale face breaking into a smile. Dimples lit up his cheeks. "I'm sorry. I was a little surprised. I'm used to being called Marcus. Anand is my spiritual name. I don't use it often."

They walked into a small living room filled with pictures of Anand with a slim, dusky Indian woman and three boys.

Max sat opposite Anand on a cane chair. Soft, vaguely familiar music played in the background. Anand removed his baseball cap to reveal a shiny bald head. He said something.

Max leaned forward, straining to hear his soft voice and understand his hard-to-place accent.

"Did I send you my address?" repeated Anand.

"It was on the email footer," said Max.

"Ah, but sometimes even I can't find my own house here," he said, dimples lighting up his face again.

Max smiled. Indeed, the driver had circled around for ages. Again and again they were told to "go straight and take a right," which Max quickly realized was a euphemism in India for "I don't know," perhaps because Indian people hated not to be helpful. Finally he had asked the taxi driver to park in front of a hotel. It had taken him an hour of walking through the maze of streets to find A-18. The streets followed no alphabetic or numerical convention. A Block stood next to M Block, and 18 was next to 232. It was a miracle he'd found it.

"There is no method here," said Anand. "People choose whatever house number they want for numerological reasons."

"Have you lived in India long?" said Max.

"Yes."

"Is that your wife in the pictures?"

"Yes."

"Is she Indian?"

"Yes."

An uncomfortable silence followed.

Max shifted in his chair. To fill the space, Max talked about his travels in India, his search for the Brazilian doctor, and the trip up the Himalayas.

Anand nodded from time to time, but his large eyes remained silent. Max didn't know if he had followed his account.

"Where are you from?" said Max after another bout of silence.

"Slovenia."

"How long have you been in India?" said Max.

"Fifteen years."

"Those are your boys?" said Max, pointing to the pictures of the three boys on the wall.

Anand nodded.

"Very beautiful family," said Max.

"Thank you."

"Do they live here?" said Max.

"Yes."

"What do you do?" said Max.

"Web design."

"Do you work from home?"

"Yes."

Max sat back in the hard cane chair. How could a man with such a warm, smiling presence be so shy? The soft beats of the surrounding music changed to a deep, resonant chant. Max was inexplicably drawn to the music. Even though the words were in Hindi, he was sure he'd heard the song before. Anand nodded his head to the rhythm and closed his eyes. Max forced his attention away from the chanting. Two-thirty PM. The driver was waiting outside. New Delhi airport was six hours away. He could still make it comfortably in time for the flight to London at midnight if he left now. One last try. Max leaned forward.

"Where did you meet the doctor?"

Anand opened his eyes. "The Tibetan Himalayas."

"Recently?"

"Twelve years ago."

"Have you seen him since?" said Max.

"No."

"Do you know where he is now?"

"No."

"How can I find him?"

"I don't know."

"Do you know anyone who might know?"

"No."

"So there is no way to find him?"

"No."

"Then why did you think you could help me?" said Max.

"Did I?"

"You wrote in the email you could be of some help?"

"Yes. I told you I saw him in the Tibetan Himalayas," said Anand.

"That was twelve years ago."

"Yes."

Another false turn. Max's heart sank. Maybe it was all for the good. Max would be back in New York the day after next. He was overcome by dread. The beats of the background music deepened, tugging at his heart again. Max closed his eyes. A sudden chill went through his body. He was falling into a deep, bottomless void. Blackness. A blinding flash of light. Max opened his eyes with a start. Goose bumps covered his forearms. He gripped the chair tighter.

"This music, what is it?" said Max.

"Hare Krishna chants," said Anand.

"I think I've heard them before," said Max.

"Heard them or felt them?" said Anand.

Max didn't know if he was more surprised at the question or that Anand had asked one. He paused, considering. "Felt them, I guess. I haven't heard any Hindi song before," he said.

The dimples returned. "I thought so," said Anand.

"Why?"

"These songs express deep love for the divine, an urge to break free from the cycle of birth and death, this trap of nature, and become one with Him," said Anand.

Again, something pulled at Max's heart. "But why would I feel them?"

"You've heard this sound before, if not the song," said Anand. "Your past lives led you here."

Max's stomach turned. "I don't believe in reincarnation," he said.

Yet he'd seen himself in the faces that roused him from his near-fatal sleep in the mountains—the same mountains that seemed to be calling him back.

"But reincarnation is pure science, isn't it?" said Anand. "Thought is energy, desire is energy. Energy cannot be created or destroyed, it just changes form. So our thoughts and desires just find a new physical body when this one wastes away."

He leaned back in the chair, seemingly exhausted by the long explanation.

"Shouldn't there be more hard evidence for it, then?" said Max.

Anand shrugged. Believe what you want to, I couldn't care less, his expression said. He closed his eyes again and nodded to the chants. Max thought he had offended him. He changed the subject.

"How did you meet the doctor?" said Max.

Anand opened his eyes. "I have to go to the temple now," he said softly. "Please make yourself comfortable here if you want to rest from your travels. My wife will be back anytime, and the kids a little later."

"No, I must go . . ." Max stopped. The chants tingled in his spine. "Can I come with you to the temple?" he said, surprising himself. Usually he steered as far as he could from organized religion, with its elaborate rituals and demands for belief.

"Yes."

THEY WALKED DOWN the narrow street past the haphazardly arranged houses—some made of wood, some concrete; some one floor high, some five or six floors high. Rickshaws, motorcycles, and cars zoomed past them. Anand seemed blissfully unaware of the traffic and noise.

They reached the ramshackle hotel at the end of the street where the cabdriver was parked. Max paid him and let him go. They walked two more blocks and stepped into a small brown oval-shaped temple. Up a flight of stairs they went, entering a large room with a white marble floor surrounded by statues of gods and goddesses. One muscular goddess had four snakes sculpted around her thick neck. Another blue-colored god had a contemptuous smile on his face, another a lion under her feet;

yet another had a bow and arrow in his hands, with his tongue hanging out. None looked calm or inspired peace.

On chairs in front of the statues sat a corpulent man with a sitar and a gaunt, disheveled woman playing a musical instrument that had a flap and piano-like keys; they were belting out loud, toneless songs. The twenty people sitting cross-legged in front of them bobbed their heads to the melody. Or the lack of it.

Anand joined the group on the floor. After a moment's hesitation, Max accompanied him. Fresh from the disastrous hike, his knees and ankles felt stiff and heavy, like large blocks of stones. He crossed and uncrossed his legs.

Anand closed his eyes and nodded to the music.

Max tried to do the same but couldn't. It didn't take a musical genius to know that the singers couldn't strike a single melodious note and their instruments were badly tuned. They wailed and shrieked, their voices gruff and hoarse, sometimes so carried away by the melody only they could hear that they forgot to play their instruments, which was perhaps better.

Max waited a few songs for Anand to get up. He didn't open his eyes.

The singers screeched on. Max fidgeted.

The singers moved from the duet to solo performances. The sitar player in his tight sequined kurta shut his eyes and screamed, triple chin rolling, loose folds on his neck and waist flying in every direction. The spindly woman in her white sari looked on encouragingly, then sang herself in a low, whiny voice. Max's skin crawled. A grating sensation went up his spine. He was in a medieval torture chamber.

. . .

FINALLY, A BREAK. Everybody got up to leave—except Anand. And Max. Max stared at Anand's closed eyes and peaceful face in disbelief. This sounded nothing like the deep, sonorous, oddly stirring music he had heard at Anand's home. What was he hearing in it?

A fresh batch of unsuspecting listeners sat down on the floor. They too left after the next break.

Max excused himself two hours later when he thought he would burst out in tears and start throwing things around if another sound came from the fat man's lips. Out in the busy street, he paced around. Four-thirty PM. He could still make it to the New Delhi airport just in time for the midnight flight if he left immediately. But something felt incomplete. Anand's calm, silent face must have something to say. He had to give it another try.

MAX WALKED BACK into the temple. Anand hadn't budged from his position. Max sat next to him. The fat sitar player was sweating profusely. Perhaps now he would stop from exhaustion. The woman wiped the man's forehead with her handkerchief. It gave him a shot of new energy. He shouted even louder than before. Max listened to the lyrics. He could make out a few familiar words in the din. Ram, Krishna, Om. But they were being uttered so tonelessly that even the fierce-faced goddess riding a lion would likely recoil and cover her ears with all her ten hands. Perhaps that was the point. Scare God into submission. Force Him to grant all your wishes; otherwise you'd never stop shrieking.

After two more hours of song, Max was in agony. He had missed his flight. The singing-shouting continued unabated. Groups of people came and left, but Anand didn't move. This was so much worse than being lost in the mountains. At least he could do something there. Here he was helpless. He breathed slowly and stared at the statues, wishing he were sitting in front of his computer in New York instead. His fingers itched to write a killer Array formula that cracked open rows of Excel data, to set up a VLOOKUP that found missing variables in a large database—something, anything that spit out an answer when asked a question. Why was the path to truth so obscure, so clouded?

Anand nudged him. "Are you ready to go?"

Max hid his relief. "Whenever you are. I'm fine," he said.

The dimples again. "You are enjoying it?"

"Yes."

"Okay then, just one last song," said Anand.

They listened to three more songs before heading outside.

ANAND SMILED WIDELY on their walk back. His shoulders swung. He put his baseball cap back on.

"The male singer is a trustee of the temple, so they have to let him and his wife sing whenever they want," said Anand. "He is a local businessman. The people who came to listen all want some favor or the other from him."

"Did you want a favor as well?" said Max.

Anand paused. "I guess you could say that."

"Did you think they were good?" said Max.

Anand laughed. The creases in his face almost touched his eyes. "They were good for my purpose," he said.

"To express love for the divine?" he said.

"I don't think God would be able to sit through that for four hours," said Anand.

Max stared at him in disbelief. "So why were we there?"

Anand lowered his eyes. "My sincere apologies. Just a whimsical little test to check your patience," he said. "Your eyes were very restless when you came."

"Why does that matter?" said Max.

They reached the house just then.

THE STRIKINGLY ATTRACTIVE woman from the pictures was sitting reading a magazine in the living room.

Anand made the introductions. Leela's face had an easy, comfortable smile and Max warmed to her despite his irritation with Anand.

"Max is looking for the Brazilian doctor. Remember him?" Anand said.

"How can I not? You'd leave me in a flash if you see him again," said Leela.

"Now Max wants to be his disciple," said Anand.

"What is it with you men and always looking to shirk responsibility?" she said. "All three of your boys are out playing cricket instead of studying now."

"You have a minute?" Anand asked her.

They excused themselves and left the room. Max heard them talk in the other room. A door opened and closed. Anand came back with a piece of paper in his hand.

"Here," he said, handing Max a yellow parchment.

Max looked at an address.

"His name is Ramakrishna. A great sage. He is the man you seek," said Anand.

Max's spirits lifted. "Is that the doctor's spiritual name?"

"No, I told you, I don't know where the doctor is. No one has seen him for years. I don't even know if he is alive or not," said Anand. He hesitated. "Besides, I hope you don't mind me saying this, but you are not ready for him yet. You have passion, you have energy, but you are a wild elephant now. Your mind isn't tame enough to walk the glorious path."

Max's face flushed. Was his incompetence so obvious? He looked down at the paper.

"Where is he?" said Max.

"A long way from here in South India," said Anand. "I have written directions on the back. Take a train from Haridwar to Madurai in Tamil Nadu. It should take fifty, maybe sixty hours. From there, a twelve-hour bus ride to a small town called Pavur. After that, a ten-kilometer hike to a village without a name, then another thirty kilometers or so through the fields to his home. There won't be any rickshaws or taxis in the village, but you can find something, perhaps a tractor. If you can't find a tractor, follow the mud trail from the village and keep walking until you see huts. It's probably Ramakrishna's place unless something else has gone up there, which is unlikely, since it's all dry, fallow land."

"How long is the course?" said Max.

Anand laughed. The shyness left his face. "This isn't your usual Indian ashram with guru goons making foreigners shriek devotional songs in ecstasy," he said. "It's just a saint teaching what he knows, and he barely speaks any English. There are no courses or programs. You live with him. He accepts no money or donations. You go there as a beggar, a monk, accept whatever alms he gives you in the form of his teachings and leave when your hands are full. All he'll ask for in the end is that you never speak of him and point people his way only if they are serious seekers."

"And you think I'm a serious seeker?" said Max hopefully.

Anand shook his head. "I don't know," he said, deflating Max. "I've been trying to figure you out. Most Westerners who come here want easy answers. That's why I also fell into the Hare Krishna thing, chanting, love, all the simplistic stuff that gives you some happiness but doesn't last. But something in your eyes, in your going to the high Himalayas in this crazy winter, makes me want to believe that you can be more." He sat down on the chair opposite Max. "I asked Leela for her opinion as well. I haven't given the address to anyone in some years. I guess I shouldn't have without knowing you better, but I told myself, if he passes my impromptu test, I'll tell him."

Max stared at the paper again. "Have you been there?"

Anand nodded. "I didn't last even a week. I wasn't meant to be a yogi in this life. Ramakrishna helped me realize that."

"Yet you are happy," said Max, looking at the pictures of the smiling family on the wall, all with big dimples on red cheeks.

Again, the dimples lit up. Anand thrust his shaven head closer. "A painting of the moon gives us joy, but it isn't the moon, is it?" he said. "How much more joy would there be in seeing the moon versus its painting, in feeling the warmth of the sun and not its reflection in the water? I'm merely seeing the painting, Max; you have a chance at seeing the moon."

"What does that mean?"

"One day you'll know," said Anand. "At least I hope you do. And maybe you'll come back and show me the moon too."

Max shook Anand's hands. "Thank you for trusting me," he said. He got up. "I'll make my way there immediately."

Anand laughed. "You can't go there in these clothes," he said.

Max looked at his muddy, torn cargo pants. "I have a cleaner pair in my backpack."

"No, I meant that it's very hot there," said Anand. "You won't last an hour in those heavy shoes and clothes."

Max still felt cold from his hike. "I'll manage," he said.

"Trust me," said Anand. "I'm talking safety, not comfort."

Max would never take another warning lightly in India. "But I'll never get shoes and clothes my size here," he said. "I can barely find shoes that fit me in the United States."

The dimples returned. "Ah, my friend, but there is one place, and luckily, it's on your way," said Anand.

12.

Two days later, Max was in a youth hostel on the second floor of a run-down building in Mumbai. Every bone in his body hurt from sitting cramped and sleepless for forty hours on a hard wooden seat of the Dehradun-Mumbai Express Train. He had paid for a reserved seat in the second-class compartment but barely enjoyed that privilege as two ticketless women had wanted to share his six-foot-long seat. "Kindly adjust, please. Kindly adjust, please," they had said, their heads bobbing. And they had been hard to refuse with infants in their arms and large smiles on their sweating faces. He had gotten along famously with them. One woman had thrust her baby into his lap while she went to the platform to refill her water bottle and had almost missed her train. The other had torn a puffy Indian bread into long strips every few hours, dipped it into a vegetable curry, and shared it with him. He had finally stretched out on his seat when they left at Surat station, six hours before Mumbai, but at the very next station, sixty or seventy pilgrims in black skirts and white painted foreheads entered the train banging drums and chanting prayers en route to their patron saint's birthplace in Mumbai. In the train corridor, they lit up a small ritual fire using dirt rags. Max could still smell the gasoline and sweat from the train on his clothes over the whiff of marijuana in the hostel lobby.

He pressed the bell on the vacant reception desk again.

Rock star–long hair flying, a young Indian in his early twenties rushed in from the adjoining room. "Yo, sorry, friend. These Israelis are driving me mad," he said. "You need a room?"

Max shook his head. He showed the kid the piece of paper Anand had given him.

"My friend said this place is close to here and you can give me directions," said Max.

The kid looked at the paper. He removed his glasses and stared at Max. "Who told you about it?" he said. He blew air on the lenses and put the foggy glasses back. "Foreigners can't go there, friend. It's not safe. I won't feel right pointing you there."

Jesus, why was everything so difficult in India?

"I'll be careful," said Max, trying to keep his voice even. "Just tell me where it is."

The kid pointed to pictures of three bronze monkeys on the peeling yellow wall behind him, one with its hands in front of its eyes, another with hands on its ears, and the third with hands on its lips.

"Mahatma Gandhi's three monkeys. See no evil, hear no evil, talk no evil," he said. "Please don't make me talk of bad things, friend."

The kid reminded him of Omkara, with his intelligent eyes and cheeky grin. Max bent down and removed his hiking boots and socks. His foot odor overpowered the smells in the room. He lifted his right foot up and pointed to the torn white patches in his red skin.

"See these blisters," he said. "I have to buy new shoes. Where else can I find my size?"

The kid pinched his nose. "You are worse than the Israelis," he said. His smile brightened his eyes. "I'll tell you if you promise to buy new socks also. I didn't know anyone's feet could smell so bad."

He drew directions on the back of a paper and handed it to Max.

"If you get killed, make sure no one posts a bad review about this hostel, okay?" he said.

Max smiled. His head began to spin. He leaned against the wall on his side. His eyes were growing heavy, his mouth stale. The skin on his face felt rough and torn.

"I think I'll take a room for one night after all," he said.

"Good idea," said the kid. "You look like shit and smell worse."

He rummaged in the drawer of the table and handed Max a key.

"One floor up. It's my best room, friend," he said. "I don't know why, but I have a feeling you need it more than all the Israelis and Russians put together."

• • •

MAX CAME BACK DOWN after a shave and cold shower. He went to the brightly lit dining room next to the reception area to get coffee before he headed back out into the humidity and traffic. A group of Israeli backpackers with scruffy faces, matted blond hair, and bead necklaces around their necks sat around a plastic folding table. One strummed a guitar, another read a magazine, and a third smoked a joint. Four more loose, long-limbed bodies occupied red cushions at the back corner of the room, playing cards.

Max made himself coffee and sat down on a vacant chair at their table. He shifted in the uncomfortable plastic chair. His butt still hurt from the fall in the mountains and the endless train journey. Five PM. If he bought shoes in the next couple of hours, he could take the night train and reach Madurai by morning. Would he be in time to catch the morning bus to the village? If he couldn't catch the bus, he'd have to . . .

"Want a hit, man?" The blue-eyed, light-haired guy opposite him offered him a joint.

Max hesitated. He had sworn off drugs in high school when he'd seen a friend of Muscle's, Andre's elder brother, who often invited them for block parties thrown by local drug lords, burst a blood vessel in his eye while injecting heroin into the eyeball for a faster kick. The smoke hit his eyes. Max rubbed them. His fingers felt stiff, his elbow joints creaky. It would feel so good to numb the pain. And this was a joint, not a needle.

Max took it. He inhaled deeply, pressing his tongue against the roof of his mouth to hold the harsh smoke. His forehead exploded.

"Good shit, eh?" The Israeli smiled, yellow, stained teeth glinting.

Max nodded weakly. "Marijuana?"

The Israeli shook his head. "Afeeṃ," he said. "Opium."

Gusts of cool air circled through Max's body. His knee throbbed. Light pulsed through his brain like the dots and dashes of Morse code. The Israeli's face blurred. Behind him, above the hippies playing cards on the red cushions, hung a picture of Gandhi. Max's gaze fixed on his bald head and dimpled smile. He'd liberated millions from their bondage. *Give me answers too. Please. Free me. Please.*

Max took another drag. The knot in his back loosened. He moved his jaw, upper teeth touching his lower teeth. Something clicked in place. He felt hollow, silent, free of pain.

His mother must have been at peace on morphine.

Max's heart pounded. Jesus, he had quit his job to smoke opium in India like a fucking hippie. "I have to go," he said. His throat felt dry and cracked.

"You are from America?" said the Israeli.

Max nodded. A kernel popped in his temples. Everything drifted into a haze again.

"Americans. Always in a hurry, always places to go, dollars to make, wars to fight," said the Israeli. He lifted his arm and spun it around in concentric circles. "Just like my country."

Max tried to get up. He pressed his arms against the table, but his feet remained rooted to the ground.

"Learn peace in India," said the Israeli. "The whole world's problems are caused by man's inability to sit quietly by himself in a room."

Max's right arm extended in autopilot when the Israeli offered him the joint again. Another hit. Guitars twanged. The world lifted up. Max was relaxed, floating; he had become the light he was chasing. The music stopped. People got up. A bell rang. Doors opened and closed. Voices. A train to Hampi. Stopover in Goa. Max tried to concentrate.

"We have to go, man. Here, keep the rest," said the Israeli. He handed the half-burned joint to Max. "You are too tight, man. Loosen up."

Max looked up and thanked him. Hot ash dropped on his fingers. He felt nothing. Someone had switched on the radio set mounted next to Gandhi's picture. A news anchor announced in a clinical voice the bombing of a Nigerian mall. Max pictured the shrapnel exploding, cutting the skin of a small curly-haired black girl, drawing red, angry blood. The girl's blue face pressed against a store's shining glass window. Max's throat choked. Why did it happen? Why was she born if she had to die so young, so violently? Where did life come from? Where did it go? Didn't these questions bother anyone else? He looked around wildly. No one was in the room. He put his head down. The small girl's image disappeared. He breathed easily again.

"Is that weed?"

Max looked up. A woman his age with a shining face and soft brown eyes stood above him. Her long, flowing black hair touched his face. Was she real?

"You look very stoned," she said and laughed a light, musical laugh.

She came around the table and sat opposite him. Her skin was milky white, her body so light and fluid that she looked as if she had consciously decided to reduce her weight on earth.

Max offered her the joint. She reached for it. The sleeve of her long white shirt moved. Her wrist had a bright red tattoo of two sticklike figures locked in an embrace.

"Have you been here long?" she asked.

Max shook his head. The world settled again.

"Where are you coming from?" she said.

"The Himalayas," he said.

"It must be freezing there," she said. "I was in Goa. You should head there before the crowds descend for New Year. The sun is warm, the beaches heavenly right now. I've never had better fish, and their feni, the coconut-sap alcohol, is to die for."

She took a drag from the joint. Max felt the same emptiness in his stomach he often felt with dates in New York when they talked passionately of restaurants and bars.

There was an entire childhood between them.

Once you've known hunger, you ate only to fill your stomach. Alcohol loses its pull when you see your whole neighborhood crippled by addiction. Unheralded in every youthful drinking story was a broke-ass motherfucker like him who had cleaned up the vomit in the bar's bathroom with a rag. Not that this was a date. He had to get on with his journey. Too much time had been wasted already.

"Wow, this is strong," she said, pulling her abdomen in. She licked her lips. "It's opium. Where did you get it?"

"An Israeli," he said.

"This isn't Indian," she said. "It's exported from Afghanistan."

"How do you know?" he said.

"I was posted there in the army," she said.

Max looked at her with renewed interest. "Her Majesty's Army?"

She nodded. "American?"

Max nodded. "We are allies," he said.

She laughed. Their eyes met. Max put his feet firmly on the ground and pushed himself up.

"I have to leave for a market," he said.

She put the half-burned joint in the ashtray. "Can I come with you?"

Max hesitated. She was so pale, so beautiful. "They say the place is not safe for foreigners," he said.

"All the more reason you need me," she said. She made a symbol of a gun with her hand. "Oh-oh-seven. Lavin. Anna Lavin."

MAX AND ANNA made their way down the crumbling hostel staircase out into the narrow Colaba Causeway, which was lined with vendors selling everything—clothes, statues, books, jewelry, food. People begged, pushed, pleaded, threatened them. Buy something, please. You are beautiful, madam, your skin is so light, you need Ayurvedic face cream. You are so tall, sir, you need a gentleman's hat. Do you need a guru? Train tickets to Goa? Hashish? SIM cards? Meditation? Cell phones? Enlightenment? Discounts on everything. Max floated past them, his world still wobbly, eyes stinging with sweat in the hot, humid, smoky air. He touched Anna's arm lightly, guiding her, though she seemed completely at ease in the madness. She rolled up her sleeves. The couple embracing in the red tattoo on her wrist shimmered in the brightly lit streetlights.

The directions took them out of the busy street past a public park, where a sea of young boys played cricket in white shirts and pants, through a maze of narrow streets to a small tenement of sheds. They walked toward the huts, dodging the overflowing gutters and food waste, steering clear of the mangy stray dogs. The air was filled with the smell of burning plastic. They had entered the other Mumbai.

Six bony men smoking outside one of the makeshift huts looked up at them with glassy, vacant eyes.

Max repeated the name of the market.

They walked in the direction the men pointed. Half-naked kids rummaged through heaps of garbage—wastepaper, glass bottles, cardboard boxes, plastic cups—bursting out of the overflowing plastic bags that lined the street. They took a turn into an alley.

Improbably, the alley opened into a large green field the length of a football stadium. It was packed with people.

"Jesus," said Anna.

Thousands of men and women in shirts, pants, long Indian kurtas, shalwars, and saris thronged to rows of small hut-shops, shouting, screaming, bargaining. Max's heart beat faster. They were the only white faces in the sea of brown. He concentrated to rid himself of the shaky, out-of-focus feeling.

"What is this place?" said Anna, sounding a little breathless.

"A black market for stolen goods," he said. "Apparently, you can get anything you want in the world here."

Touts in stained white shirts, their thin, pockmarked faces shining with sweat, descended upon them. Buy. Buy. Buy. We have everything. What do you want?

Max touched Anna's hands. "Do you want to head back?"

"No, no, this is . . . strange. Amazing," she said.

Max and Anna walked toward the shops, the touts forming a loose circle around them, shouting bargains on antiques, electronics, drugs, aggressive but unthreatening. A six-foot Ganesha statue for three dollars. A hundred Vicodins for five dollars. A Kharma Enigma music system for a thousand dollars. Viagra pills for ten cents. An original Van Gogh for five hundred dollars.

A group of urchins raced past them chasing a giant black rat with a white belly. They flattened it against the wooden beam of a hut-shop and poked it with their thin sticks, laughing when its scared eyes bulged. The rat crumpled to the ground, dead. Bored, the kids left it and ran away to search for more rats.

A toy shop with a life-size panda covering its facade. A shop selling golden blond wigs, hundreds of them strung up on wooden beams inside the hut. Another filled with religious amulets of all faiths. A taxidermy shop with frog skeletons placed atop crumbling wooden tables. There seemed no method or organization in the arrangement of shops. Shops with printed umbrellas proclaiming *I Love New York* next to ancient Indian drug and spice stores with bags of roots and leaves, each shop impossibly filled with people bargaining and buying at rapid speed.

A short man with studious glasses emerged from a taxidermy shop with a stuffed deer on his shoulders. He was elbowed by a woman carrying boomerangs and Spider-Man masks, incongruous against her starched white sari and the red mark on her forehead.

The evening darkened. Yellow lightbulbs and white flashlights came on in the shops. Spicy food smells filled the air.

Max worried the market would close down. "Shoe shop?" he said to the men following them.

A sudden silence followed by a cacophony of shouts. "Giant shoes, giant shoes, giant shoes, giant shoes."

A ripple spread through the market. Touts shouting to shopkeepers, shopkeepers to other shopkeepers. Within minutes, a pregnant woman came running breathlessly through the crowd. She caught his hand. "Come, come," she said.

They followed her, wading through throngs of people, stopping at a hut selling bangles—hundreds and thousands of them in red, green, yellow, golden, blue, every hue of color, suspended from strings on wooden beams, fixed on nails on the mud walls, strewn across a table covered by a white cloth. The woman pulled a wooden box from under the table and threw the lid open to reveal plus-size rubber and canvas shoes, sandals and flip-flops. Nike, Adidas, Crocs, even Tom's shoes.

"You like?" said the woman.

Max nodded, speechless. Some of those shoes could fit men much taller than him. Yet he hadn't seen a single man in India taller than his six foot six inches.

"Can I take a photo?" said Anna. "No one would believe me if I told them."

The woman shook her head. "Not take photo. Take shoe."

Max put his hands in the treasure box, sat down on the mud floor, and started trying on shoes. He had the luxury of choice. Four or five pairs fit him perfectly. Max bought a pair of black Nike running shoes for one US dollar and put them on. He put his weathered Merrell boots in a plastic bag to take back with him, then hesitated. From the Grand Canyon to Kilimanjaro, the shoes had been with him for years. But they hadn't worked in India. Nothing had. He had to let go of everything he knew to move forward. Max gave the woman his hiking boots.

"How much you want?" said the woman.

"Nothing," said Max. "Keep them."

She stared at him. "Okay. No problem." She put the shoes into her wooden box.

They stepped out of the hut.

"I want Marmite," said Anna.

Again a human wave surged through the market. Another man tugged them to a shop. Soon Anna had a small glass bottle of black Marmite—available for sale only in England and Australia.

"Barry M Dazzle Dust," she said.

The British cosmetic was in her hands in ten minutes.

Next Max got new socks, T-shirts, and even running shorts that actually fit him.

Anna clapped her hands together. "I thought I had seen everything, but I've never seen anything like this," she said. "They sell tiger claws and elephant tusks in Togo, but none of the other stuff."

A man with a light mustache and a bright red scarf around his neck grasped her hand. "Animals, madam, come with me," he said urgently.

They looked at each other, then followed him.

Max's feet breathed easily again in his new running shoes and socks. Past the clutter of shops they went, ignoring the solicitations of touts selling Parisian fur coats, Jamaican coffee, Portuguese porcelain, and even a black moon rock. They reached the far end of the field. There the crowd thinned and the din quieted. A herd of thin cows slept on the withered grass. Max stopped.

"Please sir, come with me," said the man, his lips quivering.

He looked small and unthreatening. They followed him through the darkness, stopping at a thickly crossed barbed wire.

The man flopped down and went under the wire. "Please, please. Trust," he said, sensing their hesitation.

They flattened themselves against the mud field and crossed over to a dark street. A turn. Another row of shops with yellow wick lamps and blue-white flashlights. Cries. Smells. So many of them.

Each hut-shop was full of animal cages stacked on top of each other. Max's heart raced. Mewing cats. Yelping puppies. Aquariums with colorful fish. White signs with black English lettering. "Pets!" "Science Experiments!" "Exotic Animals!" "Protectors!" "Predators!"

There were more cages with parrots, sparrows, cockatoos, mynahs, crows, other blue and yellow birds, crying, cawing, shrieking. Smells of wet, mangy bodies, animal waste, and the sweaty humans standing in front of them. They walked past the cages in a daze. The shops were smaller, even more crowded than the ones in the large field. A woman walked past them with a wicker basket full of hens, another with twelve squawking parrots tied to a stick with a string, a man with an aquarium filled with sparkling blue fish, another with a burlap sack with a moving, squealing, indeterminable animal in it.

"Come, come, come fast," said the man.

Their morbid fascination pulled them forward.

Sheep. Rams. A deer with antlers. How could the animals survive in this heat? They took a turn in the middle of the huts. The lamps dimmed. The men standing in front of the cages were tall and heavily built, unlike the thin Indians he had seen thus far.

A glass jar with six large turtles paddling in knee-deep water, colliding against each other. Max stared, fascinated, at another closed jar with a bundle of yellow and black snakes locked in an embrace, unnaturally quiet. A ten-foot cage with a moving black mass in it. Jesus, a black bear. Another cage next to the bear with two zebras flicking their hind legs restlessly, nuzzling against each other, a terrified look on their faces.

This couldn't be legal.

Grunting followed by a sharp growl. Anna dropped the bottle of Marmite on the mud field. Her face was red, forehead lined with sweat.

"All animals. Everything. What do you want, sir?" said their guide.

The zebras cried.

Another growl.

Max's pulse quickened. "Let's go," he said.

He found Anna's hands and turned back. Their guide followed them. He caught hold of Max's shirt.

"Do you want tiger? Leopard? What? We have everything," he said. He bared his teeth and made a hissing sound. "Snake venom? Cure for sex disease, for all disease."

"Nothing, nothing," said Max, extricating himself from his grip.

"*Arre, faqir ho, sahib,*" said the man. "You are beggars, sir."

They retraced their steps quickly, walking with their heads down, ignoring the terrified squeaks, yelps, and mews, under the barbed wire, through throngs of people in the field, past the naked children sifting through the garbage in the alley outside and the stoned men in front of the huts, onto the main road. Civilization again. Max had never been more relieved to hear the pervasive Indian sounds conspicuously absent from the market: the honking and roaring of vehicles, the scream of sirens, the blaring music from the roadside religious processions and marriage parties.

"What was that?"

"Don't talk," said Anna. "Just kiss me. Please."

Max pulled her red face toward him and kissed her on the lips. She took a deep breath and pulled away.

"God, I'm sorry, I'm acting hysterical," she said. "For a moment, I was sure the bear would break open its cage."

"I didn't mind at all," said Max.

A woman on the sidewalk tried to sell them jasmine garlands to put on each other. Max took Anna's hands and walked through the Colaba market, toward their hostel.

"God, that was a zebra, wasn't it?" said Anna.

"And snakes?"

"That taxidermy shop had a stuffed elk," she said.

"And so many shoes and clothes my size?" he said. "I can't find such variety in a big and tall store back home."

"My fiancé was as tall as you," she said unexpectedly. "He was killed in Afghanistan six months ago."

Hats for you, tall sir? Ayurvedic cream for you, fair lady? Half price only. The man selling cosmetics and hats from the afternoon was back with deeper discounts. Max bought a hat, the mindless act of giving money and getting something regular in return making him feel in control again.

"I'm sorry, I should have told you before," said Anna.

"We just met," said Max.

She put her hand through her hair. Again, Max caught a glimpse of the tattoo of the couple on her wrist.

"You got this after?" he said, pointing to the tattoo.

"Before. We were together since secondary school," she said, her brown eyes dropping.

Max hugged her. "I'm sorry," he said.

"No, I must thank you," she said. "I've been traveling since I left the army six months ago but haven't felt alive until today."

His heart lifted. "I haven't felt more comfortable with anyone in years," he said.

Anna kissed him lightly on the lips. "Should we head back?" she said.

Max put his warm, sweaty hand in hers. They cut through the Colaba Causeway, dodging tuk-tuks decked in rainbows of colors racing past them, and made their way back to the hostel.

"HOW LONG ARE you planning to stay in Mumbai?" she asked as they climbed up the stairs to the hostel on the second floor.

He pressed her hands. "How long do you want me to stay?" he said.

Anna smiled. "I'll have to know you better to decide, won't I?" She walked him to his room.

"Are you sure?"

Anna nodded.

Max's groin tightened. He felt a familiar rush of blood. He opened the door to the small room with its dim light, peeling paint, and hard wooden bed. Water had seeped onto the bedroom floor from his bucket shower in the bathroom earlier that afternoon.

"We can take a hotel," said Max.

She walked into the room on the tips of her toes. Max hardened. He followed her inside. She sat on the bed.

"Is this for me?" She smiled, looking at the bulge in his pants.

She unzipped his cargo pants and fondled him. Max blanked his mind, trying not to come immediately. She put him in her mouth and sucked vigorously. Max put his hands on her head. Her back arched. He bent forward, unbuttoned her shirt, and fondled her warm, full breasts. She sucked harder.

Max pushed her against the bed. He took his shirt off and kissed her thin, angular body. The smells of her perfume mixed with the smells of the market. He entered her. She moaned, moving her arms up against her head. In a frenzy, he thrust harder. She thrashed around wildly. Max came with a cry.

SHE NESTLED IN his arms, her eyes wet with tears. He put his arms around her warm, naked body. The red tattoo on her wrist glistened with sweat.

Anna whimpered.

"It's okay," he said, ruffling her hair.

Max stared at the dirty pink bedsheet, feeling the familiar emptiness after the overpowering sexual urge had drained.

How long do you want me to stay?

He was fronting as some kind of a lover boy now. Just who was he? He had come to India to find the end of suffering and here he was fucking a vulnerable woman with a dead fiancé.

Max held her tight. Icy mountains. Afghani opium. Exotic markets. Zebras. Tigers. Sex. This was India. There was much to see, more to do. But he wasn't a hippie on a sightseeing trip. He had wasted too much time already; he had to get his act together. His backpack, soaked and dirty, lay propped against the bathroom door. Inside the zipper at the top was the address Anand had given him. Now he understood why Anand had been reluctant to share the address with him. Max didn't have the seeker's focus.

He touched the tattoo of the couple embracing on her wrist. "Anna," he said.

She opened her eyes. His chest tightened.

"I have to leave."

She smiled, covering her breasts with the bedsheet. "To get dinner?" she said. "I'll come. I could do with a good nosh up."

Max pulled himself up. "I have to get on with my journey."

Anna stared at him blankly. "Why so suddenly?"

He got up from the bed. "I didn't get a chance to tell you before," he said. "My mother died. I came to India to find truth, some insight. But again and again I'm just not . . . moving forward."

"I know what it feels like," she said. "You're just taking a break."

Max put on his pants. "No, I wasted many years after college like this," he said, tying his shoelaces. "I'm still the same person, still looking for things and experiences, getting carried away easily. I have to get away from all this."

She sat up, pressing the bedsheet against the curve of her body. "Where will you go?"

"I know of an ashram down in the south."

"And you have to go alone?"

Max nodded. "I need to learn to be silent. I need to become someone different altogether."

THE YOGI

The Yogi is superior to the ascetics and even superior to the men of knowledge. The Yogi is also superior to those who perform action with interested motive. Therefore, O Arjuna, be thou a Yogi.

—LORD KRISHNA, *THE BHAGAVAD GITA*

13.

At least he wasn't lost, thought Max. No one could get lost here. Everything was flat land, not a crop, farm, or shelter in sight, just orange earth and the narrow yellowish-brown dirt track on it. He poured another half a bottle of water on the towel around his head and gulped the other half down, his eighth liter since morning. Walking in the hundred-and-ten-degree heat made him a little dizzy, but he wasn't worried. He had packed enough food and water to survive a week if things went wrong. The shoes were his only mistake. Even the Nike running shoes were too thick for the scorching earth. His feet were full of blisters now. He should've gotten sandals instead. Not that they would have been much better. Avoiding physical discomfort in India was harder than seeing God face-to-face.

He ate yet another melting, gooey chocolate bar, one of the twelve he had bought in a shop outside the Pavur bus stand. His backpack straps cut into his shoulders. Four hours of continuous walking in the relentless heat. At this pace, he had at least six more miles to go to Ramakrishna's ashram. He didn't regret his decision to walk the twenty miles from the village. Not yet, at least. He had needed to overcome the sinking inadequacy he felt after his Himalayan misadventure. So he trudged along in the blazing afternoon sun, marveling at how quickly he'd gone from shivering in the Himalayas to sweating buckets in Pavur. It wasn't just the weather that had changed. The people in the South seemed smaller, darker, and quieter. They ate more rice and gave less advice. No one asked him why he wasn't married or judged his travel plans. They'd probably give him the same blank good-natured smiles they had during the journey if they saw him now—stripped down to just his underpants. Not that anyone was looking. He hadn't seen one sign of life in his fifteen-mile walk yet—no man, animal, or insect. Just hot wind and him, the last life in the universe. The heat seemed to have burned everything else to dust.

Two more hours of walking. Still nothing. His heart beat faster. He would turn back after forty-five minutes sharp, so he could walk back to the village before dusk. Half an hour later, he saw four thatched huts in the distance. Tears stung his eyes. He thanked the red sun above and sat down on the burning earth. A small round black beetle, the first life-form he'd seen all day, scuttled by. He put his T-shirt and pants back on, wincing as the rough cotton touched his sunburned skin. He removed his shoes and walked the remaining distance barefoot. The hot earth pressed against the blisters on his feet, yet it pained less than wearing shoes.

Max knocked on the wooden doors of the four thatched huts one by one. No one answered. The guru must be out in the fields. He took off his backpack and sat down on the long bench in the space between the huts, resting his head on the bare wooden table for a moment before going in search of him.

A TOUCH ON his back. Max looked up with a start. A thin, lightly bearded, middle-aged Indian man with big, silent eyes stood by his side. Max couldn't take his eyes off him. The man's smooth, unblemished skin radiated a white light.

"I'm sorry. I think I fell asleep. Are you Ramakrishna-ji?" said Max.

Ji, the Indian suffix of respect he had read in the guidebook but struggled to use, came without effort now.

The man nodded.

"I've come from far to see you," said Max.

"Did you walk from the village?" said Ramakrishna.

He spoke in perfect English but pronounced his words softly, politely, reminding Max of Viveka. Just fifteen days ago, but it felt like a different lifetime.

Max nodded.

Ramakrishna closed his eyes. "Mahadeva. Strong, self-willed, and obstinate," he said as if to himself. He opened his eyes. "You may rest now, if you prefer."

Max put on his shoes and followed him toward one of the huts. A toned, auburn-haired white woman in her late twenties swept the dust off the packed orange mud in the courtyard. She looked up at them through her scholarly horn-rimmed glasses.

"This is Shakti," said Ramakrishna, extending one long flowing hand in her direction. "And this is Mahadeva," he said, gently touching Max's shoulder.

The woman nodded at him without expression.

Mahadeva. Max's eyes burned from the salty, stinging sweat that poured down his temples. The blisters pressed against his shoes. No, he didn't need a new name. The woman resumed sweeping with complete concentration. Max stared at her. He wasn't a typical Westerner with a daddy complex looking for a guru to control his life. If he was going to learn something, he could learn it under his own name. What did this name and identity business matter in the spiritual world anyway? He'd bring it up once he knew the guru better.

Max stooped but still managed to bump his head against the hut's mud wall. A chunk of dried grass and twigs fell on his neck. Max wiped it away and entered the thatched hut.

Two colored pieces of cloth partitioned the bare hut into three parts.

"Hari is on the left, the middle is empty. You can take the space on the right if that is convenient," said Ramakrishna.

The roped wooden bed on his side of the partition was covered with a clean white sheet, freshly made as if they were expecting him. Had Anand called? But he hadn't seen a single phone cable anywhere in his twenty-mile hike. How did the man know he was coming then? Max shivered despite the heat.

"May I get you food?" said Ramakrishna.

Max shook his head. All he wanted just then was to be alone and put his head on the thin pillow.

"We stay silent here for nine out of ten days. This is the fourth day of this cycle. If you need something, please come to me in the other hut. Tomorrow I will explain more if you prefer," said Ramakrishna.

Max thanked him. He left. Max flicked the switch for the small lightbulb on the ceiling. No light came on. He took his shoes off, examined his swollen, blistered feet in the light shadow of dusk, and lay down on the hard rope bed. The mud walls and the straw roof gave some respite from the heat. He sweated less. A gecko darted toward the dark bulb on the ceiling. Max closed his eyes to stop himself from crying. He felt so lonesome.

A SHARP PINPRICK awoke him. Buzzing. A mosquito. Max clapped it. A hundred more attacked him, stinging his face, hands, and arms. He wrapped himself like a mummy in the bedsheet and closed his eyes.

Malaria.

Max sprang out of bed. He hadn't had any of his antimalarial pills since arriving in India. He'd be fucked if he fell ill in this wilderness. Max got the pills from his backpack and gulped two down with a bottle of water. Two-forty AM. Morning was still a long time away. Max went back to bed and slept immediately, unbothered by the buzzing, stinging mosquitoes.

The wall shook.

Max woke up groggily.

Someone rapped on the partition wall again.

Three-thirty AM. Who was it at this hour?

"Mahadeva," said a deep voice.

Were they all psychos? Like a mad cult? They could kill him in a ritualistic sacrifice and no one would ever know except perhaps Anand, who could be part of the cult himself.

The mud wall shuddered again.

He clenched his fists, then remembered Ramakrishna's glowing face from the night before. Relax, don't be an idiot. He opened his fists. "Yes, I'm awake," said Max.

"Time for yoga asanas."

Now? Max got up and pulled the separating sheet aside. A broad-shouldered muscular giant with curly hair and bright green eyes stood in the middle room.

"Hari?" said Max.

The man nodded.

"Okay, coming," said Max.

He took a cue from Hari's red T-shirt and loose pants and pulled out a cotton T-shirt and baggy shorts he had bought in Mumbai.

MAX WALKED OUT into the black night lit up by two oil lamps kept on the long wooden bench. Ramakrishna sat cross-legged in the packed mud wearing a bright white tunic and an orange cloth around his waist. Three rubber mats lay in front of him. On one sat Hari, on the second, Shakti, and the third was ostensibly for Max. Max sat down on the thin gray mat, mirroring Hari and Shakti's cross-legged pose. His thighs screamed. He shifted position, pushing his knees out and bending forward, but remained uncomfortable.

"First we do pranayama, expanding one's vital energy using the breath," said Ramakrishna.

He demonstrated while he instructed, likely for Max's benefit. Inhaling deeply, he thrust his abdomen out, then pushed it in sharply. He repeated the in-and-out motion two hundred times. Immediately after, he retained his breath for ninety seconds. They repeated the cycle three times, retaining the breath for longer and longer, going up to three minutes.

Max sputtered and swallowed, trying to follow along. He managed the in and out motions but couldn't retain his breath for more than a minute and a half at a time.

Next, they applied bandhas, or energetic locks. Max had read about this ancient yogic breathing practice to improve blood circulation in a book he had picked up in London. Now he followed Ramakrishna's instructions closely. First, Max took a deep breath in, then pushed his chin against his throat so that inhaled air couldn't come up the neck. Simultaneously, he pulled his perineum—the region between the genitals and the anus—toward the spine so that the breath couldn't leave his abdomen. The fresh inhaled oxygen was now trapped in his torso. As the logic went, until one released these energetic locks, the oxygen circulated slowly, deliberately, in and around the heart, liver, lungs, intestines, bladder, and pelvic area, rejuvenating every nerve, every vein, every cell in them. Oxygen was energy. Energy was life. If one applied bandhas long and well enough, the oxygen would revitalize the cells, slow the body's aging process, even reverse it. The yogi's body would become a complete, self-generating system in itself, not succumbing to age, sickness, or decay; the yogi would conquer time, as it were. Maybe that's why Ramakrishna's face shone like a lamp and the Brazilian doctor's perennial youth was mentioned in every blog post. But there was a logic flaw somewhere because . . .

Blood rushed to Max's face and his heart thudded from the influx of fresh air. He just couldn't think anymore.

"Lie down, my child. Corpse pose," said Ramakrishna.

Max lay on his back, spreading his hands and legs apart like a corpse, stealing a glance at his able compatriots, who had moved on to the next breathing exercise.

NEXT HE LEARNED sun salutations, a series of stretching and bending exercises that worked every part of the body from the tops of the arms to the backs of the legs, in an elegant dance.

After ten, eleven, twelve sets, his heart again threatened to burst out of his chest.

He lay down, watching the others complete eight more sets. This was so different from the one yoga class he had attended at a studio in Chelsea. It had been taught by a slender, smiling woman chanting Oms and urging the class to go deep within and feel their vibrations and energy fields. He had dismissed yoga as too soft and New Agey. Now he was dizzy from the effort. His stomach felt hollow and the nagging ankle and knee pains from the hike had flared up.

The "warm-up" was now over, said Ramakrishna. They were ready to begin the asana practice.

Begin? They must be an hour in already. A wave of dread surged through Max. The black night had given way to a full sun. Hot air stung his eyes. Orange mud, rivers of sweat on the mat, miles of desolation around him—how many days could he do this? Where would it take him? He hadn't traveled ten thousand miles just to sculpt his muscles.

"We'll start with Sirsasana, the headstand," said Ramakrishna.

Shakti and Hari bent forward, planted their elbows on the ground, propped their head between their palms, and lifted their entire body up, standing inverse in a straight line.

I'll never be able to do that.

Max knelt down on his mat, his mind an agitated knot. He didn't need to stand on his head. His body was fit. He had quit his job to learn Eastern philosophy, life's why and how, not to twist and turn his body. He'd leave that day itself.

"You can also try this. Just be here. Thoughts cannot depart to other dimensions in asana."

Max looked up at shiny-faced Ramakrishna. He wanted his stillness, his certainty.

"Now, place your elbows on the ground, chest width apart, and interlock your fingers."

Max followed Ramakrishna's movements. He planted his elbows on the ground, then his wrists and his head. His back arched. He walked a few steps forward. His legs lifted from the ground. Just a few inches up, not all the way straight up like Shakti and Hari's, but at least he was in the air.

"Just stay here. Feel the weight on your elbows. Tighten your abdomen. Don't go any higher today."

Max didn't want to go anywhere ever. Cool waves of air went down his body. He felt silent, awake. He closed his eyes.

"Now come down slowly."

Max came down to the mat. Shakti and Hari were still in the air, balanced on just their elbows and heads. Max took a deep breath and looked up at the blazing sun. He'd been similarly outclassed before. In his second week at Trinity, the English teacher had asked everyone to read aloud their homework essay about a family vacation. Other kids had written about visiting indigenous tribes in the Amazon, going on museum tours in Florence, building churches in Guatemala, and rescuing elephants in Tanzania. Max had written about a lunch his mother and he had in the Boathouse Lakeside restaurant in Central Park after saving up for a year. His classmates had stared at him in surprise and he'd had a crushing feeling in the pit of his stomach that he would never be able to catch up with them. But he had. He just had to work harder than everyone else.

FOR THE NEXT two hours, Max worked in the same state of feverish suspension he had worked years ago to get into Trinity and Harvard. He drowned out all his thoughts. There was no future, no past. This moment was all there was. This was his one chance, so he had to give it all he had. He followed the others, going from lifting his body supported only by the tips of his shoulders to inverting into a plowlike position with legs stretched beyond his head, arching the upper back like a cobra, lifting his legs up like an insect, and making them taut like a bow. Up and down, backward and forward they went, stretching and elongating the spine, exhaling stale air, inhaling streams of fresh air, rejuvenating all parts of the body. He kept pace, picking himself up when he fell behind, and fought the pain to hold each pose like Ramakrishna insisted.

"Hold the pose, hold the pose. Longer, longer," said Ramakrishna, soft but firm. "Asana means steady pose. You build concentration by holding. Hold. Concentrate."

They lay down in corpse position at the end. Max relaxed, loosening his mind, thinking about what he was doing once again.

Ramakrishna made them apply the two bandhas once more. Max understood the logical flaw that was bothering him now. Hemoglobin carried oxygen to the blood cells. Trapping air in the abdomen wouldn't increase hemoglobin production. The oxygen held in his torso wasn't going anywhere else in his body. Ramakrishna told them to stop after five minutes. Max lifted his head. Seven AM. The class was over three and a half hours after it had started. He got up. The discomfort in his spine was gone. His knees didn't hurt. He walked a few steps. The blisters on his feet didn't press against his skin. The pain from both yoga and the twenty-mile walk from the previous day had receded. He shook his head. It couldn't be the bandhas. How could the trapped oxygen travel all over his body? He was thinking about body chemistry again when Ramakrishna called him to his hut. Hari and Shakti disappeared without looking in his direction. Hari and Shakti. Funky names. Now he had his own funky new name to deal with.

MAX SAT CROSS-LEGGED facing Ramakrishna on the mud floor inside Ramakrishna's thatched hut.

"May you be feeling well?"

Max nodded. "I've barely done any yoga before."

Ramakrishna smiled, making his face glow so much that Max almost had to turn away.

"You have done yoga before," he said. "These postures are but one very small part of yoga. Breathing attentively is yoga. Complete absorption in your work is yoga. Thinking about others instead of yourself is yoga. Anything which makes you forget your small self and become one with the infinite is yoga."

Max was strangely tongue-tied. As always, he had questions, but Ramakrishna's presence was so peaceful, so complete, that Max didn't feel like listening to his own rambling, dissatisfied voice.

"You did asanas well. You have a gift," said Ramakrishna.

Max tried to hide his astonishment. He felt lumpy and light-years behind Shakti and Hari.

"Your eyes are restless, though," said Ramakrishna.

Max stiffened. Coming from a soft, polite mouth, the words felt like a slap. He looked at the fissures in the mud wall of the bare hut.

"So much agitation. So much loose energy. If you are unable to silence the mind, you will make very little progress here," he said. "Do you plan to stay here for a few days?"

No, I want to go back to the world where people thought I was calm under pressure, not someone with restless eyes syndrome.

Max nodded.

"Very good. I will learn a lot about asanas from you, even though the idea may strike you as unreasonable now," he said, his back erect as a column while Max stooped and shifted, trying to find the perfect alignment to sit comfortably cross-legged in. "We do asana practice from three-thirty until seven every morning, then again in the evening from three to six-thirty. In the day, we work in the fields. After dinner, we do three hours of meditation before bed at ten."

And sleep?

"Four or five hours of sleep are enough for a yogi. As you progress, even that will be too much. You can use that time to read some of the books that people have left behind if you choose."

How had he known the question that Max hadn't said aloud? Could he read his mind? He tried to empty his mind of all his rambling, restless thoughts.

"Many things will happen to you here, Mahadeva, some hard for the rational mind to understand. Take them for what they are, signs pointing toward the path, not the path itself," said Ramakrishna. "Look for answers within. I can see you like talking, debating, questioning. Nothing agitates the thought waves more. That's why we speak only once in ten days here, the same day we deliver food to the village. You can do any chores you want in Pavur town that day as well."

Contrary to Ramakrishna's impression of him, Max wasn't intimidated by the silence. Lately he had become more and more aware of the inability of words to express thoughts that truly mattered. Complete silence appealed to him. Today was the fifth day of the cycle. He had five full days to show his worth.

"We deliver food?" said Max.

"Half of whatever we grow goes to the village, no matter how little or how much we produce," he said. "Going beyond the narrow reaches of family and friends and feeding a stranger before feeding yourself is necessary. It purifies you, simplifies your life."

Max nodded. He paused. "Actually, I'm sorry, I meant do we walk to the village to deliver the food?"

Ramakrishna smiled. Again, his face blazed, lighting up the dark hut. "Walking will also become simpler soon. But we don't walk to the village. The food sacks are heavy. One of the village tractors will come by."

"I've never worked on a farm before," said Max.

"It requires some strength, some dexterity. You have a little of both," said Ramakrishna. "Your posture is loose and you are heavy. As you shed weight, become tighter, it will become easier."

I'm not fat. I'm a marathoner. But the face in front of him seemed to speak only truth without caring how it sounded. Max straightened his spine.

"May you have other questions?"

Max started to say something, then stopped. He didn't want to be judged for his restlessness again. Ramakrishna smiled. He probably knew what Max wanted to ask anyway.

"What is the point of all of this? Just what exactly are we trying to achieve?" said Max in a rush.

Ramakrishna shrugged. "People tell me different things. I don't teach anything, Mahadeva, I just live here. So you alone decide what you want and understand what you get. For me, yoga is both my path and my goal."

"And the name, Mahadeva, is it necessary? Can you just call me Max?"

"I will defer to your wishes on that, Max. However, Mahadeva is a good name. It means the powerful one," said Ramakrishna.

But Max wanted to transcend his ego, not transfer it to a different name.

Throw away the trinkets. Be a yogi, Max. "Mahadeva is fine," said Max.

"That is all," said Ramakrishna. He closed his eyes, then opened them again. "You should know I have not reached the end of yoga myself. My mind is not still enough to perceive the subtlest truth within. You have to decide whether you want to learn from an imperfect teacher."

Max's heart fell. If Ramakrishna hadn't reached transcendence yet, what chance did he have?

"We each have our destinies, Mahadeva," said Ramakrishna. "If you have walked on this path in another life, you may make more progress in a day here than I make in a lifetime."

Max nodded. If nothing else, he would gladly settle for reading people's thoughts like the man in front of him could. "I will stay. Thank you for taking me in."

14.

Max, now Mahadeva, squatted on an Indian toilet, nervously eying the frogs playing in front of him and bending as much as his screaming thighs would allow. He gave himself five days there. Just until the silence broke. That's it. Twenty percent would be done at the end of today, forty percent the next day. Then he would have crossed the halfway mark and the reverse countdown would start. He'd learn some basic yoga. Enough to practice in slightly more livable conditions, perhaps in Varanasi or a bigger city like Delhi or Bangalore. No, he didn't need much comfort, but these conditions weren't fit for humans. Perhaps they were fine for yogis who had transcended the limitations of space and time, but he had become so addicted to comfort, he didn't even like the idea of a cold shower in the blistering heat.

Max peered suspiciously into the large drum of water in the bathroom hut. Large black specks of something floated inside. Probably gecko shit. Because other than geckos, mosquitoes, frogs, and the plentiful red ants, every spot of the packed mud floor and walls was scrupulously clean. Thrusting the bucket inside the drum, he scooped out clean water. He poured the first mug of water on his torso. His heart jumped to his mouth. He hopped from left to right, right to left. How could the water under the scorching earth be so cold? Inhaling and exhaling slowly, he poured the water below his chest this time. Again, he jerked back, breathless and gasping.

What a privileged little fucker he'd become. He had lived without heat in the most severe of New York winters. He had taken cold showers in Trinity's gym every morning before going to class. Where had that Max gone? He poured another bucket of water on his head without worrying about breathing. His head pounded. But he didn't care anymore. Again and again he poured the water, filling more buckets from the drum until he had washed off all the dirt, grime, sweat, and dead mosquitoes.

Shivering and wet, he ran into Hari with his broad, freckled brown face when he came out of the bathroom.

Had fun? His green eyes seemed to smile.

Yes, Max nodded.

Hari pointed to the hand pump near Shakti's hut.

Ah, so the big drum needed to be replenished with water. Of course there was no housekeeping service in this luxury hotel. Max took the bucket to the hand pump. He had seen hand pumps before in his travels and in movies, though he had never operated one. He picked up the handle tentatively and gave it a little push. Nothing. He raised it up higher and pushed harder. A thin trickle of muddy water came from its mouth. Now he understood its function. He placed the bucket under the pump's mouth and lifted the handle higher, pushing it down with all his strength. A gush of water ran out, filling a tenth of the bucket. Ten thrusts more were needed to fill just one bucket. He walked back across the mud yard to the bathroom with the full bucket and poured it into the drum. Slightly less than a quarter full. He smiled. What a complete idiot he was. He had used seven or eight buckets in his zeal to get clean. Now he had to fill them up one by one by one and carry them to the bathroom drum until the drum was full again. Half an hour later, he had learned a lesson. Water is precious. It's even more precious when you replenish it yourself.

Soon he learned the same lesson about food. Every day they worked for hours in the blazing sun, sowing, plowing, harvesting, and cooking each grain of food themselves. Max plowed the hard earth; Shakti watered, fertilized, and spread the mulch; Ramakrishna harvested the day's crop; and Hari removed hard stalks and weeds with sharp knives. Then they cooked, Ramakrishna working the huller to remove the millet chaff, Shakti slicing and setting dry wood on the fire, Hari cooking the food, and Max cleaning the dishes. So they went, changing responsibilities every day, united in their quest to break the hard, fallow land and make it yield enough for them and the villagers. Max adapted quickly to eating millet, a cheap rice substitute that looked suspiciously like what the cattle were fed at his uncle's farm in Greece; eggplant; and a slender green stick-like vegetable called drumstick. Sometimes they combined the three into a curry, sometimes they ate them separately, but it was always these three crops every day in the two meals they had, for the dry land bore nothing else. They tasted like . . . nothing. Just flat, soft, and chewy cud. But Max felt heavy and full after eating them, which when he thought about it was enough.

15.

On his fifth morning, the eighth of the ten-day silent cycle, Max didn't move from his bed when he heard Hari shuffling next door. No, he thought, I can't keep at it another day. He was done. It wasn't the hard work in the fields that got to him, though. He actually liked it. Farm work was real work, not pushing paper around or running numbers and creating presentations for pre-alignment meetings before alignment meetings. A thrill passed through his aching, sore muscles every time he forced the plow to break the unforgiving earth. The sun peeled his skin, the wooden plow handle rubbed his palms raw, yet it was miraculous, almost divine, to picture a shoot emerging from a mere seed, breaking the earth, becoming a plant, and sustaining the one that had sowed it.

Neither, he learned, was he tired of having the same food every day. The passionate discussions on restaurants and menus had always grated on his nerves in New York. Here food was simple, focused, the way it was in his childhood. You ate what came your way, grateful to have a meal at all. It restored your energy and you thought no more of it. Nor did asanas faze him much. He could sense his body changing in just a few sessions—his spine crackled, his hips opened up, and his lower back felt hard and strong. Always a light, anxious sleeper, he was sleeping better than he had in years, perhaps because his mind didn't wander in a thousand directions all day the way it used to back home. Asanas, pranayama, field work, cooking on the wooden fire—everything required single-minded absorption, so that when it came time to sleep, his mind had been trained to think of just sleep and not the activities of the day.

Yes, he could've made the ashram his home for a bit—if it were not for the silence, that is.

The silence turned more and more oppressive with each passing day. Not the absence of chatter but the presence of the vast, unending sameness. Just five days in, but each minute felt exactly the same. The scorching sun, the huts, the three impassive faces around him, and the infinite orange mud. Nothing changed. Even more than change, perhaps, he missed control. He wanted to do something to shatter the atmosphere. Order pizza after meditation, sip a Diet Coke on the burning farm, joke with Shakti during asanas, ask Hari where he had got his green eyes—anything that broke the heavy silence. It didn't feel human. They were just programmed circus monkeys doing acrobatics under the command of a bearded, shining face ringleader. For four days, he had jumped through all the hoops. Now he was done.

Three-thirty. Hari's heavy feet shuffled out.

Today Max wouldn't get up. Hadn't Ramakrishna said everything was one's own choice?

He turned on his side.

Heavy inhalation and exhalation sounds outside. They had begun pranayama.

He turned again.

No, he wouldn't get up.

The sounds stopped. They must be holding their breath.

How long would they keep holding? He counted one hundred and fifty seconds, then one hundred and ninety seconds, two hundred and ten, *four full minutes.*

Jesus, they were still holding.

Were they holding longer because the weakest link in the chain was absent? But he hadn't shown them what he was capable of just yet.

Max jumped out of bed. Today he would hold his breath until he choked and died.

He joined them for the next round.

They continued the rest of the practice as usual.

FOR THE REST of the day, Max kept planning to quit but didn't. He wondered if Ramakrishna had drugged his food so he became a bovine, unthinking, unquestioning little hamster, just like the other two. His irritation at Jesus-face Ramakrishna turned to annoyance at himself. The problem wasn't the silence. It was that *he* wasn't silent. Ramakrishna was right. His mind was on fire. It violated every yogic precept Ramakrishna had talked of, claiming it wanted enlightenment when it craved pleasure, coveting the comfort of chatter, committing violence when it thought negatively about Ramakrishna. His mind knew no contentment, no peace, no maturity.

And meditation was the greatest charade of all. He had thought he would learn quickly. That's what he had come to India for, after all. He'd read in his yoga books that the human form was incomplete and that the end of suffering lay in reaching a union with permanent consciousness within. But for the three hours he sat cross-legged with his eyes closed trying to empty his mind of thoughts and think of consciousness, he was tormented by the same images. He, twelve years old, putting his black jacket over eight-year-old Sophia's head when the cops pulled a bent, blood-soaked old woman from a sewer opposite their building. "She looks like a turtle," Sophia had said later. Max hadn't been able to stop her from seeing the dead woman. Neither had he been able to stop kids from bullying her in PS 65 after he went to Trinity. Her eyes would be full of tears when she came back from school. Just like Keisha's eyes were when he left her. He'd been so cruel to Keisha. Her family wasn't as poor as the rest of the people in their neighborhood and had owned a grocery store and even their own house on Cauldwell Avenue. For years, Keisha, Sophia, and he had studied together in the basement of her house, away from the gunshots and firebombings of Mott Haven. Her father had talked to him about men building colonies on the moon one day; her mother had cooked for him. He wouldn't have made it to Harvard without their support. In return, he had robbed them of their joy, their life forever. What right do you have to seek peace when you've caused so much pain to so many people, Mahadeva? Max, I'm Max, he repeated to himself.

Just two nights left, eighty percent over, twenty percent to go, it's over, soon now. No, he was helpless. Without any masks to wear, without the need to front as someone, he had fallen apart. He couldn't rein in his mind no matter how much he tried to focus on the space between his eyes or observe his breathing. This just wasn't his path. But where would he go next? New York was too soft; India was too harsh. What did little Goldilocks want?

THAT NIGHT HE dreamed that the water in the hand pump had turned into sulfuric acid. He opened his eyes. A wave of hot bitter liquid surged from his abdomen into his chest. It wasn't a dream. Ramakrishna had forced sulfuric acid down his throat. No, it was . . . He stumbled out of the hut and puked his guts out in the squat toilet a few yards away from their hut. As he stood over it, vomiting, a grayish-black snake with white bands, ten feet long, slithered away from the toilet bowl toward the open door.

Fuck, there's a snake in the toilet, a snake, screamed Max—silently.

He'd almost stepped on a snake. His stomach contracted and heaved. He vomited again, then squatted on the toilet, and relieved his bowels. So the Delhi belly had struck finally. Or more accurately, the desolate-ashram-with-mud-in-the-hand-pump belly. Why had it taken so long? It should have happened days ago.

He put his hands against his heated face and staggered up, faint and spinning. Where would he get medicine here? He was dead. Ramakrishna and Hari were waiting for him when he walked outside after scrupulously cleaning up every smear of vomit from the bathroom floor with a rag kept in the corner and washing it with clean water from the drum.

"How bad is it?" said Hari.

Finally I made you break your silence, I did, I did, I did, Max exulted, dizzy and incoherent.

"There is a snake," said Max and tried to say more, but the words wouldn't form in his mouth.

They supported him to his bed and Ramakrishna made him drink a foul-smelling green liquid. Max gulped the hot potion down without protest.

"Rest today, rest all day," said Ramakrishna, putting his hand over Max's burning head.

Max nodded and slept.

His watch alarm went off at three-fifteen. He switched it off. As he did, his head exploded, his body burned. He was going to die. But hadn't he read that a permanent consciousness beyond birth, suffering, and death lay within him? *Concentrate on that.* Oh, but his stomach hurt so fucking much. He turned to his side and tried to sleep again. His stomach rumbled again. Max rushed to the bathroom.

RAMAKRISHNA WAS SITTING in his usual cross-legged position in the courtyard on his way back. Shakti and Hari would join any time now. Today Max officially had the day off. He went back to his hut. Moments later, he heard Hari shuffling out.

Max turned on his other side.

Soft voices outside.

He turned again.

Ramakrishna had begun his instructions.

No, he couldn't miss this. He sat up in his bed and coughed away the burning feeling in his throat, then joined them in the courtyard.

You don't have to, said the expression on Ramakrishna's face.

I want to, was Max's unvoiced response.

Max's palms sweated with every pumping of the first pranayama. Shivers ran down his spine. His throat gagged at the end of three rounds. He coughed and had to hurry to discharge the greenish-yellow phlegm in the bathroom. As soon as he did, a pleasant, cool sensation went down his throat and the bitter bile aftertaste subsided. He joined the others and sat back down.

Likely in response to Max's condition, Ramakrishna taught them that day a new breath lock, the Uddiyana Bandha, an abdominal purge. They stood up, leaned forward, and forced the stale air inside the torso out, then pulled the abdomen inside the rib cage with a powerful physical contraction. Fifty or sixty times they went, churning the abdomen from left to right, then right to left, again and again, faster and faster like an eddy swirling at maximum speed. At the end of three rounds, Ramakrishna taught them to practice the Maha Bandha, or the Great Breath Lock, a simultaneous application of all three breath locks—chin, abdomen, and perineum.

Max lay down quivering on the floor after applying the Maha Bandha, too spent to do even a single asana.

He closed his eyes and didn't open them again until class ended. When he got up, he wasn't dizzy anymore. Instead, gusts of fresh air circled through his body. His stomach felt light, his skin pleasantly warm. He walked around shaking his head in disbelief. His mind couldn't accept what his body told him.

He felt fine.

It was a delusion, an exaggerated exuberance from the oversupply of oxygen in the head. Circulating your abdomen like a madman for an hour couldn't cure something that needed days of rest and medicine. Max went to the bathroom and tried to puke. Nothing. He squatted down. Nothing. Not only was he cleansed of his illness but he felt lighter. He would live another day. Tomorrow he could leave, if he chose.

MAX AWOKE THE next day with tense excitement. Today he could talk—and leave. The brilliance of the asanas and pranayama exercise was unquestionable, he knew now after his symptoms didn't surface again. But how long could one keep up with the complete silence? Ten more days, perhaps even a month if he pulled in every ounce of reserve, but it had to end sooner rather than later. He had thought that he could handle any hardship because he'd grown up in a kind of urban purgatory, but he was wrong. The self-imposed silence here felt more oppressive than the gunshots and screams of his old neighborhood. Surely he'd find someone like Ramakrishna elsewhere in India and build to excellence in more hospitable conditions.

Silence would break after the three-thirty AM asana class. His last class. Max walked to the warm courtyard in the darkness, surprised not to feel the exhilaration he expected after anticipating this moment for days. He sat in his usual spot for the breathing exercises, feeling stronger than he'd ever felt. A lifetime of waste seemed to have been purged from his system. Ramakrishna had done him good. Never before, never again perhaps, would he learn from a man of this stature.

As the class progressed, hour after hour, each pose felt smoother, more intentional. Then the final bow pose. His last asana in the ashram. Max lay flat on his stomach, pulling his legs off the ground by holding an ankle in each hand behind him. He straightened his arms and pulled his legs higher until only his navel touched the ground. His lungs filled up. Warmth spread through his spine. His neck strained. The blazing sun above was so close. He pulled his legs with all his strength. Suddenly his navel lifted a little off the ground. A rush of air went to his head. His navel touched the ground again.

For a moment, he had flown.

Stunned, he looked up at Ramakrishna standing beside him. Ramakrishna's face was impassive as usual.

Of course he hadn't flown. It must have just felt like it. Right?

"You are better today, I see," said Ramakrishna.

That was when Max knew he wouldn't leave. Not until he reached a shadow of Ramakrishna's greatness. Selflessly opening his doors to strangers; offering everything his land produced to others before taking a morsel himself; a mind restrained and composed, not restless and hungry. Max had come to India to become a yogi, a Ramakrishna. How could he think of leaving for petty comforts like hot showers and mindless chatter?

Max got up, breathless, his face warm, his body pulsing with streams of energy. He had never felt this way after asanas. He felt giddy. *Maybe he had flown.* The air was electric with possibility. He breathed deeply to calm himself down.

Max faced Ramakrishna, struggling to put his thoughts into words. "The pranayama cured me," he said finally.

He wanted to say more, to thank Ramakrishna for allowing him to stay there, to express his gratitude for the gift of Ramakrishna's teaching. But as usual, he fell silent in his presence and couldn't look into his eyes.

"You cured yourself," said Ramakrishna.

"Yes, you learn fast," said Shakti with the freckles and reddish-brown hair, joining them. Her severe, impenetrable face softened when she smiled. The severe black-rimmed glasses now looked cute. She spoke with a thick Italian accent. "I am here six months and I do not make headstand as straight as you. I saw you the first day. You have not even practiced asana before, have you?"

Max shook his head.

Shakti raised her hands up in the air and threw her head back. "Wow," she said.

"You must have in a past life, for sure," said Hari in a Middle Eastern accent, joining them in front of Max's yoga mat.

Max smiled. In India, talking about past lives seemed as common as discussing the Yankees lineup back home. He felt a sudden pang of guilt for saying good-bye to Sophia so hastily. Now that he had decided to stay here, would he get a chance to call or email home?

"You can walk from the village to Pavur. You will find everything you need there," said Ramakrishna.

Max's pulse quickened. He tried to empty his mind of any lingering negative thoughts.

"I go there today also," said Shakti. "We go together."

RAMAKRISHNA FOLDED his hands and excused himself. Max stood with Shakti and Hari in the courtyard, chatting, laughing, the sun no longer oppressive, the day alive with potential. They shared the basics. Shakti, previously Lucia, was an Italian astronomer, who was using a one-year university sabbatical to find out who she really was. Hari, previously known as Ahmed, an Egyptian film actor, had quit the movie business after a fortuitous encounter with Buddhist meditation. Hari had been at the ashram for nine months. In a few minutes of talking to them, Max felt more understood than he had by people he'd known all his life in New York. They were burning with the same ineffable questions that he had. One day the fire had raged so strong that they had left career, love, and life behind to answer them. But neither seemed troubled by their choice. Hari, in particular, looked completely at peace in the ashram and hadn't been to the village or surrounding town for months. He wanted to direct his prana, his vital energy, inward and not fritter it away the way the world did, in travel, in conversation, in frenzied movement that tried to quell the restless mind but further agitated it—quite like the activities Shakti and Max were planning that day.

"So okay, we get ready. The tractor arrives any time now," said Shakti and laughed a surprisingly girlish laugh. "Tractor arrives any time now—so many months and I still laugh when I hear. How my life changes."

16.

The old man who had driven in the big faded red tractor from the village to the ashram welcomed them with a warm, toothless smile. They adjusted themselves and three bags of produce—two with millet, one with drumsticks—on the narrow metal front seat.

Shakti had pulled her hair into a ponytail. She wore a light purple dress and a beaded orange necklace with matching earrings, the dash of color giving a radiant glow to her tanned skin. Max was glad he had picked up a new pair of khakis in Bombay. Between the hikes and the bus and train journeys, his cargo pants were falling to pieces.

Shakti said something.

It was lost in the din of the tractor's motor as it rumbled

toward the village. She moved closer to him. He gripped the seat tighter to avoid flying off the open-air vehicle.

"How is your first week?" she said.

Max pulled the spare T-shirt he carried tighter around his head to protect against the beating sun. "A good experience," he started to say but stopped when it struck him how precious speech was.

"I'm struggling," he said. "Badly."

Shakti's eyes narrowed. "But you look like you adjust well," she said. "Eight or ten people came in last six months and they all leave in first week itself. You feel uneasy when that happens, so I think both Hari and I are happy to see someone who can last."

"I can't meditate," said Max.

"You have not meditated before?" she said.

Max shook his head.

She raised her hands in the air. "You are crazy. People come here after many years of making yoga and meditation," she said. "I practice for nine years, Hari for much longer, and even people who come and leave practice for many years. And you just drop in from nowhere? How do you even find this place?"

Max explained his saga over the roaring motor.

"Incredibile," she said. Loose strands of hair flew in all directions. "No one knows of this ashram. A monk in my village in Italy who tells me about Ramakrishna says path to him opens only when you blaze in desire for truth for many lives. But you just come here like it is winter skiing holiday."

Not exactly, thought Max, remembering the glaciers he had crossed barefoot on his way to Bhojbasa.

"Past life. Good karma." She shrugged.

Max stared at her sure, angular face. "You believe in that, being an astronomer and everything?" said Max.

"I believe because I am astronomer," she said.

"How?"

"Yoga is *figo*, the real thing. You will see soon. It is science," she said. "When I was in university ten years ago, I analyze gravitation, energy fields, solar systems, and I find everything is more similar than different. I think there is one principle in universe. I started doing yoga around same time and understand yoga philosophy says exactly that." Her black eyes got bigger under the glasses. "Centuries before modern science, the yogis say origin of the universe is one vibrating energy. In the beginning, it shimmers alone, then it goes from one to many, manifesting the whole material universe: space, time, the sun, the moon, the oceans, landforms, everything."

"Like the big bang?" said Max.

"Yes, yes, just like big bang," she said, adjusting her glasses. "Only science makes original energy dry and without attribute. Yogis say it vibrates with life, energy, intelligence, good, bad, everything—the sum of all attributes. That makes sense to me. I struggle with scientific view that an intelligent universe like this one creates itself out of unintelligent molecular mass in a fraction of a second. It just can't be. After that, I study more ancient yogic text. The yogis in 10 BC are like scientists. Not just scientists, like . . . mystic also. They analyze nature. They go within man. They find that like nature, essence of all life is also same alive, intelligent energy. Insects, animals, you, me, everyone—our core is same. Call it God or consciousness or whatever you want. But underlying us all is just one energy. We just don't see it as that because it is covered by layers of individual thoughts and desires," she said.

Max had read this before, but after a week of silence the dots connected more fluidly. He understood Ramakrishna's words better now. Yoga stilled the fluctuations of the individual mind's helpless thought waves, allowing it to see the one unchanging energy, the unborn, un-aging, un-ailing, sorrowless, and deathless state within that Viveka had talked about. If indeed all this was true.

Shakti poured half a bottle of water on her head. It dripped from her hair to her slender neck and down her bare arms.

"I like yoga science very much," she said. "No praying, chanting, singing. No nonsense about suffering is good or God is all-powerful. Yoga also says God, this energy, is both the field and the knower of the field. But he doesn't need to be all-powerful. Inside the field, life runs by same impersonal cause-and-effect laws as nature. You think bad, do bad karma, you get suffering, no God helps. You work hard, you move forward and evolve like Darwin's natural selection. Until one life after many lives of moving forward, you become a human. Now you have sophisticated intelligence for first time. You find this up-and-down, ever-changing nature of life incomplete. You go inner, you do yoga, silence your mind, lose identification with your thoughts, desires, the whole sense of I, and become the One."

Max regretted not having discussions like these since he was twenty and stoned in his suite at college. Where had the last decade gone? One job, then another, dinners in fancy restaurants, trying to become a part of a world he didn't belong to, draining precious prana.

The tractor slowed. Thatched huts appeared in the distance. The bumpy dirt track became smoother.

"How do you know all this? I want to learn these things myself. What books do I read?" said Max.

"Why are you in such hurry? You just started," she said, knotting her hair again.

"I don't know. Why should I wait?" said Max.

"You are very American. Hurry, hurry, hurry," she said. "Just meditate on it, bud."

Max laughed. "How do you speak such good English?"

"How do you speak such good English?"

"Well, I mean . . . you know, I grew up in America," he said.

"Well, I mean . . . you know, I grew up in Italy," she mimicked.

Max reddened. "I'm sorry. I didn't mean it like that," he said.

Shakti threw her head back and laughed. "I was just making a joke. I know Italians don't speak English well. But I did my master's at Princeton. I learned better there," she said.

The tractor stopped next to the village well. They jumped out. Shriveled, blackened women in colorful saris sat in a circle around the well, gossiping, laughing, looking unbothered by the blazing sun. Naked children played with marbles next to them. Ahead in the fields, men pulled large, heavy plows and women watered the millet plants. Max didn't feel apart from them anymore. He could picture their lives better now, squeezing the barren earth for every grain, the difference between a good crop and a bad crop meaning life or death. Life back home with its doormen, gluten-free diets, and soy and nut allergies felt soft, easy, and entirely useless.

A weathered old man came out of one of the huts. Max helped

him take the sacks to a storage place at the back of the hut. The man folded his hands and thanked him.

"Pavur has telephone and even laptop with Internet dial-up. You want to walk?" said Shakti when he came back, sweating.

"Isn't it six miles away?"

"Ten kilometers, yes, about," said Shakti.

Max groaned.

"Inhale, exhale, inhale, exhale," said Shakti, mimicking Ramakrishna.

Max laughed.

"Seriously, it helps. Just exhale long to count of six," she said.

Once again, pranayama worked its magic. The careful, long exhalation meant an automatic long inhalation, which brought a fresh supply of revitalizing oxygen into his body. He wasn't the breathless, sweaty mess he'd been when he had walked from the village to the ashram.

HALFWAY INTO the journey, Max gave up the studied breathing. He could walk easily the rest of the way.

"You said I should meditate on the consciousness within," he said. "Isn't meditation about emptying the mind of thoughts?"

Shakti exhaled loudly. "First, you practice concentration," she said. "Slowly your mind becomes sharper and sharper. Now when you meditate on something, you just think of that thing only. No other thoughts left. You meditate on consciousness, you become pure consciousness. This is goal of yoga. It can take many years, many lives. You can't jump or hurry like American."

"If meditation is the goal, why do we spend so much time exercising every day?" said Max.

"Asana and pranayama are just to keep your body fit," said Shakti. "If body is not silent, how can mind inside be silent?"

Again, it made sense. In the three hours he sat for meditation, he constantly crossed and uncrossed his legs, stooping and fidgeting in an effort to find a comfortable position. No wonder his mind was so restless.

"Why doesn't Ramakrishna teach us all this?" he said.

"Did you hear anything about him before you come here?" she said.

"That he is a great man," said Max.

"Nothing more?"

Max shook his head.

"I hear other things," she said.

Aha, spiritual gossip. "What things?"

"He will not like we talk about him," she said.

"Come on, it's just us," said Max. "Not like word is going to spread in this desert."

"So okay, he comes to this village many years ago—fifty, maybe sixty, no one knows for sure—when he is a young boy, thirteen or fourteen years old," she said. "Without any help, he builds a hut thirty-five kilometers away from the village. He lives alone there since then. He says he learned yoga from his guru, but no one has ever heard or seen his guru. No one knows his parents. No one sees him with any family ever. No one sees anyone visit him except his students. Who is he? Where does he come from? How does he learn what he knows? Why does he teach?"

Max stared at her. "I don't know. What does that mean?"

"Villagers say he is reincarnation of Jesus," she said.

The savior was back. Max thought of the wild-haired homeless men camping on the green benches in Central Park who promised Max when he ran past them that Jesus was coming back soon. Some things never changed whether you were running in New York or melting in a remote South Indian village, where a missionary had likely traded food for belief.

"That's such bullshit," said Max.

"I agree a hundred percent. That is not yoga science. Jesus has realized oneness. Like Buddha. Like Muhammad. Like anyone can. He is not born again in the world," she said. "I think Ramakrishna is very successful yogi in past life. Not enlightened, though. This life maybe he gets full liberation. He knows yoga from past. That's why easy for him to do, difficult for him to teach. You will see. He can do very difficult yoga pose himself but cannot tell you how you can do it step by step. Same in meditation. He can sit in meditation for hours, but he cannot explain how you can meditate."

They reached small, dusty Pavur. Men rode long black bicycles at a leisurely pace around them. A cow lingered in front of a mom-and-pop store, its nose touching the chips and cookies dangling on a string from the shop's facade. Next to the store, men wearing skirtlike white cloths around their waists sat on their haunches smoking beedis, thin leaf-wrapped Indian cigarettes. Opposite the store, a stray dog urinated on a shuttered shop advertising mobile phones.

Attracted by the glass bottles of soda on the counter of the mom-and-pop store, Max and Shakti bought a Pepsi each, then quickly gobbled chocolate biscuits and Lays chips, enjoying the sticky, sweet, salty, familiar taste of home. A clot of kids gathered around them. A ragged kid touched Max's arm and mimed being struck by an electric shock from his unfamiliar white skin. Max and Shakti laughed with his companions and bought them each biscuits and drinks. Their thin brown faces lit up. Max shuddered involuntarily. Years ago, he had gone to a Trinity girl's Sweet Sixteen party. The girl's father had flown in a band from New Orleans and showered her with gifts from cars to diamond necklaces. Max's heart had filled with rage that Andre's mother had to beg money from her neighbors to buy him a wheelchair while this girl test-drove a shiny new Mini Cooper. Was that karma? he thought now. An unbroken chain of cause and effect continuing from one life to another, bringing pain or pleasure as one deserved until one broke out of the cycle for good. It felt even more unjust. Could he really believe that the kids in front of him with their angelic faces and easy smiles had been mass murderers in their previous life? In a fit of guilt, he bought them another packet of biscuits each. They cheered.

"Do you want to see Internet or make phone call?" asked Shakti.

Max's stomach tightened. Was Sophia fine? He'd never forgive himself if something happened to her. *Chill.* She wasn't a kid in the projects anymore. She was probably having brunch with her tree-hugging friends in hipster Brooklyn.

"Internet is great," said Max.

They turned into a narrow mud road that had along it an empty tea shop, three shops with assorted clothing, and two general merchandise stores. Pavur's main market ended there. Shakti pointed him to one of the general merchandise stores and went to the adjoining one to make her phone call. He stooped and entered a shop with half-shut steel shutters. A hairy man stood behind the counter. His mouth opened on seeing Max.

"Giant," he said.

Max smiled. Behind the man were shelves filled with paint, hammers, pliers, nails, wires, fixtures, and bulbs. Biscuits and assorted fried Indian snacks lay on the counter. Hardware and snacks, an odd but soothing combination. Work hard, eat well. But he didn't see any computer in sight.

"Internet?" said Max.

The man nodded and went to the back of the shop. He came back with a small laptop covered with dust. Without wiping the dust off, he opened the cover, put it on the counter, and hooked up a modem and a USB cable.

"Now, okay," he said after ten minutes and gave the laptop to Max.

The Internet Explorer was slow, his Gmail even slower. The connection went in and out for half an hour before it eventually connected in basic html. Max scanned his email. A note from Sophia.

> **Maxi, I'm really worried you are never coming back . . . you don't give up. Ever. But this time you aren't chasing Trinity or Harvard or private equity, you're asking questions that have no answers . . . I just think you'll never stop looking. Don't do this, Max.**

Max wrote quickly to Sophia before the Internet went out again.

Don't be crazy, Sophie. I'm just traveling for a bit. Chill, ok?

No email from Andre. It didn't surprise him. Andre wouldn't feel right telling Max he was making a mistake once again when Max had paid for his college and living expenses for years. The silence between them had grown even before Max left New York. They weren't equals anymore. Was any relationship pure? Even friendship was complicated. Max returned to his email.

A long note from Anna. She was thinking about their night together and how they had shared something special. Why had he been so abrupt? Would they see each other again? Their brief encounter seemed such a distance away. He closed the email and went on to the next.

Notes from friends. The word had spread that he had quit his job to travel. People were surprised, shocked, even glad that one frog had jumped from the well. They sent updates of their own lives.

Just five days in silence and he felt overwhelmed by this sudden influx of information. He inhaled and exhaled six times and shut down his email.

OUTSIDE THE SHOP, he wished he had written a longer email to Sophia and had at least acknowledged Anna's message.

"Someone looks like they are missing their girlfriend."

Whoa, could Shakti also read his mind? Max turned around. She flashed him a cheeky, flirtatious grin. A tall, toned, auburn-haired astronomer with a cute accent and cuter glasses, Shakti was the ultimate geek fantasy. Yet he felt only a distant, detached sort of attraction for her, and one he had no desire to pursue. All he wanted was to start making progress in his quest. He had left behind far too much to fritter away his time.

"I don't have a girlfriend," he said.

Shakti walked up and high-fived him unexpectedly. The owner of the hardware-snack-Internet shop stared at them curiously.

"Good for you," she said. "I should break up too. This path is lonely. No one understands. My parents will disown me now because I don't believe I am born because Adam and Eve had apple for breakfast. My boyfriend thinks watching football leads to enlightenment."

Max laughed. He felt his tension break. "You'll find someone in India," he said. "Like Hari, the handsome film actor."

"I do not think he knows difference between Ramakrishna and me," said Shakti.

"Is he very serious?" said Max.

"He has lived with Ramakrishna two times before. I think this time he makes promise to himself that he will not leave the ashram until he achieves enlightenment," she said. "He never comes to town. He never talks for more than a few minutes even on the tenth day."

Max wanted to be like him.

Shakti pulled her hair out of her ponytail. "For last six months, I speak so little. I feel happy you came. Do not go away soon."

Their eyes met.

"I need to buy some snacks," said Max, looking away.

"Why?"

"I'm still adjusting to two meals a day. Sometimes I feel hungry in the night," he said.

They walked up the mud street and turned toward the snack shop.

"Be careful about food," she said. "Ants, insects, other things may get into them."

Max paused in front of the dangling biscuits. He remembered the snake from the night before. "I saw a snake in the bathroom. Are they poisonous?"

"What color was it?"

"Grayish-black with white bands."

"That's a krait," she said matter-of-factly. "Very poisonous. It won't bite unless you tease it, though."

Max recoiled. "I would never tease a snake," he said.

"Yes, but a half-open packet of chocolate biscuits in your bag?" she pointed out.

Max lost his appetite. "Come on, snakes don't eat biscuits," he said.

"How do you know? Do you have snakes in your bathroom in New York?" she said.

Max laughed. "I don't, but I wouldn't feed them biscuits if they were in my tub," he said. He turned around. "But now I'm not hungry anymore."

THEY CHATTERED AND laughed as they made their way back to the village. On the tractor ride back, Shakti asked him how long he planned to stay at the ashram.

"I don't know. As long as it takes," said Max. "You?"

"I have to decide soon," said Shakti. "My sabbatical ends in six months in July. I don't know whether I work toward enlightenment after that or I join back university, marry, and make family. I am more than thirty. If I miss the time, I never have it later. For a man, it is easy."

Max didn't think it was any easier for him. He had quit the job he had worked all his life to get. He was racked with guilt about leaving Sophia. Yet in the moment of sudden silence when he felt his navel lift off the ground that morning he had seen a glimmer of something. Still far away, but more complete, more real than anything he'd known before. Even so, he felt a hollow emptiness in his stomach when they approached the lonesome huts. It was dusk and Max felt more alone than ever. Another ten days of heavy silence. No talking, no comforting sounds of laughter, just the all-encompassing joyless strife toward eternal joy.

Indeed, sir, the yogis don't want any contact with people.

Max thought of Viveka quietly wiping the snow from the roof of his cart and Ramakrishna's silent face in the morning. He also would have to find peace within himself.

17.

Max awoke sweating for the fifth night in a row. His heart clutched. Another nightmare. A dark-skinned man electrocuted himself by climbing up an electric pole standing on the corner of a busy street. His face turned grayish-blue. His flesh burned. People screamed when his rigid body fell to the ground. It was like the first night. In that dream, a young man with close-cropped hair had set himself on fire. Max's ears still rang from the screams of people surrounding the man. On the second night, a group of women in black headgear wept around a dead body. The next night was less gruesome. A thin old man sat in front of a television in a dark house and ate from a cracked bowl of rice, smiling eerily. A horrifying image each night, all different but each tugging at his heart, making him cry out in pain and grief.

Yet he was also just a little distant from the people he saw—unlike the Scottish Catholic priest, the woman looking skyward, and the man kissing the amulet whom he had seen during his near-fatal hike up the Himalayas. These people weren't him in past lives. They were familiar yet separate from him. Was he remembering forgotten images from the gang wars in the projects because his meditation had deepened?

On the first day of the ten-day cycle, he had sat still and meditated on the infinite consciousness within just as Shakti had suggested. But it hadn't worked. His mind still distracted easily. The object of concentration was just . . . too infinite. He needed something tangible to concentrate on. Perhaps a symbol of the infinite, he reasoned, and focused in his mind on the image of the Buddha, the man who claimed to have crossed the boundary from the finite to infinite. The Buddha's contented eyes and inward-looking gaze occupied his attention. He didn't cross and uncross his legs, stoop forward, or bend backward. Soon Max's mind migrated from the man to his qualities. He now concentrated on the Buddha's blazing determination instead and felt inspired after every meditation. Something clicked. It was as if he was becoming a small part of what he was meditating on. And as his meditation became more certain, his asana practice evolved too.

That day, the sixth in the cycle, during asanas, he felt a sudden urge to bend his knees when he was standing inverse in Sirsasana, the headstand. He bent his knees but instead of coming down, he arched his back and slowly brought his legs behind his back. Lowering his feet farther, he touched the back of his head with his toes. A satisfying stream of blood rushed to his spine. He removed his wrists from the ground and caught hold of his big toes. He'd been in that pose for just a few seconds when he was struck by the impossibility of his whole body bent backward in a circle supported only by his head. God, he would break his spine. He was crushing his neck. He was choking. His eyes watered. He panicked. He pulled his feet up in a rush, flailed, and fell—into the able hands of Ramakrishna.

"Relax, breathe, relax," said Ramakrishna.

He glided Max down gently.

"Push your chest out," said Ramakrishna.

Max thrust his chest forward and exhaled. He opened his eyes. His spine tingled. His head buzzed. The world felt fresh, different, alive. Both Hari and Shakti were staring at him.

"What is that?" mouthed grim-faced Shakti, who hadn't acknowledged his presence with as much as a nod since the silence started.

"Sirsa Padasana, touching your head with your feet," said Ramakrishna. "One of the toughest poses in the eighty-four classic asanas. Excellent for strengthening the spine, but do not attempt on your own yet. Please ask me to help you if you want to try."

Neither Shakti nor Hari wanted to try. Max didn't either when he realized what he had just done.

TWO DAYS LATER, something similar happened when he was in Salabhasana, the locust or grasshopper pose. He lay facedown with his hands clasped under his stomach, chin touching the floor, eyes looking ahead, legs hoisted up, feeling none of the lingering back pain he had experienced in the initial classes, when some impulse made him kick his legs up higher. Without instruction, he pulled them higher and higher until they were vertically above his head and just the top of his chest lay on his upper arms. It didn't feel comfortable, so he arched his legs farther back and brought them down so his heels rested in front of his face. He straightened his knees. His chest lifted from his arms. He stared incredulously as he was inverted into a circle once again. From the corner of his eye, he saw Shakti and Hari stand up and watch him.

Lift up your legs. Now. His spine would snap any moment. But it didn't. He was shocked by how natural the position felt. Until he started to choke. His chest was exploding. He lifted his legs in a rush when Ramakrishna stopped him.

"Go back," said Ramakrishna.

Max pulled his legs back in front of his face. He was staring at his heels again.

"Hold," said Ramakrishna. "Circulate the breath, don't exhale."

Max lay upturned for a minute, maybe more, following Ramakrishna's instruction, feeling the fresh oxygen reach the depth of his abdomen. His panic subsided. He could do this for longer. He closed his eyes.

"Now exhale and come up," said Ramakrishna.

Max released his breath slowly. He lifted his legs back, softly touching the ground without thuds or crashes. His body shook with energy. A stream of warm air flowed from his pelvis to the top of his head and back down to his pelvis. His head buzzed. The world was his to take. He could do anything. He breathed deeply to calm down.

Hari and Shakti broke into spontaneous applause. Ramakrishna smiled broadly.

"Viparita Salabhasana, the inverse of the locust," he said. "The ancient yogis derived all asanas from nature. The grasshopper has the strongest abdomen among insects, hence the pose. Do the Salabhasana regularly for abdominal strength, but try the inverse only if your flexibility is exceptional."

Max didn't think his flexibility was exceptional. He struggled with some basic poses like sitting forward bends and half spinal twists, poses that Hari and Shakti did with immaculate grace. How had he known these advanced poses that Ramakrishna hadn't taught and he'd never seen? Please, not past lives again. No matter the science, the whole idea of reincarnation was still too much of a cliché. A hippie came to India, did some backbends, and started seeing events from his past life. But something else was happening; something physical was changing in him. His body pulsed with energy after the bandhas. He didn't sweat buckets in pranayama as he used to just a week ago. He worked for hours in the burning sun, softening and breaking each piece of hard earth as if it were alive, a physical foe, but slept only two or three hours every night. For the rest of the night, he was awake, reading books other travelers had left behind on yoga, spiritual searches, Buddhism, and Zen—and of course, sweating from his inexplicable nightmares.

Max didn't sleep at all the night before silence broke. One moment he was meditating in the courtyard, the next moment someone was shaking him. He looked up at Ramakrishna.

"Do you want to join us for asana class today, Mahadeva?"

"Now?" said Max, surprised.

Ramakrishna smiled. "Same time every morning."

Max skipped a breath. It couldn't be morning. He had just sat down to meditate. He saw Hari and Shakti sit on their yoga mats. Had he really meditated the whole night? *Nine hours straight from seven PM to four AM?* He couldn't sit cross-legged for that long, let alone meditate. It must be his body's subconscious response to avoid the nightmares.

"I'm coming," he said.

His mouth was dry. He circulated the saliva in his mouth.

Back in his hut for a change of clothes, he felt no tiredness, no watering of eyes, no nervous energy pulsing through him. He felt none of the side effects that he experienced from sleepless nights back home. It was as if he hadn't needed sleep at all.

MAX REMAINED DISTRACTED through asana class that day. When silence broke at the end of class, he was surprised he didn't want to go to town. The idea of talking to Shakti, checking the Internet, hearing from Sophia, getting new information from the world, overwhelmed him.

"Hurry, get ready," said Shakti, laughing. "Tractor comes any time."

Max hesitated. His body quivered from the morning asanas. He just wanted to be alone, silent, still. A hollow fear arose in his gut. What was happening to him? The nightmares, the sleeplessness, this desire to keep silent after nine days of silence, it wasn't normal. Too much, too quick. He had to get away from this bubble.

"Yes, coming," said Max.

They followed the same steps—the tractor, the walk through the same unending orange land in the same heat. Max talked, laughed, tried to feel like himself, but his thoughts were occupied by his heels in front of his eyes in Viparita Salabhasana.

HE CHECKED HIS email again. A note from Sophia marked *Urgent.* He opened it immediately.

> **I need to know you are safe. Just tell me you are still in India and have not wandered off to Tunisia . . . this has gone on too long, Maxi.**

Puzzled, he opened another message from Andre.

> **Sophia is worried u r in Tunisia because u always wanted 2 go to Africa again. I told her even u r not so stupid. Write back Ace.**

Similar messages from Keith and Tina, his friends from Harvard.

What was happening in Tunisia? He couldn't load the online *New York Times,* CNN, or Yahoo!, so he asked the shopkeeper for the name of the national newspaper. The *Times of India* website loaded slowly. The cover page came up amid a hundred pop-up ads.

A smiling photograph of a Middle Eastern man with closely cropped hair. Another picture of women wearing black headgear walking on a street.

Max scanned the headlines, a distant, vacant chill rising in him: HUNDREDS OF PEOPLE PROTEST IN TUNISIA'S STREETS.

BEN ALI THREATENS STRICT ACTION AGAINST DEMONSTRATORS. ANOTHER MAN ELECTROCUTES HIMSELF IN SIDI BOUZID.

He opened the links mechanically. Brown faces shouting in protest, policemen in black fatigues with rifles in their hands, a jeep overturned, a burned man in a hospital bed, another man's grayish-blue electrocuted body.

He had seen every image before.

They were the people from his dreams.

Day 9 of the civilian rebellion in Tunisia. The revolution had started the same day his nightmares had.

Max rubbed his face. His skin had gone cold.

"Very sad in Africa, sahib. But good also. You wait and see, same thing will happen in India," said the shopkeeper.

Max contracted his abdomen and exhaled deeply. Numbly, he wrote back to Sophia and Andre.

I'm in a small Indian village and nowhere near Tunisia. This place is a million times safer than New York so don't worry for a second.

Again he went back to the *Times of India* website and studied the chronology of the protests. No, he couldn't have read of it before. There was no inkling of an uprising in Tunisia before a fruit seller burned himself in front of a government building. He couldn't have guessed it from his trip to Africa. After Kilimanjaro, he had always wanted to go back, but only for a walking safari in a jungle. He knew absolutely nothing about Tunisia and its politics. What was happening?

"My mother tells me about Tunisia. She is worried. She

doesn't know India and Tunisia are in different continents." Shakti was standing behind him, watching the screen.

Her smile disappeared. "You look white like ghost," she said. She bent down. "You have friends and family in Tunisia?"

Max shook his head. His throat was dry. It was just simple déjà vu, wasn't it? Nothing to be alarmed about. Right?

"The pictures are hard to see," said Shakti.

Max turned around. "What pictures, Shakti? I saw the whole thing. I felt it," he said. "I smelled the man's burning flesh. I heard the women shouting in the street. I saw a man electrocute himself. And I saw other things that aren't in the newspaper. A man eating his dinner, smiling when he watched an overturned jeep on TV. A teacher writing the electrocuted man's name on a school blackboard."

"What do you mean you see it, feel it?" she said.

He stood up, wanting to be alone again. "I don't know. I've not been myself for a few days," he said.

THEY WALKED DOWN the narrow mud road.

"I saw those people in my sleep every night since it happened," he said.

"Your sleep?"

"In my dreams," he said. It sounded strange. "They were the same people, I'm sure."

She stared at him. "So it happens to you. I do not know anyone who experiences it directly."

He stopped. "Experienced what, Shakti? What happened?" he said.

"You see *scorcio*, like . . . a glimpse of single universal energy we talk about," she said. "You merge into it for a moment and see biggest wave on its surface."

Max wiped the sweat off his face. It couldn't be. It was too . . . too New Agey.

They walked again, passing the snack shop. Shakti wanted a Pepsi. The thought of sweet drinks, salty snacks, any processed food made his stomach churn. What was happening to him? He forced himself to buy and gulp down a Pepsi. They walked back to the village.

The only way he could have merged into this single universal energy that connected all beings—assuming it even existed—was through meditating on it. And that was impossible. He was a novice. He couldn't even contemplate the infinite. He was still using the Buddha's image as a surrogate, and even that kept slipping from his mind as it digressed to other thoughts, unspiritual thoughts such as a presentation he had screwed up at work, fucking Anna, his guilt about Keisha, and his mother's dying face.

"Have you ever had such dreams?" said Max when he calmed down.

"I don't know. Maybe. I don't dream much," she said.

Max sensed something, probably her disappointment at not having a similar experience, unpleasant as it was.

"It means your meditation is working," he said. "Only people whose minds are not at rest dream, right?"

Shakti shrugged and kept silent for the rest of the walk back.

"VERY HOT," SHE SAID on the tractor and covered her face with her white handkerchief.

Max understood now why Ramakrishna insisted on silence.

He had made Shakti question her own practice by opening his big mouth. A part of him wanted to apologize, but a larger part of him just wanted to be silent forever. Strange things were happening. He needed to go deeper, to their source.

Shakti removed the cloth from her face. Her usually animated eyes were quiet. Max's heart broke. All day, he had been chattering about his progress in this or that.

"I am sorry," he said.

"For what?"

"I'm just insensitive," he said.

The tractor arrived at the ashram.

"No, I am sorry. I am small," she said on their walk to the huts. "I work hard, but nothing like this ever happens to me."

"If it's any help, it was no fun to smell rotting, burning flesh."

"It sounds more fun than my sleep," she said. She smiled. "I want to see dead people too."

Max laughed. They said good-bye. She went to her hut and he entered his. Hari was sitting cross-legged on the floor, his back ramrod straight against the mud wall on his side, meditating with the usual silent, determined look on his face. He opened his eyes as Max walked gingerly past him.

"I'm sorry," said Max. "I didn't mean to disturb you."

"No, no, I was thinking of going to sleep anyway." Hari uncrossed his legs and got up from the floor. "I hope you had a good day in the village."

"I guess," said Max, suddenly understanding Hari's decision never to leave the ashram in a way he hadn't before. "I don't think I'll go again. All these unnecessary sights, sounds, information, the phone, the Internet, it just unsettles you. "

"This dewdrop world is just a dewdrop. And yet. And yet."

"Sorry?"

"A Buddhist poem," said Hari. "The world pulls you in despite its incompleteness."

"You seem to be resisting the pull quite well," said Max.

Hari went to his bed. "So you think," he said. "I have a three-year-old son back home in Egypt. Not a day goes by when I don't think of him."

Max's heart welled up on seeing Hari's moist green eyes.

"Sleep well," said Hari, pulling the bedsheet over his large frame.

"Thank you." Max went to his side of the hut and lay on his bed for a minute, then sat up erect and meditated. Max was lucky. Nothing bound him to the world he had left behind. He would give it all he had.

18.

From then on, Max banished all doubt and surrendered himself more fully to every part of the day. He didn't have more prophetic dreams, but he changed in smaller, more meaningful ways. One day he didn't suck in his breath while pouring cold water on himself in his daily bucket shower, now reduced to half a bucket. The next day he removed the cloth he put on his head in the fields. His scalp burned but he felt nothing. That night he stopped applying Odomos, the insect repellent cream that Shakti had given him after his malaria pills finished. The mosquitoes ravaged him, but it didn't matter. The following day he didn't curl up his fingers on the scorching yoga mat to avoid the stinging, burning sensation on his fingertips. His fingers and toes baked in the heat, turning pink and blistered, causing pain to his body but leaving his mind unaffected. It was as if the part of his brain that processed discomfort and pain as bad had receded into a distance, still there but not as active anymore. Something similar happened with most things that once bothered him: the frogs that danced in front of the squat toilet and even the squat toilet itself, the gray-black snake that slithered in and out of the huts from time to time, Hari's loud snoring at night, the specks inside the water drum. He still saw them, felt them, but the part of his mind that judged those sights and sounds as inconvenient or unpleasant was quiet.

This in turn made his asana practice stronger. He didn't judge which pose he liked, which he disliked, which he could do well, which he couldn't do well. He didn't want Ramakrishna to hurry up with the spinal twists or hold the headstand longer. As a result, he observed Ramakrishna more closely and made minor adjustments that galvanized the flow of energy in his body. His body became fluid, malleable, and more receptive to Ramakrishna's instructions. If only his mind would do the same.

Often he would wake up in the middle of his night with his heart beating wildly. "My life, my life," he would repeat to himself. Those images again. Sophia, three years old, brown head, curly hair, and cute lisp saving a piece of Werther's candy their mother's employer had got from Germany for him when he returned from school by holding it in her mouth. Her outstretched hands and dimpled smile. The small gooey candy dripping with her saliva. Staying up all night to tutor her so she'd get into Trinity too. His mother's eyes widening when he handed her their tickets for Greece from his first real paycheck as an intern at a hedge fund. The pride on his mother's face when she walked into his doorman building in Manhattan for the first time. Andre's first time out in a wheelchair after three months of lying in a hospital bed. They had taken him straight to see the bright, shiny Rockefeller Center Christmas tree. Tears of joy had rolled down his cheeks. Max's throat would tighten. What was he seeking? He'd been happy before. Couldn't he surround himself with friends and family the way the world did and be happy again? Life was meant to be lived, suffering to be experienced, not run away from. He was being brainwashed into joining a cult.

His anxiety would spiral the next day, coming to a head in the hour-long break they had between lunch and the afternoon asana class. With no work to distract him, his mind would spin doomsday scenarios. He'd be broke and unemployable soon; he was squandering his most productive years; all this wasn't real life; he'd regret this time forever. He remembered himself studying all night in a corner of the living room, obsessed with nailing the SATs while the world crumbled around him—the stock market crash, his mother's being out of a job, losing welfare, nights when they went to bed hungry, the terrifying prospect of homelessness, crack entering the projects, his friend Pitbull's throat slit in a gang fight, Andre's going to jail, waves of arson in the neighborhood. Nothing had come in the way of getting a perfect SAT score. Where had that Max gone? Why had he dropped out of the world he had worked so hard to get into? So his thoughts would swirl until pranayama began. Then he regulated his breathing, his mind calmed, and his body felt connected to the universal energy again. He didn't fear suffering. He wasn't craving happiness. He was seeking something quite different... completeness. The way out of the predictable rhythm of birth and death. Joy, grief, anger, guilt, love, passion—he had experienced everything in events past and lives before. A perfect state existed beyond all of these, and he would reach it. It was the law of nature. The eagle had flapped its wings high, experienced everything the world had to offer. Now it was time to bring the wings down, go inward, complete its journey. Max would push through another day.

DAYS PASSED, a month, then more. Max went to town only when he wanted to be with Shakti. Otherwise he felt more and more repelled by the sights of living and the sounds of commerce. Emails from home left him indifferent, even a little sad. Sophia wasn't enjoying substance-abuse counseling anymore. Addiction seemed endless, and what she was doing wasn't making a dent. She was trying to figure out what to do next. Jason, a friend from work, didn't like the increased government financial regulations after the recession and was planning to join a technology start-up. Keith and Tina were planning to buy a house in New Jersey to have more space after the baby came. Everyone wanted a different life but in a narrow realm. Did they ever feel dissatisfied with the same ebbs and flows that billions had experienced before them and billions would experience after?

Yes, of course everyone did, Shakti would say in one of their rare trips out. Who hasn't had that strange feeling of something indefinable still missing from one's grasp even in moments of great achievement? The evolutionary journey from animal to man is one of higher and higher self-awareness. At its peak, man realizes that his mind is always vaguely discontented and is crying for something beyond the world of people, objects, and achievements. Only then begins the journey of involution, of seeking completion within. Until that awakening dawned, he would keep repeating the cycle of seeking, desiring, fulfilling some of his desires, not being able to fulfill others, all the while feeling that familiar gnawing incompleteness. Max didn't know if he had experienced any deep awakening. All he knew was that he felt more and more alienated from his life back home. He had left New York in December. It was April now, and nothing was pulling him back.

ONE EVENING, while meditating in the courtyard, Max had an overpowering urge to speak to Hari. He opened his eyes. Hari was absent from his usual position on the mat next to him. Max was surprised. Hari never skipped evening meditation. Max closed his eyes. Hari's sharp green eyes and rugged, handsome face filled his mind. He opened his eyes again. Still no Hari. Max fidgeted through the remaining hour. He paused in front of the partition sheet when he went back to the hut. No sound. Hari must be sleeping. The hotter it got every day, the more exhausting working in the fields became. Max wouldn't disturb him.

Max walked back to his own side of the hut. He tossed and turned. After an hour, he lifted the dividing sheet and entered Hari's section.

Hari was sitting on his bed, staring at the wall.

"Hari?"

He turned toward Max. His green eyes glowed in the lamp's light. "Mahadeva, you know?" he said softly.

Max was surprised he had broken the silence. There were still three days to go in that ten-day cycle, and Hari seldom spoke even on their days off.

"Know what?" said Max.

"I'm leaving later tonight. The tractor will come around midnight," he said. "It should have been here by now. You have a watch, don't you? What time is it now?"

"Twelve-fifteen," said Max, without turning around to get the watch buried somewhere deep in his backpack.

Twelve-seventeen, to be precise. Though during meditation he remained suspended in timelessness for longer and longer, he had developed an acute sense of physical time in every other part of the day. He didn't care about the time, but he always knew it. Down to the minute. A recent phenomenon he couldn't explain. It was scary. He had thought of asking Ramakrishna for an explanation when he had first noticed it. But he had pictured the saint's smile and his eyes shining with the words he'd likely repeat from the first time they had sat together in his hut: many things will happen here, some hard for the rational mind to understand. They are signs pointing toward the path, not the path itself. Don't be distracted. Thus, Max accepted it as a by-product of his improved concentration and didn't dwell much on it.

"He must be running late," said Hari.

"Are you leaving for good?" said Max.

"I don't know, but I won't come back for a while," said Hari.

Despite his newly acquired distance from his emotions, Max felt a pang of sadness. He liked Hari in spite of the fact that they didn't talk much. His quiet competence in the fields inspired Max. Outside the fields, Hari's kindness shone through in small gestures, such as his waiting for Max outside the bathroom when Max was struck with the stomach flu and always shining a flashlight if Max came back late from meditation and he was awake.

Max shook Hari's hand. "I will miss you. Thank you for your kindness."

"I will also. Sharing the space with you has been easy. It's seldom so effortless. People have many complaints when they first come," said Hari.

"Why are you leaving?" asked Max.

Hari shifted in the bed.

"You don't have to say," said Max.

"I'm not ready for the summer here," said Hari, his green eyes dropping. "I tried before, but I couldn't do it. This time I worked much harder to prepare, so I thought it would be different. But I can feel in my gut that I'm still not ready. And now with everything Shakti told me about what's happening in the Middle East, my heart is not here. I worry for my son even though I know he's happier with his mother in her big family than he can ever be with me. I have to make myself much tougher before I come back again."

Max wondered why the strapping film actor, who beat the hard earth into submission in real life and likely beat villains on film, needed more toughening. He wondered what happened in summer. The heat would get worse, of course, but he'd always seen Hari perfectly composed, even as the hot winter had given way to a burning spring.

"Why?"

"Summers are tough here. You will see," said Hari. He paused. "But you'll get through them. You are meant to be here."

They heard the dull engine of the tractor arrive outside.

"I hope you'll come back soon," said Max.

Hari got up from the bed. "I hope so too. It gets harder each time," he said. He picked up his backpack. "My father wants me to run our family business back home in Egypt, which I've avoided for many years. My son's mother wants me to be close by. They're both right, of course. It's hard to explain why I keep coming here to them—and to myself."

They walked out of the hut.

"Did Ramakrishna tell you why I was leaving?" asked Hari in a hushed whisper in the courtyard. "I requested that he not share it with you or Shakti so I didn't worry you."

Max shook his head. "He didn't say anything."

"How did you know I was leaving then?"

"I didn't. Just a coincidence," said Max.

Even as he said it, he knew it wasn't true. He had known Hari was leaving. He had sensed it, felt it deep within his bones, the same way he had felt the need to flip over his pillow three days ago. A rusty red scorpion with open pincers had fallen out of the pillowcase. Max had lifted it on a piece of paper and thrown it outside the ashram boundary without fuss.

"Stick to it. You'll do much," said Hari.

Max walked with him to the tractor. Hari got on it. The driver put it in gear, and without looking back or uttering a sound, Hari drove off into the darkness.

19.

April gave way to a sweltering May, and Max began to understand why Hari had left. The sun burned the land as if it were just a few feet off the ground, not millions of miles away. The monsoon that was expected in early May never showed up. Crops withered. New seed refused to bear fruit. The earth turned harder than concrete and broke into little dry pieces.

The three of them kept up their daily routine in the beginning, but the prospect of physical hunger soon overcame spiritual hunger. They eliminated the afternoon asana class and worked longer in the fields, spreading out to farm softer land, breaking the earth with axes and the backs of plows. Eggplants and drumsticks required more water, so they planted only millet. Only a few of the new millet plants broke through the ground. They lavished them with fertilizers. Still the crops languished, for they lacked the most crucial ingredient of all: water.

The hand pump dried up. Max helped Ramakrishna drill the bore well supplying the pump deeper. Both of them continued to drill every day until the drill stem cut through their torn, callused palms and their heads spun in the heat. After days of continuous effort, they would be rewarded with a small trickle. They poured three-quarters of it on the field and stored the remaining for drinking. With little water available for anything else, they roasted millet and the last of the eggplant and drumsticks directly over a wood fire. They rationed their drinking water to three glasses a day. None of them had bathed or washed their clothes since the water dried a month ago.

The rain remained elusive through June. Max knew he would break soon. Only once before when he was seven years old had he experienced this helpless hunger. It was in the aftermath of the 1987 stock market crash, when his mother could find few cleaning jobs and their savings had run out completely. But they had managed to fill their stomachs with mac and cheese and apple juice in soup kitchens every night. Here all they had was the meager rations they produced. Max felt dizzy and disoriented all day. The skin on his face, neck, and back cracked and peeled. His mouth dried up. He didn't have a drop of saliva left to moisten his lips. Every day he stared longer and longer at the wooden gate that separated the ashram from freedom. Any minute now, he would walk out. He was free. He'd come back later when the sun didn't beat so hard and the thin stream of water coming out of a hundred-foot-deep well didn't feel like a miracle. But he would look at Shakti working in the fields with a determined look on her mud-streaked face and he would be ashamed at his softness. She was like his mother. Sturdy, determined, relentless. Again and again the same image of his mother would come to his mind. Her face gaunt and colorless, her torso bent with pain, and her legs swollen with lymphedema, yet shuffling around on her crutches in his apartment, insisting on cooking Sophia and him a Thanksgiving dinner just days before she died. Max could transcend his body's limitations too. The constant hankering for food, water, and other petty comfort tied him to the physical plane, obstructing the path to transcendence. He could overcome it.

MID-JUNE. STILL NO SIGN of the monsoon that had been expected six weeks before. The eggplant died. The drumstick crop shriveled but still yielded a little. They reduced their food to two cups of roasted millet and a small serving of dry drumsticks a day. Max lost weight rapidly. He made more holes in his belt with the awl-like tool they used in the fields.

One day he stopped pumping his stomach in the middle of the afternoon pranayama.

He wasn't sweating as he usually did in the afternoons. Fuck. He was so dehydrated he didn't even sweat a drop anymore. Ramakrishna and Shakti were thrusting their abdomens in and out. Did they realize they were in the middle of a drought? They couldn't burn energy like this. It was dangerous. He couldn't be part of this madness anymore. He lay back down on his mat and didn't do the rest of the pranayama or any of the asanas.

The next day Shakti stopped as well.

Max stared at her thin body in the fields that day. Was she trying to keep up with him? But he was trying to keep up with her. They would both kill themselves like that. That night he didn't come out for meditation. He lay still on his bed just as his exhausted body told him to. When he went to the bathroom, he saw that Shakti's mat was empty as well. Max came back and slept. He saw his mother with a crumbling cookie in her pale, bony fingers. Sophia stretching out her hand to offer him the melting candy. Swirling, spinning blackness.

One day this will all come back to you, Max.

Max awoke with a start. His throat choked. Keisha, black eyes brimming with tears outside the clinic in Tarrytown. He had forced her to ride up the Metro North with him so that no one would see them. Just as he had pressured her to abort their child. His chest filled up. Max hadn't wanted to be a father at seventeen like all the other guys in the projects. He had wanted to go to college so his mother's sacrifices didn't go to waste. The mud walls of the hut closed in on him. Max covered his eyes with his hands and tried not to cry and lose water.

You did what you had to, Max, but one day this will all come back to you.

She was right. It had come back. This was his penance for destroying Keisha's life. She had grown up in a strict religious family. They hadn't told anyone about the pregnancy or the abortion, but her guilt had likely made her run away from home. *Was she even alive?* Max couldn't stop the tears anymore. Keisha was so bright, so beautiful. She could've run with the drug lords, with their BMWs and Mercedes-Benzes and worldly talk. All the girls wanted them for boyfriends. Instead, she had dated a poor white kid who was trying desperately to be cooler than he was. He didn't even have to front with her. She had seen how much he enjoyed math and chemistry and had encouraged him to study. Where would he be without her? Yet he'd turned away from her the moment he got into college. How different her life would have turned out if he hadn't entered it. The pain he had caused was coming back. He had to bear it. He turned over and pressed his aching stomach against the hard bed.

NOT A DROP of rain fell in the next two weeks. The rain was now eight weeks late. Their well water all but disappeared. Even the millet dried up. They cut their food intake further. Max passed the week in a hazy stupor. He woke up with a dull pain in his head every day and did a little pranayama to fill his empty stomach with breath. His guts hurt from severe constipation. He worked listlessly in the fields, feeling nothing—not heat, not exhaustion, not even pain when the millet stalks cut deep grooves in his dry skin, just hunger.

For the rest of the day, he lay on his bed, caked in sweat and mud, images of eighteen-year-old Keisha's sharp, shining face filling his mind, stopping him from walking toward the gate.

"ANY DAY NOW it will come," said Ramakrishna, looking skyward at the flaming sun after completing their spare lunch in the tenth week of the drought on a day when silence broke. "It always comes. Sometimes early, sometimes delayed, but rain comes."

He looked so unfazed, so oblivious, that Max couldn't take it any longer.

"I have money," he said in a raspy voice he almost didn't recognize. His dry, cracked lips hurt when he spoke. "We can get food and water."

Ramakrishna shook his head. "I am your host. I cannot accept anything from you. And whatever we have is enough for us."

The hunger roared within Max. He opened his mouth to protest but faltered as Keisha's small, slim body clouded his eyes again. He looked away. Shakti was picking the last of the millet seeds delicately from her plate. A lump formed in Max's throat. He coughed. "It's not enough for me," he said evenly.

"My doors are always open for you. Might it be easier for you if you come back after a few months?" said Ramakrishna.

Max felt his face redden. He stared at his blistered toes on the burning red mud and breathed slowly. "It's just food. Why does it matter where it comes from?" he said.

Ramakrishna was shaking his head even before he had completed his sentence. "No, no, that is the way it has to be. And we do have enough to live. Fasting is good. It gives the digestive organs a rest. It cleanses the system of toxins. You develop patience and self-control. One who conquers hunger conquers all the senses. Nothing binds him to the material plane then."

"But this isn't fasting," said Max. "We are starving."

"All I can offer you is my share. Please have that from tomorrow," said Ramakrishna.

He got up and wiped his plate with dried, burned leaves and left it at its usual place outside the hut.

Max stared into Shakti's sunken eyes. "I'm going to leave," he wanted to say. He knew if he capitulated, she would too. Shakti wiped off a strand of dry hair from her face and looked away. Hot wind stung his eyes. She must be working through her own past as well. He wouldn't get in her way. All his life, he had made easy choices. Now no longer. Max wiped his plate dry and left.

. . .

FROM THAT DAY, Ramakrishna ate only half a cup of millet a day.

Max apologized and requested him to have more.

"No, no, your talk was good. I was getting lazy from habit. I have lived on much less before," he said.

ANOTHER WEEK PASSED. Max began to worry more and more about Shakti. She had lost at least twenty pounds in the last two months. Her face had lost its color. Her red hair looked dull and her eyes bloodshot.

One day she didn't wear her glasses and stumbled through the fields as if she were sleepwalking. Max had never seen her remove her glasses before. She didn't wear them again the next day. Her swollen eyes popped out of her sunken face. Twice she stopped and adjusted her glasses. Only there was nothing to adjust. Her thin fingers moved up and down her eyes weakly. Max started to panic. It took all his strength to restrain himself from talking to her.

Later that afternoon, he woke up from a thick sleep to hear Ramakrishna and Shakti arguing in the courtyard. Max walked out of his hut. Ramakrishna was shaking his head. Shakti's expressions grew more and more animated. A tear trickled down her face. He had never seen Shakti cry. She must be asking for more food and Ramakrishna was refusing as always. Didn't he know her by now? She was too proud to break silence and ask for more unless she needed it to live.

Enough. This had gone on too long. The tight knot of Keisha's images loosened. He'd never forgive himself if something happened to Shakti. It was time to tap into the emergency rations they'd been storing away. No matter how meager the crop they produced daily, Ramakrishna had put a portion away for later. It made perfect sense. If the rain didn't come in another week, the dry land would turn to cement. Thus far, hunger had been tough to bear. Another week and it would be the difference between life and death. Shakti had likely reached that point. What kind of a saint was Ramakrishna if he couldn't see that?

Shakti went inside her hut. Max walked over to Ramakrishna.

"Shakti looks really sick. We should use the emergency rations," said Max.

Ramakrishna looked puzzled.

"The supplies in storage," said Max with rising impatience. He went to the kitchen hut next to Ramakrishna's. "This," he said, pointing to the four brown sacks, two with millet, one each with eggplant and drumsticks.

Ramakrishna shook his head. "No, no, no. This is for the village. We will give it to them when the tractor comes next."

Days of hunger and deprivation rose in Max like an angry force. He coughed to clear his throat. "No, you can't do that," said Max. "Shakti is dying."

"I think I told you in the beginning, whatever we produce, we give half to the village," said Ramakrishna.

Max felt an urgent physical need to lift Ramakrishna by the collar of his long Indian kurta, force him against the wall of the hut, and shake the idiocy out of him. He backed away a step. He couldn't trust himself not to lift his hand.

"No, I helped farm too. We can't give our food away," said

Max, shaking. Tears stung his eyes. "We can't help anyone if we can't help ourselves. This is madness."

Ramakrishna's eyes didn't waver. His face had lost none of its luster in the days of deprivation. "This is how it has to be," said Ramakrishna. He turned around.

Max could no longer restrain himself. He grabbed him by his shoulders. "She is dying, don't you understand?" he said, shaking him. "Shakti could die. We can't let her die. Please."

"Don't be crazy, Max. I am fine."

Max turned around.

"Your glasses?" he said weakly.

"A screw comes loose," she said.

"You were asking him for food?" he said.

"Not for myself," she said.

She was having the same discussion with Ramakrishna as he had just had. Max took his hands off Ramakrishna's shoulders.

Shakti turned to Ramakrishna. "Can we cook now?"

"I'm . . . I'm sorry," said Max.

"Not at all," said Ramakrishna. He paused. "I know this is difficult, but what we have is enough."

THEY ATE THEIR scant meal in Ramakrishna's hut, tucked away from the blazing sun.

"I want to leave," said Shakti at the end of the meal.

Ramakrishna nodded. "A tractor will come on the third day from today. You can leave then."

No tractor had come for the last month, probably because the village was enduring the same drought. But they didn't ask how he was sure one would come in three days. They just knew it would.

Max hesitated. "I will leave too," he said.

"I understand. My door will always be open should either of you want to come back," said Ramakrishna.

Shakti smiled at Max when Ramakrishna left, then burst out in dry sobs. Max wanted to cry too, because he knew she wasn't crying for the hunger or the thirst. They would pull through another week. She was crying for the loss of a guru who had given them a glimpse of truth and could light the entire path for them. But leaving, they both knew, was now inevitable. Max put his hands in hers and held her close, feeling her burning skin under him. They had never touched before. Ramakrishna had never explicitly forbidden them, but touch meant desire, a narrow craving that tethered one to this limited life. But today, to touch another burning, throbbing body was to feel alive again. For everything around them—the land, their crops, the spare insects, even the resident frogs and geckos—had all shriveled and burned to death.

20.

The tractor came early in the morning on the third day. The driver had aged considerably from the last time they'd seen him a month ago. His dry, papery skin was covered with thick grooves, his lips were cracked, and he seemed to have shrunk to half his size. Max shook his burning hand, relieved they were carrying food for the village. He felt ashamed for throwing a tantrum. But Shakti and he were starving too. Just loading the food sacks and backpacks in the tractor made his head spin. They bent down and touched Ramakrishna's feet, then folded their hands, thanking him for his teaching and hospitality. Max felt a pang of concern about leaving him alone without emergency rations. But he knew Ramakrishna would manage as he had for all these years. They drove away in the sputtering tractor.

The tractor ran out of fuel a few miles before they reached the village. The farmer apologized. There was no gas in the village. They would have to walk. He himself was too tired to walk. Could they ask the villagers to make something from the food sacks they were carrying and send it back? He lay down under the tractor to protect himself from the blazing sun. Max promised he would come back himself with food. They hoisted their backpacks and loaded the food sacks on their heads, beginning a slow, stumbling walk to the village.

They stopped for a break midway and sat down on their backpacks, sweat pouring down their temples. Max licked his lips. Salt. He licked some more. Any food would do. Soon he would eat more. Chocolate biscuits and orange juice. Apples, bananas, rice, bread. Blood coursed through his veins. Max took off his shirt and wiped the sweat off his face.

Shakti looked around. Seeing just miles of desolate land, she removed her T-shirt and sat in her bra.

"Where you will go next?" said Shakti, opening her ponytail so that her hair fell over her naked, tanned shoulders.

Max cupped his hand over his eyes to shield them from the blinding sun. "Not back home," he said. "Maybe Varanasi. I read that it's India's holiest place. Anywhere I can find a teacher half as good as Ramakrishna. You?"

"Back to Milan," she said. "My sabbatical is almost over. First, I thought I would not join the university, but now I want to."

"Come with me," said Max.

She shook her head. "I feel like this for some time now. I do not want this. I want life. I want family. Imperfect. Comfortable. Beautiful."

Max's eyes watered from the hot wind. He would probably never see Shakti again. An aching loneliness filled him. Yet another friendship left halfway. "Even I don't know if I want liberation," he said.

"You do," she said.

Max had the sudden urge to pull her sure face closer. "Will you have a family with your boyfriend?" he said.

"Maybe yes. Maybe no. Finding a man is not difficult for me." She smiled.

She tossed her hair back, a stream of sweat dripping from the side of her neck to her naked torso. Max stared at the tops of her soft white breasts against her tanned skin.

"Not difficult at all," he said. "You are beautiful."

"Yogis do not look at woman like that." She laughed.

"I'm not a yogi then," he said.

He came closer. His lips found hers. He tasted water, salt, and blood in her chapped skin. He put his hands on her waist and pulled her closer to his naked chest. Her burning skin pressed against him.

"I am messy. I am dirty. I smell. I do not feel attractive," she said.

"I love your smell," he said.

He spread his shirt below them, put her on it, and tugged her cargo pants off. He buried his face between her legs, smelling sweat mixed with dry earth. She moaned. He moved up and down her lean, hard body, licking, kissing, touching, nibbling, biting, his desire fueled by starvation.

He stopped and lay down still on her, feeling her writhe below him. She circled his cracked sore nipples with her tongue, caressed his raw skin, rubbed her fingers over his dry, torn hips, and drew blood from his cuts. He gasped with pain and pleasure and entered her.

They fucked hard as the sun beat upon them.

Again and again they went up, down, his face in her buttocks, her mouth working his penis, fucking, sucking, living, the months of abstinence and denial seeping away from their hard, weary bodies until their skins peeled from the unforgiving wrath of the sun and they cried out in pain.

He shifted position and took her from behind, aroused once again by the red-brown hair falling over her shoulders, the fullness of her breasts and her hard waist.

They screamed together when he came.

They collapsed into each other's arms, a sweaty mix of dust and blood, and lay there still and silent, unconcerned with the beating sun.

"I want this every day. I like this. I do not like yoga," she said after a while.

"Come with me. We can have this every day," said Max.

She got up, pushed her hair back, and started clasping her bra.

Max forced himself up as well. A thousand prickly, throbbing, alive sensations coursed through his body. "Come with me," he said again.

She snorted. "I give us one week, maybe two. You will disappear after that. You want yoga, not sex."

He put his shirt back on and tousled her hair. "How do you know everything?"

"I do not know everything, but I know you, Max. I see you work. I see you do yoga. You are a *parivrajaka,* an eternal traveler, a yogi with no home who will not rest until he sees God face-to-face," she said. "I am not like that."

She looked at her watch. "Almost eleven. If we do not start now, we will burn up, walking six miles to town."

They put on their backpacks and lifted the sacks above their heads and walked back to the village. Max was heady and light. The images from his past that had been tormenting him for months had receded. He felt Shakti's touch on his skin, a loose strand of her auburn hair below his eyes, the smell of her sweat. He stole a glance at her determined, sure face. His eyes stung. She was beautiful.

21.

Something felt different. Max hadn't been to the village in three months, choosing to stay in the ashram even on days silence broke, so he couldn't put his finger on it. What was it? He looked around. Everything was just as he remembered. The thirty-odd huts in a neat semicircle, the giant well in the center of the huts, the shop selling cigarettes and sundry items on the far right, the weaver's shop on the left, the fields with their hardened earth ahead. Why did it look so different, then? It struck him then. He couldn't hear a sound. The village was completely silent. There was no one around. No women huddling at the wells, no children playing with marbles, not a single farmer plowing the fields, no weaver working in the shop. No words, no whispers, no sign of life.

"Where is everybody?" asked Shakti, her words a shout in the eerie silence.

They approached the hut where the man who usually took their food sacks lived. The wooden door was open. A man lay on the mud floor. His skin looked like the earth—patchy, dry, and black. The man raised a bony hand in greeting. It took Max a moment to recognize him as the erect, proud man who had greeted him the last time they had come with the crops.

Max and Shakti put the sacks in front of him.

His withered, dry face broke into a smile. He said something. Max bent closer. He wanted Max to call the others in the village. They knocked on all the doors. Fifteen or twenty women and a couple of old men shuffled out. Heat and hunger seemed to have driven their modesty away. Their rags showed most of their burned, blackened bodies, their hair was unkempt, and their movements were slow and unsure. They had entered the land of the living dead.

The women stared at the food sacks with bright eyes. They smiled through their cracked lips and stained teeth. Three of them lifted one of the sacks and carried it inside to the tall man's hut. The others came closer to Max and Shakti and touched their feet, mumbling their gratitude.

Max stood there staring at the food sacks he hadn't wanted to part with.

"Where are all the men?" said Shakti.

They learned that the men had gone to Madurai, the nearest city twelve hours by bus from Pavur, to find work after farming became impossible in the village.

A middle-aged woman pointed fiercely to a hut on the far

left, gesturing that they should go there. The tall man tried to dissuade her, but she persisted.

They walked through the scorching land and entered the hut. The rancid smell of human waste. Two thin boys, five or six years old, whom Max had often bought snacks for and joked with, were huddled together naked on a bed strung together by ropes. They breathed heavily, making loud, scratchy sounds. Max looked away from their scared eyes.

The woman folded her hands. Her eyes begged them to do something. Again and again she raised her arms, praying and begging.

They had been fucking less than a mile away.

Max indicated she should give them the food they'd brought immediately. But he knew the futility of his suggestion. The three sacks of food would be three meals for one day for a village in the throes of a drought. There wasn't enough food to go around. Today two kids would die, tomorrow some more and then a few more. Hunger, starvation, death were right at his doorstep. How could he have been so selfish, so oblivious? Ramakrishna had been right. They'd had more than enough to eat. Max gripped Shakti's hand.

"Let's go," he said.

"Where?" she said.

"Pavur. Somewhere. There must be an ATM or a bank nearby. I have money," he said.

She started to say something, but her words were drowned by the anguished cries of the woman. They walked out of the hut, past the two-hundred-foot well, which didn't seem to contain a drop of water, away from the charred bodies collecting near the hut they had kept the food in. Limp, weary hands waved at them.

A middle-aged man ran toward them with obvious effort.

He lifted his shirt and pointed to his waist.

Max didn't understand.

"Help. Kidney. Buy kidney," said the man.

The man wanted to sell his kidney for money. Max had read about impoverished donors selling kidneys to needy, rich people. It hadn't struck him with any urgency then. Just as droughts hadn't.

Instead of pity, anger surged within him. Didn't this happen every year? How could these people be so unprepared, so oblivious? Why did they choose to live here?

The man fell on Max's feet, pleading.

Max brushed him off. "No need. I will get money," he said.

They turned around and walked out of the village.

"How many villages will you give money?" said Shakti on the dirt track to Pavur.

He stared at her.

"There are small villages all around," she said pointing to the huts along the road. "It is the same everywhere. How much money can you give?"

His initial irritation disappeared. Shakti was right, logical as usual. What he gave wouldn't be a drop in the ocean for this village, let alone the millions of people dying of starvation in the hundreds of villages all over the world. Half of this world lived on less than a dollar a day. Just because he had seen a few kids die didn't mean it began or ended here. Why did it happen? The questions hadn't changed since he had begun his journey.

"I also think they put on little show for us," said Shakti.

Max understood. The villagers knew they were coming that day, so they hadn't made any effort to hide their needs.

"I read before I came here. Drought and famine are very bad in India but no mass deaths anymore. We were worse off than the villagers. The government sends water tankers to the village every few days. At Ramakrishna's ashram, we had nothing," she said. "Farmers' problems are inflation and debt, not food grain itself."

Max figured the villagers were likely taking on debt to tide themselves through the drought and the men were working menial jobs in Madurai city to pay them off. So the villagers probably had a little more to eat and drink than they had shown. Maybe the boys on the rope bed would breathe less heavily if Max and Shakti weren't around. Sure, he was being manipulated, but it changed nothing. Misery was written large on their faces. The cycle of hunger and debt and more hunger and more debt would go on.

"The planet can't support so many people. There has to be an end to this cycle of birth, death, and rebirth," said Max.

Even as he articulated this half-formed thought, he realized he was running away from the one man who could show him the end of suffering. Why? To have more drumsticks and eggplant? While he was busy angling for an extra bowl of millet and fucking in the fields, the world had continued to spin in its uncaring way. He had come so close to seeing a glimmer of the truth but been distracted once again.

"I'm going to go back to Ramakrishna," he said after a minute. "I'll withdraw whatever money I can from the ATM, buy supplies for the village, and walk right back."

Shakti tied her bandanna around her hair. "I think that is wise," she said.

"Will you come?"

She shook her head. "Nothing changes for me."

"Yet you say it's smart for me to go back?" he said.

"The path of liberation is like poison in beginning, nectar in the end. The path of the world is nectar in beginning, always poison in end," she said. "Quoting as it is from Bhagavad Gita."

"So come with me," he said.

"I do not want to think about the future. I want nectar now," she said.

A boy waved at them from a hut on the side of the dirt track. Max waved back distractedly. "And I should have poison?" he said.

"I think you cannot help it," she said.

A light, empty feeling arose in his gut. He was afraid of going back without Shakti. "Is it safe to live with so little food?" he said.

"If Ramakrishna is okay all these years, you will be okay too. You are strong like him. I try to keep up with you all these months," she said.

"I was keeping up with you," he said.

They arrived at the bus stand. Shakti bought a ticket for the bus to Madurai. They kept their backpacks down and hugged. Tears fell from both their eyes. She touched his face.

"You'll be fine," she said. "All these ups and downs are just small waves in the yoga of your discontent."

"The yoga of my discontent?"

"In the Bhagavad Gita, Arjuna's sorrow shows him the path to unite with the universal consciousness. That's why Bhagavad Gita begins with Arjuna Vishada Yoga, the yoga of Arjuna's despondency," she said. "Your discontent with the world as it is will lead you to your union."

She waved at him and went inside the bus. Max waved back, a lump forming in his throat. He willed himself to feel nothing. It had to start from here. The narrow need for comfort and companionship had to be burned in the fire of a broader, universal love. The bus left. Max walked over to the shop with the phone, feeling an aching sadness in his heart.

MAX CALLED HIS BANK, concentrating on remembering long-forgotten security questions, and maxed out his ATM's international withdrawal limit. He left the shop and withdrew $2,000 in rupees from the ATM next to the bus stand, enough for the village to survive the season if they bought the essentials of grains and lentils. On his way back to the village, Max stopped in front of the hardware store with the Internet connection. He hesitated. He had to break free from the pull of the world, go deeper within. But he couldn't stop himself from entering the store.

Biscuits and chips strung on the façade, shelves full of machine parts, and the proprietor sitting on a chair in the relative coolness of the dark shop interior—everything seemed glaringly opulent in contrast to the sparseness of the ashram and the village. He connected to the Internet, barely noticing how slow it was. To touch the cold metal of the laptop, to know how to operate it, and have an email account itself made him aware of the vastness of his privilege.

Petty, irrelevant noise entered his silent life as soon as he opened his email. Jobs being changed, houses being bought, babies being welcomed. He skimmed through everything quickly, stopping only at an email from Sophia.

Maxi, I got admitted to Stern . . . I know you'll be surprised I'm going to B-School but I gotta make some money! Else I'll end up back in the projects . . . I've realized now I was just trying to be different from you. Send me news. Oh and I've met someone! He's great . . . he's helping me think through a lot of things.

Max was surprised. Sophia had always been so driven by purpose and meaning. He couldn't see her working in a corporation. Was she okay? She didn't seem as self-contained and thoughtful as she usually was. He didn't quite like the sound of the guy she had met.

Max walked back to the shop with the phone. He dialed Sophia's number from memory. It went to voicemail. Max disconnected the phone. He wouldn't call her again. If he wanted to become the universal, he had to transcend this narrow love, these binding attachments that fed one's sense of self. Not that she needed him. She was twenty-six and going to graduate school, not a mother of two trying to feed her children in the middle of a drought.

Outside the shop, Max began throwing his clothes out of the backpack with a vengeance. He returned to the village with a bag full of powdered glucose, water bottles, biscuits, fruits, lentils, and rice—and just enough diesel for the tractor ride to Ramakrishna's ashram and back.

IN THE VILLAGE CHIEF'S HUT, he succumbed to the villagers' insistence of sharing a portion of their meager rations. They treated him like a messiah. *I'm nobody,* he wanted to scream at their dried, torn faces. Just someone born in easier circumstances he didn't work for in this life. A bony, charred young woman served him potatoes and biscuits. She looked roughly the same age as Sophia, but this woman's future would be as black as her past. Could he help her? Could anyone? Who knew if her pain was the effect of actions from lives past or just a random act of nature? All he knew was that the world was imperfect and an ancient path promised perfection. Now he would walk the path afresh to get answers back for all. Max looked at the woman's sallow face and couldn't taste the potatoes anymore. He had lost his taste for food forever and was glad for it. So fleeting and capricious was the joy of the senses, these external pleasures. Nothing would distract him in his search for the permanent truth within.

Max made his way back later that evening once the driver had his fill of the cooked food Max brought for him. Ramakrishna greeted him at the gates with his silent smile. Despite Max's protestations, he insisted on sweeping the floors of his hut and making his bed just as he had done the first time. It was as if he was welcoming a guest other than the one who had left.

22.

The rain came three weeks later. First a trickle, then a torrent, breaking the land open and making it soft and malleable again. They planted six columns of new seeds after the first rain, adding rice and tomatoes to their usual three. The bore well filled. The hand pump worked again. Crops sprouted, as did insects, and with them came frogs and snakes. New life. Despite the now-abundant food and the luxury of being able to choose between rice and millet, Max stuck to eating one meal a day. And he did well with it. His strength returned, his constipation eased, and he found that he could do asanas and field work with more intensity than before.

The monsoon brought new visitors. A Portuguese couple who had cycled for eighteen months from Portugal through Spain,

France, Italy, Croatia, Bulgaria, Turkey, Iran, and Pakistan and finally into India. Ultimately they realized the futility of endlessly chasing new sights and sounds, abandoned their plans of going to Nepal, sold their bicycles in India, and embarked on the more perilous journey of looking inside. They lasted two weeks.

They were followed by a Sri Lankan artist who wanted to make herself an instrument of the universal creative force. She left in a week, as did the Indian software engineer who had started to feel life was an elaborate charade. Others came and went. Max talked to them eagerly in the beginning. Soon, though, he fell silent like Hari, became reflective like Shakti. With each passing face, he understood more and more what dying would feel like. He'd remember a collage of faces and smiles—and bid them a final good-bye, knowing he hadn't unmasked the eternal truth. New faces would keep coming. The chatter would go on. None of it would take him closer to his goal of completion, of reaching a spiritual whole with the infinite. Every moment now was dedicated to learning, giving, dissolving his small self. Nothing else mattered.

Now he worked in the field without thought of enjoyment or pain and surrendered his body to the universe's will in his asana practice. His actions were that of a yogi, neither white nor black, just colorless. He was determined to break the cause-effect cycle, produce no reactions, no impressions, neither good nor bad. Slowly he was untethering himself from life.

His meditation deepened. One day he saw a bright yellow light in the space between his closed eyes. Liquid warmth surged through his body. The next day the light became brighter. Bells chimed somewhere within him. Max opened his eyes. The chiming stopped. The bells tolled again when he closed his eyes. Deep, sonorous, melodic, tugging at his heartstrings. Bright yellow light pulsed from his head to his body. Was this the divine—unknown lights and mystical sounds, the feeling of complete warmth and peace?

"Don't be distracted. Don't get attached to lights and sounds. They are just signposts that you are on the right path, not the end of the path. Keep working hard." The words Ramakrishna had said once long ago remained in his head.

So Max did exactly that. He slept less and less, sometimes two hours a night, sometimes not at all. His dreams ceased, probably because his mind was at rest. More blinding lights appeared with the passing of the months—yellow, orange, red—and they stayed for longer and longer. Late one night when he was meditating in his hut, a hollow, guttural sound originated in the bottom of his spine. The sound traveled up and down his spine before reverberating in the depths of his heart. Max felt weightless, floating, dissolving into the sound. Radiant white light filled the space between his eyes. The light disappeared. He was submerged in infinite black space. From the blackness emerged the sun, moons, galaxies, stars, and hundreds of red planets. They whirled rapidly in a circle, crashing against one another, and turned into large glaciers, mountains, oceans, and flat land. Max shuddered. All of creation lay within him. He opened his eyes to a bright morning.

Ramakrishna hadn't shaken him out of his meditation for asana class that day. Perhaps he knew that Max had felt for the first time the presence of the creating energy, the causeless cause within him. For Max realized the sound that emerged in his spine was Om, the root in every sound, the word that had vibrated in the act of creation. He had read of the mystical Om in books at the ashram, but he had never experienced it until that day. Om vibrated again and again within him in the days that followed. Soon Max's nagging worries about his future began to disappear. This body, this mind that tormented him wasn't him. The Dutch yoga teacher and the mother of two from Texas, who were staying at the ashram that week, were no different from him. Clay made pots, pans, plates, bricks, and houses, but the real nature of all of them was the same clay. One consciousness vibrated everywhere, in everything. Om, the vibration of that consciousness, filled his body and mind, slowly dissolving the images lingering in his mind. Keisha's face became hazier. Shakti standing at the bus stop, waving good-bye, shimmered and disappeared. His mother's yellow, contorted face and Andre's limp, lifeless legs were mere wrinkles on the surface of the pot. Their real nature was unaffected. Other faces touched, hands held, promises made, conversations had—all were receding, disappearing into the growing void within him.

Max relied more and more on himself for his asana practice. The sum of all knowledge was within him. A twist there, a bend here, a little shifting of his toes, some responsiveness to the cosmic will, and he got into asanas that he didn't think were possible. Ramakrishna would tell him the names later: Kapotasana, the dove; Valakhilyasana, the heavenly pose; Gherandasana, the sage's pose; Kapinjalasana, the partridge pose—and others whose names Ramakrishna didn't know but whose existence he didn't doubt because Max was being taught by the all-knowing consciousness within.

. . .

MORE MONTHS PASSED. Once in a while he checked his email. Andre emailed to tell him he had graduated from college and was working with troubled kids in the Bronx. Sophia didn't end up going to Stern after all. She decided to travel with her new boyfriend to Europe for a few months to figure things out. Max had never seen her so lost before, but he tried not to worry about her. After all, he had left the land he knew for a greater knowing too. One full year ago. It was December again. Max had never felt more at peace. The space within him was growing, filling him with a strange silence. Boundaries of space and time were breaking. He worked hard in the fields, did asana and pranayama, and meditated like before, but none of the activities felt distinct from the others. Something within him remained silent. The body worked, the mind concentrated, but he was unmoved. Complete. The same in every contortion of the body, in every fluctuation of the mind. Winter. Spring. Summer. Another drought.

This time he was alone with Ramakrishna. He understood now why the saint remained unaffected. The sun was not an enemy, the land not an unrelenting ingrate. They were beautiful, majestic, all part of one system, linked by the karmic cycle of cause and effect, action and reaction. The first summer it had caused him sorrow. Now his lean, hard body, likely forty or fifty pounds of unnecessary weight lighter than when he had first come to the ashram, remained unaffected by the drought. It craved nothing for itself. He felt the villagers' hunger like his own, and this time Ramakrishna and he had more rations to spare for them. Max delivered them every week until the rains came again.

In town one day in August, Max checked his email for the first time in many months. Not a single note from Sophia. *Are you okay, my dear? Did you go to Europe? Are you still with that guy?* Max checked to see if Andre had written about Sophia but there was just a single note from him.

> **U inspired me 2 get out of my head, ace. I looked up 2 u all my life. Christ, what happened 2 u ace? U were going places. Get ur life back. I'm always here 4 u.**

No word from Sophia. Max was flustered again. Why was the bond with his sister so hard to transcend? Nothing weighed him down anymore, not the body, not its petty need for comfort, not the pull for sensory stimulation. Only his little sister held him from losing himself completely to the blissful void. He banished the image of the little girl with curly hair sliding down an iron slide in Central Park and stopped himself from walking into the phone shop.

On his way back to the ashram that day, he didn't fall into the state of spontaneous absorption that was coming over him more and more naturally those days. *Sophia, my dear, are you well?* He forced himself to concentrate on his breath.

23.

The next night, the noise of footsteps broke Max's concentration. The ashram had filled with temporary visitors once again that monsoon season, and a Bulgarian man and two German girls were staying with them. Max closed his eyes and resumed his meditation.

Heavy breathing. A muffled shout. More footsteps.

Max got up and walked toward the bathroom.

The tall, bald muscular Bulgarian stood outside the bathroom hut, his eyes narrowed, jaw tight, sweat pouring down his temples. He held an aluminum trekking pole in his thick hands.

Max raised his eyebrows.

"Snake inside. Large cobra," said the man.

Reluctantly Max broke the silence. "It'll be gone tomorrow," he said. "Go to sleep."

The Bulgarian wiped the sweat from his jaw and stared at him. "You crazy, man? I have to use bathroom," he said, his eyes blinking. "Also I cannot sleep next door with that big bastard right here. They are poisonous. You be dead in minute if it bites. You don't worry, man. I done this before in mountains."

Max knew this thick Bulgarian wouldn't last the week. The rains had picked up. With the rains came insects, frogs, and more snakes. If you didn't trouble them, they never troubled you. The same living energy coursed through them. Much like humans, they were driven by desire, the desire to eat, procreate, live, and evolve, not to bite and kill what wasn't food for them.

A slithering sound came from inside.

The Bulgarian's bald pate shone with fresh sweat. He pushed the door wide open. "Just see the bastard," he said.

The snake was ten feet long with yellow-brown skin, fiery black rectangular patterns, and a large head. It looped around the squat toilet, its beady eyes gleaming, tongue flicking in and out.

"Move back," said the Bulgarian. He tightened his grip on the trekking pole. Sweat dripped from the back of his head to his thick neck. The snake must have heard or felt him. It raised its head up and spread its magnificent hood.

Max stood rooted to the ground watching the snake's shiny, smooth scales and oily brown skin. It was beautiful, magnificent, shaking with life force.

The Bulgarian raised his hands seemingly to bring the pole crashing on the snake's head.

"Stop," said Max. "Please stop."

"What, man?" said the Bulgarian, turning his head around in apparent confusion.

Max didn't answer. The void within him expanded to include the wondrous life-form in front of him. *He was the snake.* The majestic twisted body that didn't know why it was born, why it would die, why it struck everyone with repulsion and fear. *We are one*, said Max to him. *I understand you. Just go outside for now. Slowly, lower your hood, unwind yourself from the toilet, come straight toward us, move forward to the bench in the courtyard and outside the boundary of the ashram. Don't come back for a few days. Are you listening to me? Do it now.*

The snake put its hood down. It untangled itself from the toilet and moved toward them.

"Back," said the Bulgarian and lifted the pole again.

"Stop," said Max. He caught hold of the Bulgarian's sweaty right arm and pulled it down.

"What are you doing, bastard?" said the Bulgarian.

The snake came closer to them. The Bulgarian tried to wrestle his arm away. Max held his thick wrist tight, pressing hard on his veins with his fingernails.

"It hurts, man. Stop. Help," shouted the Bulgarian.

He lashed out with his left hand.

Max caught it and held both his hands behind him, still staring at the snake.

The snake slithered and curved around their feet. It remained looped around their feet for a minute while the Bulgarian whimpered. Then it uncurled itself, moved toward the lone courtyard bench, and went out of the gates of the ashram.

Max released the Bulgarian's hands.

The Bulgarian shoved him. "What the hell were you thinking,

man? Why did you catch me? We could have died, man. We were dead. Fucking fuck. We were dead," he said, hopping around.

The sweat from the Bulgarian's brows poured in a steady stream down his face. All of a sudden he stopped and stared at Max. "You knew it, didn't you, man? You knew cobra would come toward us and go out." He made a strange sound with his throat, half laughing, half crying. "Who are you? You are mad, man. You spoke to snake, right? Oh fucking Christ, where the hell am I? The silence, the snake, this Harry Potter craziness. You guys are like devil cult or something."

Max left him and went back to his bed. He wasn't sure the snake had understood, but something had happened between them—a transfer of energy, an awareness of presence, something. Whatever it was, the snake had lived. Max slept comfortably that night.

The Bulgarian left the next morning. He preferred to walk to the village than wait three days more for the tractor.

24.

The next evening, during meditation, Sophia's face filled Max's mind. But it wasn't the Sophia he remembered. She was thirty pounds heavier, her face completely white, her eyes sunken and weary. An angry blue scar crossed her pale cheek. Max opened his eyes. She was sick. He began to breathe faster.

Max closed his eyes again. Now Sophia was in a flowing, light green dress. Her limp hand lifted to swallow a handful of pills. The veins below her eyes grew larger.

Max opened his eyes again. By now he knew enough to know the image was real. Somewhere Sophia was suffering. His lungs exploded. He had known it when her emails stopped. His throat choked. The silence, the space within him, vanished.

. . .

BACK IN HIS HUT, he paced around. He walked out to speak to Ramakrishna but stopped. Ramakrishna wouldn't say much, but his eyes would speak the truth. Human attachments tethered man to this unfulfilling cycle of birth and death. *Liberate yourself from narrow individual bonds. See oneness everywhere.* Max sat down on his bed and meditated. Sophia's body was suffering. Her mind was ill. The body, the mind—they were fickle and destined to decay, subject as they were to the same laws of impermanence that bound the entire phenomenal world. But Sophia, her true essence was fine. Still laughing when she slipped down the iron slide; squeezing her date's hand at Thanksgiving dinner; eyes dancing, hands moving with abandon when she talked. She was so close he could touch her. Max opened his eyes. She had no one but him.

Max stuffed his backpack with his sparse clothes and left the ashram. The moon, a faint sliver, cast only a bare light on his path. He removed his shoes. Barefoot, he connected easily to the ridges and furrows in the hard land and let them guide him to the village. In three days, he would be back in New York. He'd stay only until he helped her recover. Nothing else in the incomplete material world would ensnare him again. The blackness enveloped him as he walked through the silent, starless night. He closed his eyes and concentrated on the space between his eyes. No new images came. Just Sophia's pale, worn face and listless eyes. *What happened, my dear? I'm coming.*

MAX REACHED THE village at dawn. He took the water from the pail hanging by the well's side and threw it over his burning eyes. A shriveled old woman with scorched purple-black skin came out of one of the huts. She called out to the others. More doors opened. Three women in saris, four or five lanky men with long white cloths tied around their waists, and a handful of naked kids rubbing their eyes shuffled out of the huts. They greeted Max with broad smiles. The kids surrounded him, pulling at his T-shirt, talking and laughing. A boy brought out a pair of sticks and wanted to play Gilli Danda—lifting the small stick in the air with the big stick and hitting it as far as it could go.

Max hit one into the distance. The kids clapped. Max smiled at them. He knew every kid's name now. They played with him whenever he came to deliver food supplies to the village. He had taught them a smattering of English and he understood some of the local dialect. A woman gave him a glass of tea. Someone or the other always served him food on his visits. Just like a second family.

Max set the stick down and began walking to Pavur, six miles away. A girl with tiny pigtails pulled at his khakis, asking him to stay. In the distance, an infant cried in an old woman's arms. Max looked into the eyes of the little girl, smiling through her cute, chipped teeth. He felt hollow; he was sinking, disappearing into space. He was breaking into pieces, melting, merging into the girl. Max had never felt such helpless love before. He stood still, allowing his breath to return to normal. The feeling passed.

Max resumed his walk to Pavur. The girl waved at him. The kids cheered.

Soon they would bind him too.

Max walked faster.

Seeking but not finding the House Builder,
I traveled through the round of countless births;
O painful is birth ever and ever again.

Something, someone, this person, that family had tethered him in every life. This time he was so close to liberating himself from the bondage to this sense of self, to becoming just a channel of the universal. He couldn't let this narrow love hold him back. Max stopped. Sophia's pale, sickly face came before his eyes again. His throat tightened. Max looked up at the sky. Hari's family had pulled him back. The need for comfort had called Shakti. Max wouldn't let his attachments get in his way. He turned around.

The kids jumped and shouted upon seeing him again. Max tried to smile. Each one of them, everyone in the world, was the same as Sophia. Tears stinging his eyes, he began to walk back to the ashram in his bare feet.

25.

Ramakrishna didn't ask him where he had been when Max came back later that day. Max remained restless throughout the afternoon. In yoga that evening, his body felt heavy and his limbs moved with effort. He paced in the courtyard after yoga, then skipped meditation and lay on his bed, staring at the ceiling.

Late that night he awoke with a start. His back was on fire.

He jumped out of bed. The fire spread from the bottom of his spine to the middle of his ribs when he stood up. The bones in his back felt as if they were being grated into a paste, then being burned to ash. He lay down and got up again. It hurt so much. He rushed to the bathroom and doused himself in bucket after bucket of cold water. Nothing helped. Max had never disturbed Ramakrishna at night, but he couldn't help himself. Whimpering in pain, he ran into Ramakrishna's hut well past midnight.

"Please help me," said Max. He was disintegrating, dying. "I can't. My back. It burns so bad."

Ramakrishna's concerned face broke into a smile. "Your kundalini has awakened," he said.

The fire flared up. Max's head spun.

Ramakrishna made him sit cross-legged on the floor and straightened his back. "Soon you'll be better, better than ever," said Ramakrishna.

Max inhaled and exhaled slowly. The fire turned into hot liquid that surged from the bottom of his spine to its middle, up the back of his neck, and down, again and again. Max removed his T-shirt and put his naked back against the hard, cold mud.

"It's not getting better . . ."

His eyes closed.

THE FLAME HAD disappeared when he awoke the next day, but his spine tingled with alternate warm and cold sensations. He stepped out of Ramakrishna's hut. The usually odorless air was alive with smells. He could distinguish each note. There was the fragrance of mud mixed with morning dew, the sweat of the two German girls, the lingering smoke from the previous night's fire, and the heavy aroma of tomatoes that had been cooked the day before in the afternoon. Each smell had its own texture. The morning colors were different too. The sun hadn't risen yet, but the dawn was a white light far on the horizon. The orange mud in the courtyard was a shade darker than the one around Ramakrishna's hut. Why hadn't he noticed these sights, these smells before, each so distinct, so wonderful?

Ramakrishna was instructing the German girls in the courtyard. Max heard every sound made by the girls, their inhalation, their exhalation, their heels shuffling below their thighs, their knees shifting on the floor. A little overwhelmed, Max joined them for asanas.

His body had changed overnight. He felt light as a feather. Warm fluid flowed from the base of his spine to all his nerves. He got up in a headstand. The blood didn't collect in his head. There was no pressure on his face, no throbbing in his heart, no pulsing sensation in his neck. He closed his eyes and fell into a meditative state. He didn't emerge from it until he felt Ramakrishna's hands on his back.

"If you want, you can come down now. An hour is quite enough for the headstand," said Ramakrishna.

An hour. It couldn't be. Max had never stayed up for more than twenty-five minutes at a stretch before, and he had built from five minutes to twenty-five minutes over the course of eighteen months. That day, though, standing on the head felt as comfortable as standing on his feet. He could have remained like that forever.

The German girls were staring at him. Again Max had the same, overwhelming feeling of seeing everything as if it were under a magnifying glass. One girl's skin was slightly torn under her eyes; the other's eyebrow hair was uneven. If he stared at them any longer, he would know every thought in their heads. Max averted his eyes and continued with the asanas.

His spine elongated and stretched; he flipped forward and backward farther than he had on his best days before without a hint of discomfort. Max had learned not to be surprised at the coincidences and intuitions and the glimpses of cosmic energy that had entered his life, but when he got into Kakasana, the crow pose, and found his whole body inverting in the air by its own accord as soon as he touched his fingers on the ground, he couldn't stop himself from looking up straight into Ramakrishna's eyes.

Just what was happening to him?

We'll speak after meditation tonight, said Ramakrishna.

Max came down. How did he just hear that? Ramakrishna hadn't moved his lips.

Yes, it is related, said Ramakrishna.

Ramakrishna had just answered a question Max hadn't framed in his mind.

Max took a sharp breath. An ocean of cool air washed down his body.

DURING THE REST of the day, Max remained in the same hyperaware state. He detected the slight movements of earthworms below the surface of the mud and moved his plow away from them. He corrected the placement of one of the thirty seeds that Anna, one of the German girls, sowed twenty feet ahead of him. His ears registered every thud of a tool against the earth and the bristling of water on the crops. His tongue tasted a hundred notes of sweet and sour in the eggplant. Everything felt stark, intense, as if he had awakened from centuries of slumber.

. . .

LATER THAT DAY in meditation, a rainbow of colors merged into him. Om resonated again and again through his body. The sun, moons, stars, oceans, mountains—the whole universe revolved around him in concentric circles. He was the beginning, the middle, and the end, the center that held everything together. Then suddenly everything was snuffed out in an instant. A deep indescribable silence arose within him. It had the tranquility of water and the stillness of air, the alertness of a predator and the repose of a rose petal, the brightness of the sun and the coolness of the moon. Yet it was none of these, for it was quite apart from the world. He remained suspended in the silence until Ramakrishna shook him gently.

The blacks of Ramakrishna's eyes shone in the yellow-white light of the courtyard lamp. Max's heart overflowed with love. He was gripped by the same boundaryless feeling he had experienced with the little girl from the village, but he wasn't overwhelmed this time. He was complete. There was just oneness. Nothing separated him from Ramakrishna. The words that were about to come from Ramakrishna's mouth were already alive within him. Max breathed slowly.

"You have received the rarest of the rare blessings. For so many lives, you have worked for this," said Ramakrishna, his voice echoing in the still night. "The universal consciousness is awake in your body."

"What happens now?"

"If you keep striving, the active consciousness will slowly move from the Muladhara chakra at the base of your spine to the Sahasrara at the top of the head, the home of the static, creating energy—or God," he said. "This final union is yoga. Individual consciousness has merged with divine consciousness. You will become the universal, God as it were. It is the end of the individual, of birth and rebirth, this endless cycle of suffering. You will achieve the very goal of the human form."

Max trembled. The bottom of his spine tingled.

"You have to work harder than ever before. Only the most accomplished of yogis achieve this union," said Ramakrishna. "You will become the sum of all knowledge. Many powers will come to you. But all that has to be left behind. Falling from this state is easy if you develop even a shadow of an ego."

Max shifted on his mat, suddenly afraid. "Will you continue to be my teacher?"

"The universe is your teacher now. Consciousness will guide you to merge with it," said Ramakrishna. "See it, hear it, feel it everywhere, within and outside everything. You have nothing more to learn from me."

Ramakrishna looked up at the black sky and waved his hands around. He didn't move his lips but Max heard his voice in his head.

It will come. All will come. You will surpass me very soon, in mere days or months. I haven't reached the end of yoga, but you can.

What does the complete dissolution of self feel like? thought Max.

I don't know yet. Perhaps you will know for me, for all of us. Ramakrishna's thoughts merged with other voices in his head.

"Come back and teach me. That will be your *gurudakshina*, your gift, for whatever little you've learned here," said Ramakrishna aloud.

Max bent down and touched the tips of Ramakrishna's feet. "I have learned everything from you," said Max.

"You knew everything. Everyone knows everything. You just chose me as a channel in this life," said Ramakrishna.

Just a day before, Max was about to leave the ashram. Even now Sophia hadn't disappeared completely from his mind.

"I was lost when I came here. I still feel a little lost," said Max.

"The awakening of the kundalini is unsettling. Stay here for as long as you like. Teach yourself how to use the power, how to keep making progress," said Ramakrishna.

Max got up, straightened his back, and felt the warmth spread out from his spine. He felt one with the great sage in front of him, the blackness of the night around him, and the moon and stars above him. His body was as light as the air that hugged him. For a moment he thought he was floating. He looked down to check.

Soon even that, maybe very soon. Ramakrishna smiled without speaking. *May you never fall from the grace of yoga, Mahadeva, may you always be a yogi.*

Max walked back to his hut. He sat on his bed and closed his eyes, concentrating on Sophia. Her pale, heavy face came into focus. He directed the light, buoyant energy coursing through him toward the middle of his forehead just above the junction of his eyebrows. His heart seemed to have become her beating heart, feeling her sadness, her longing, her sickness, then soothing her, making her still, silent, complete. A touch of color appeared in Sophia's cheeks. He concentrated harder so that nothing existed in the world except the shimmering blackness between them. Blinding white light poured from him. The redness spread up her cheeks to her nose and filled her face. Max's body burned. He lay down on the bed, his temples pounding, a blazing flame spreading through his torso. He saw Sophia's eyes lighting up. He spread his hands wide up toward the ceiling, allowing the universe to take revenge on his body for manipulating the laws of nature. The effects of Sophia's actions would now become his own. Sophia sat up on the bed she was lying in and smiled. *Strive, strive, strive for perfection. Don't be caught again in these ceaseless ups and downs, the world of polarities.* Max drifted off to sleep.

THE SAGE

Seeking but not finding the House Builder,
I traveled through the round of countless births;
O painful is birth ever and ever again.
House Builder, you have now been seen.
You should not build the house again; Your rafters have been broken down; Your ridgepole is demolished too.
My mind has now reached the unformed Nirvana.
And reached the end of every kind of craving.

—GAUTAMA, THE BUDDHA

26.

Jesus Christ, Jesus Christ, Jesus Christ, Jesus Christ."

Max turned around and smiled at the kids who were chanting and pointing at him. They'd been following him from the bus station in Madurai, the nearest big city, to Pavur, twelve hours away by bus. He glanced at his reflection in the dusty glass door of the freestanding ATM kiosk in the market next to the bus station. Loose shirt, long brown hair, light beard, sunburned skin, sharp eyes, weighing at least sixty pounds less than when he had first come to India, he had to admit he did look a little like Jesus. Although he didn't feel much like him right then. He couldn't produce gold coins from air. He couldn't even get an ATM machine to work. The ATM machine in Pavur had rejected his card, as had the one inside the Madurai bus station. He needed money for his journey ahead even though he didn't quite know where he would go next. After spending three years at Ramakrishna's ashram, he felt overwhelmed by people, smells, shops, traffic—and getting simple things to work.

His debit card was rejected once again.

Outside the kiosk, men on bicycles whizzed past busy shops, hawkers peddled their wares, and a bent old man dragged a wheelbarrow filled with brown sacks. Max fingered the card's silver strip. Had his bank frozen his checking account because he hadn't used it in more than two years? Max opened the door and walked outside to look for a telephone booth.

He collided with a tall, lean man on a bicycle who was staring openmouthed at him.

"Sorry, boss, sorry," said the man.

"Pen, pen, pen, Jesus Christ," chanted the boys following him.

Three women selling vegetables, a man selling newspapers and magazines on a cart, and a few passersby collected around him.

Max wasn't used to the attention. He hadn't gone beyond Pavur for three years and everyone there had known him. Here, he felt like an alien once again. Even so, he was surprised that the locals followed him when he walked to the phone booth. Madurai was a temple city and saw its fair share of Western tourists. Some were on the street right then. He spotted a young blond couple, an older Russian-looking man, and another white family of four, but no one followed them around or gaped at them. Was it because of his height? His ragged clothes? Max couldn't figure it out, but he did find a phone booth. People gathered around the booth to watch him. Puzzled, he turned his back to the street and concentrated on dialing the phone number listed at the back of his bank card.

"Please enter the last four digits of your Social Security number," said a mechanized voice.

In his previous life, Max would have pressed a series of #'s and 0's on the phone to bypass the prompts and connect directly to a live person. Now every thought, every action was an exercise in complete truthfulness. For there could be nothing relative in the path of the yogi. He couldn't speak a half-truth, the same way he couldn't squash the mosquitoes ravaging him or covet a more comfortable way of traveling than the lowest class available on the train. A yogi lived in absolutes. Truth, nonviolence, and austerity were his religion. It rid the body of physical craving and the mind of ego, thus reducing the pull of the world.

Max punched, dialed, corrected, then repunched and redialed his Social Security digits, birth date, and former street address on the broken phone console before finally being connected to a live voice.

His ATM access had indeed been blocked due to account inactivity. They needed the exact amounts and dates of his last three ATM withdrawals to verify his identity.

"Is there another way?" said Max. "I haven't withdrawn money in years. It will be hard to tell the exact dates."

"I realize the difficulty, Mr. Pzoras, but Capital One bank's international fraud protection policies are aimed at safeguarding customers' interests first and foremost," said the efficient male voice. "Alternatively, we request a notarized letter stating your reason for not using the bank account. We will process it within seven business days of receipt and reopen the account."

Fraud protection. Safeguarding. Notarized. Process. The words of the world sounded heavy and difficult. Max paused, trying to understand everything. "Notarized by whom?" he said eventually.

"Any recognizable US body. Like an embassy or a consulate in your country of travel," the voice said.

The nearest consulate was probably in Chennai, another ten hours away, and there would probably be more red tape there. Nor did he have money to get there. The yogic test had been performed. Max was now clear that it would utilize far less prana to perform samyama, a blend of deep concentration and meditation resulting in complete merging with the object of focus, on the withdrawal dates. In the last year, Ramakrishna had taught him to practice samyama on his body to understand the working of the cells that made up his vital organs and the interconnected masses of veins and nerves that supplied blood and nutrients to them. Knowing his body would allow him to keep it fit and functioning, making it a sturdy temple to worship the soul within. Now Max would concentrate on his memory with the same intensity.

"Could you hold for just a minute?" he asked.

Max closed his eyes, shutting out the curious crowd outside. He inhaled and exhaled, concentrating on the Ajna chakra in the center of his forehead, the storehouse of all memory. First he drowned out the lingering images of leaving Ramakrishna and the previous twenty-four hours of walking and bus journeys. Next he zoned in on the ATM trips he had made more than three years ago, and finally he retained his breath, flowing his entire living, breathing energy, his prana, toward the Ajna chakra, merging with the man who walked into the ATMs many years ago.

He opened his eyes, weak and breathless. His shirt was soaked with perspiration. He gripped the phone tight so that it didn't slip from his sweaty grip and rested his head against the stained glass door.

"December 3, 2010, 4:57 PM EST. New York. $200. December 9, 2010, 12:31 PM. Rishikesh, Indian Rupees 20,000, US $443.75. July 14, 2011, 2:19 PM. Pavur, Tamil Nadu, Indian Rupees 100,000, US $1,907.30."

"Yes, yes, yes, exactly right. Date and withdrawal amounts are both correct. I don't have the exact time or place printed in front of me. Thank you for confirming, Mr. Pzoras. Your account is now unblocked," the customer service representative said. He paused. "I can't believe you've kept the receipts all these years. I wish I was that organized," he added in a slightly embarrassed tone.

Max thanked him and set the phone down. The crowd watching him outside had swelled. Max stepped out of the phone booth and sat down on the side of the road. He felt dizzy and depleted. If remembering three dates had taken so much concentration, so much prana, how much more would walking on water and levitating demand? Yes, Max could do much if he performed deep samyama on something. But Ramakrishna was right. Pursuing extraordinary powers broke the laws of nature and distracted one from the goal. Every breath spent on clinging to the earthly realm took energy away from merging with the divine. Just like sending waves of prana to heal Sophia from afar had left him weak and feverish for months. Now he understood his urge to finally leave Ramakrishna more than a year after his kundalini had awakened. The veil separating him from pure consciousness had thinned, but to penetrate any farther into it, he would have to conduct his own experiments with truth. Only when he verified the knowledge he had received with his own experience would it fuse into his every breath.

"Photo, photo, photo."

People jostled to sit beside him on the pavement. They put their arms around him and asked their companions to click pictures on their phones with Max. One, two, ten, twenty, Max clicked pictures with kids, shopkeepers, vegetable vendors, newspaper sellers, and their customers, too weak to resist their attention. He recovered his breath after more than an hour and walked back to the ATM. This time his card worked. He withdrew the money he wanted, bought pens for the kids from one of the newspaper sellers, and began walking toward the railway station.

People rushed toward him.

"Thank you, Thank you, Jesus Christ. Come again, Jesus Christ," shouted the delighted kids, shaking his hands.

The vegetable-vending women touched his feet. "Bless, bless."

A legless beggar on a wooden cart scrambled next to him. He tugged Max's cargo pants, urging him to put his hands on his head.

The phone booth owner prostrated in front of him.

More people joined him. Now a crowd of folks lay before him.

"Stop, please stop," said Max, surprised and still dizzy.

"God, God, God," chanted a short, fat woman in a yellow sari.

Others picked up the chant. More people joined them.

The noise overwhelmed him. "No, I'm nobody. Stop, stop, please, stop," said Max.

A woman in a bright dress came forward and showed him her small phone-camera with the picture she had just taken.

"Look, you are God. Light. Shining," she said.

Max looked at the image on the woman's phone. He smiled and exhaled slowly.

Ramakrishna had taught him well. Despite the holes in his well-worn clothes, his unkempt hair and tired face, Max's skin glowed like a lamp—though it was a pale reflection of the ethereal glow on Ramakrishna's skin. There was a lot more distance to cover.

"No, not God," said Max. "Just a yogi. Or trying to be one."

He walked away from the surging crowd, toward the railway station.

THE MAN AT the ticket counter asked him where he wanted to go.

He could go anywhere. All he needed was solitude. He remembered the remote beautiful places he had visited before or heard of in India from the visitors at Ramakrishna's ashram—Dhanushkoti, Sarnath, Kaapil, Arpora. But he knew there could be only one answer. Despite it being winter again, his home, the mountains, the mighty Himalayas were calling him back.

"Haridwar," said Max.

"Second AC or Third AC?"

"General."

The man stared at him. "You can't go in General, *machi*. They are unreserved compartments. No seats. No place to sleep. Standing room only. Completely packed. It is a sixty-hour journey. Impossible."

Max smiled. "In the beginning, even the journey within is uncomfortable."

The man hesitated. "So Third AC then?"

"No, General."

The man's eyes widened. "You are not well. Do you have fever? Your face is very shiny," said the man.

"I'm well, friend, as well as this limited human form can allow," said Max. "Please let me continue on my journey to liberation."

The man stared at Max but eventually sold him a ticket.

27.

Max went back north the same way he had come, resisting the urge to stop in Dehradun and thank Anand, the Slovenian who had guided him to Ramakrishna. It wasn't time. He hadn't yet reached a spiritual whole with consciousness, become the universal. He still identified himself as Max, one who was born, grew, decayed, suffered, and died and couldn't alleviate anyone's suffering because he hadn't conquered his own. Yes, he had seen glimpses of the truth, a shimmering, blinding light dancing in the corners of the growing void within him. In those rare moments, there had been pure silence, just the One and no other. But the individual lump of salt hadn't dissolved completely in the ocean yet. He had to go deeper still.

A little depleted after his samyama at the ATM, Max used the time in the train to restore his vital energy with kapalabhati, pumping his abdomen in and out, inhaling fresh air and exhaling out the stale air with force. He smiled at his fellow passengers, unbothered by their surprised stares, the hundreds of people pushing him, climbing over him to get in and out, the kids tugging his long hair, the men and women who touched his skin, the cockroaches who crawled on him, and all the sounds and smells alive in a train carriage filled to many times its capacity. They were all him.

SIXTY HOURS LATER, early in the morning, the train reached Haridwar. Once again, as he had done a few years earlier when he had first arrived in the Himalayas, Max took a bus to Uttarkashi and stopped at a hotel, this time needing no warm blankets and hot water, his body immune to the craving for petty luxury. He had expected to wait a few days in Bhatwari until he found some intrepid motorcycle riders again, but he was pleasantly surprised to find a jeep making its last trip to Gangotri for the season.

Max reached Gangotri late one overcast afternoon in the first week of December with everything he needed for the months to come in his backpack: three gunnysacks containing millet, chickpeas and kidney beans, a stove, a penknife to carve wood, matchsticks to build a fire, one change of T-shirt and pants, gloves and a jacket if it got colder than he could force his body to adapt to, and a bedsheet to cover the ground in a cave. Once again the village was deserted and the tiny houses and shops were covered with soft white snow. The wind gusted as he started on the deserted snow-covered trail to Bhojbasa. Clouds blanketed the sun and a wall of gray loomed ahead of him. A heavy rain began as soon as he passed the abandoned forest office building two miles into the hike. Rain seeped through the holes in his sweater, drenching his thin shirt. The rain turned into a light snowfall, then a blizzard. But this time he was prepared for the wetness and cold.

Every day for the last six months, he had performed samyama on the Manipura chakra in his navel, the junction of the 72,000 root nerves in the body, and his body had revealed its most intimate workings to him. Each of the 72,000 root nerves was connected to 72,000 other nerves, all of which transferred prana, vital energy, to all parts of his body. With enough concentration, he could flow prana anywhere he wanted in the body. As he walked, he visualized the prana as a flame and his body as a vibrating stream of light and heat. He increased the prana in the nerves supplying his fingertips and toes to keep them heated. Simultaneously he pressed his chin to his neck and pulled his perineum to the spine when he walked. The two bandhas trapped the air in his torso and he rotated the air around fiercely so that it collided with his ribs, vertebrae, and sternum. The friction increased the heat in his body, making him immune to the drop in temperature outside. Now he felt no different walking up the snowy mountain than he had felt walking from the village to Pavur in the blazing heat.

HALFWAY UP THE trail to Bhojbasa, he saw six pairs of heavy boot marks and the sharp, narrow imprints of ice axes and trekking poles. Late-season hikers on their way to Gomukh.

Wanting nothing to interfere with his solitude, Max abandoned the trail. He removed his shoes and scrambled up a cliff, letting his naked feet find easy grooves in the snow. Without gloves, his fingers held tight to tree stumps and rocks. He moved quickly. The air thinned as he climbed higher. He contracted his diaphragm, allowing his lungs to go down and his rib cage to expand so that the air pressure in his chest dropped significantly. The outside air rushed in, spreading fresh oxygen through his chest. He breathed comfortably and kept climbing higher, looking for a hospitable cave for the months ahead. None of the ones he passed looked suitable. Some were too narrow to build a fire inside; some too far from a source of water; others opened right onto the edge of a ravine. He could make any of them work if he had to, but this wasn't an endurance test. He wanted to spend his days in meditation, not in foraging for food and melting snow to get water.

Night fell. The snow abated. Max walked by the dim light of the half-moon, letting his bare feet guide him. He crossed a mile-long patch where the snow was so soft that he sunk up to his thighs with each step; then it turned into packed ice again. Another two or three hours in, he ran into a withered tree protected from the snowfall by a giant rock. Max cut its dry branches with his knife and put the wood in his backpack. He climbed higher, watching carefully to avoid hidden crevasses in the white blanket.

Past midnight, more than ten hours after he had begun climbing, Max came across a suitable space. A large outcropping in the jagged mountain slanted above flat snow-covered ground, protecting it from wind. The still air smelled of pine. Yellow-gray roots broke through the snow on the ground under the projecting rock. He cut a stem with his knife and sniffed it. Mushroom or something like it. They would serve him well if his rations ran out. He looked around for water. Finding nothing, Max turned with the mountain, holding tight to the jutting stones, walking gingerly on the narrow, rocky path that separated him from the deep abyss thousands of feet below. The cliff turned sharply. He closed his eyes, concentrating on his navel, pumping prana with force into the fingertips that held the edges of the rocks on the outside of the mountain. Nothing could stop him from falling if his fingers went numb. His heartbeat increased. He inched forward.

The path opened into a large stretch of sharp, snow-covered rocks. Max let go of the cliff. He rested on a rock and breathed slowly. The red heaviness in his forehead reduced. Another mountain arose on the opposite side of the furrowed ice, fifty meters away. Six or seven natural caves lay at the bottom of the cliff. Max's spirits lifted. Yes, this could work. The mountains on either side would obstruct the wind. All he needed was a source of water and this could be home for a few months. The air smelled heavy with dew, but he couldn't see a drop of water around. He walked toward the caves.

THE GROUND BELOW him shifted. Max looked down. The ice was crumbling beneath his feet. The earth was swallowing him. He jumped back—and crashed into freezing, icy water.

A stream.

He had mistaken the thin layer of ice for solid land. Now he was drenched in icy water, but at least his water problem was solved. He pulled himself out and grabbed his dripping backpack. Rubbing his wet hands, he applied the Maha Bandha within seconds to generate heat within his body once again. He stared at the thin ice shimmering in the moonlight. Bluish-white water seeped through the cracks on its surface. Was he ready?

Max walked to the edge of the lake and concentrated on the caves on the opposite side. Closing his eyes, he inhaled and exhaled one hundred and eighty times, emptying his mind of images, letting the universe guide him forward. He retained his breath ten, twelve, fifteen, seventeen minutes, until he couldn't hold it any longer. Next he exhaled quickly, forcing out the breath left in his torso and making the torso empty like a deflated life vest. He concentrated on the prana vibrating within him and thrust it upward with force. His body was now light as a feather. Max performed samyama on his navel and visualized every root nerve of his body alive with the same stream of minute energy particles that the water in front of him was. He took a step forward. Energy merged with energy. There was nothing under his feet.

He was walking on air.

More steps.

Still nothing under his feet.

Knowing he wouldn't be able to hold his breath very long, he moved faster in space. He felt the dampness of water on the soles of his feet. He pulled his abdomen in and exhaled with force. Again he walked a fraction of an inch above the water, on air.

A few steps later, he ran out of breath. He choked and inhaled a rush of air. Immediately he felt the weight on his feet, cold water touching their bottoms.

He opened his eyes. He was less than five meters away from the shore. He could do it. Max brought his right foot forward but fell into the water. Quickly he swam to the other end and pulled himself and his backpack out. He had done it. Almost. He had walked over more than forty-five meters of water—with his backpack.

Max put his backpack down on the ice. He breathed normally and visualized the energy flowing like a river through his body once again. Millions of energy particles vibrated within his body, in the air below his feet, and in the air around him. He exhaled and forced his prana up. His feet lifted two feet above the ground. He pulled his abdomen in sharply and pushed out the air left over in his torso. He rose another foot above. Max held his breath and stood suspended in air. Cold wind touched his bare wet feet, sending tingling sensations up and down his spine. He stood in the air for a few minutes, staring at the soft white half-moon above, feeling its blue-white light alive within him. Inhaling with control and pulling his prana down, he landed softly on the snow. He was ready for the last phase of his journey.

MAX TOOK OFF his wet clothes and squeezed the water out of them. Shivering and spent, he stood naked on the edge of the lake. The cold cut into his bones. The stars were so close he could pick them out of the sky. The paw marks of an animal, likely a

Himalayan bear or snow leopard, formed an elegant ellipse on the ice below him. Soon he would be one with the sky, the stars, the tall cliffs, the white snow below him, and the animals that danced on it. This was the final step. He wouldn't leave the caves until he was enlightened, became the Tathagatha, the one who was gone, whose body remained in the world but whose mind had become the universal, complete.

He walked over the sharp rocks in front of the caves, inspecting the area. All seven caves were blocked with ice. A fifteen-foot-tall boulder with a flat surface and sharp, serrated edges stood in the middle of the row of caves. Max climbed on top of it and sat cross-legged on its wet surface. Almost immediately, he fell into a deep trance, sensing a shimmering, vibrating presence within him, around him. He understood now why the Himalayas had been the home of spiritual seekers for centuries. Every rock, every surface, vibrated with the energy of the One.

Max slid down the boulder. Putting on his T-shirt, pants, gloves, and hiking boots, he began clearing the snow from the mouth of the first cave, the tallest in the row of seven. He broke the particularly hardened lumps with his boots. The noise resounded through the hundreds of miles of silence. He scraped and kicked for an hour, slowly opening the mouth of the cave an inch. This would take a long time, perhaps the whole night, and there could be no shortcuts. If fresh snow deposited on top of the packed ice, he could be buried alive inside.

Two hours later, he had cleared the mouth sufficiently to peep into the cave. It smelled of wet earth but looked warm and spacious. A winged creature bumped against his face, screeching. A bat. The sound was picked up by other bats inside. The still air filled with shrieks. Max smiled. At least he would have company if he felt too lonesome. He liked his new home already.

Max chipped away at the packed snow for another couple of hours. The hole was now wide enough to melt the remaining snow with fire without the risk of smoke filling up the cave.

He retrieved the matchboxes and tree branches from the jacket inside his backpack. None of the matches would light. He set them aside and performed samyama on the tree branches, becoming one with them, visualizing a bright yellow flame coursing through him, the branch's wooden bark, the tip of dried green leaf. A tiny spark burst out on the wood. Not enough to light the damp wood. He concentrated harder. Sweat formed on his eyebrows. This time a huge spark flamed at the end of the branch. Still the wood wouldn't light. Max wrapped the branches in his jacket and continued scraping off the snow from the cave entrance with his bare hands.

He tried lighting them again after a few hours. The wood was still too wet. Max broke the branches into smaller pieces. No more sparks. He felt dizzy. His muscles ached. He had wasted too much energy testing his new skills. He needed to rest and restore his prana. Max looked up at the sky. Could he trust it not to snow for a couple of hours, just until he squeezed into the warm cave and took a nap? A snowflake fell on his shoulder, then another. The universe gave him his answer. He began scraping the snow once again.

He heard a slight sound on his right.

A Himalayan bear?

Max whipped around.

A man stood on top of the boulder.

Max rubbed his eyes.

Yes, it was a man. Fiery black eyes shining in the moonlight, gray hair falling to his hips, and a thin yellow-orange cloth wrapped tight around his lean, hard body. A yogi. He was staring at Max.

MAX WALKED TO the boulder and folded his hands.

The man jumped down, scowling at Max, his eyes glinting. He pulled his gray hair behind his head.

Max concentrated on the Ajna chakra in the center of his forehead, the seat of all memory of all lifetimes, accessed the reservoir of language, and spoke in Hindi. "*Mera naam* Max *hai. Main is gufa mein rehna chahta hoon*," said Max.

The man didn't react.

Max repeated in English. "I'm Max. I want to live in this cave," he said.

The man raised his right hand and touched his thumb with his bony index finger again and again.

Max didn't understand.

The man repeated the gesture with both hands.

"No, no, no photograph," said Max in Hindi. The man had likely confused him for a tourist because of his T-shirt and khakis. "Not tourist. I want to be a yogi."

The man's gaunt face softened. He turned around and went into a cave on the other end, easily pushing away the snow that blocked its mouth. Unlike Max's cave, his was covered by fresh snowfall, not packed ice. Reassured by the presence of another yogi nearby, no matter how taciturn, Max cleared his cave with renewed vigor.

The man appeared next to him again. He gave Max a piece of paper. Max looked at it in the moonlight. It had one sentence written in many different languages: "I have taken a twelve-year vow of silence." And it was signed *Baba Ramdas.*

Max touched his heart to convey that he would respect his wishes.

Baba Ramdas gave Max a fifteen-inch-tall black stick. Max sniffed magnesium. Yes, this would work better than the matchsticks. Max held it vertical and struck his knife against it.

Baba Ramdas nodded.

Max struck again and again until he got the angle right. He was rewarded with a crackling flame. Max thrust it against the wood. It still wouldn't light.

Baba Ramdas went back to his cave and brought four pieces of dry tree bark and a handful of pine needles.

Max followed his lead and made a platform with tree bark. He placed the branches on it so that the ice wouldn't wet them. Once the branches were stable, he scattered pine needles on the pile and created a spark with the magnesium stick. The wood caught fire immediately. Max threw on more pine needles and the fire rose higher. The snow melted quickly.

Max folded his hands and thanked Baba Ramdas. He tried to return the magnesium stick, but Baba Ramdas wouldn't take it. Max thanked him again.

Max stooped into the musty cave, using a burning branch for light. The bats screeched their welcome. The cave was fifteen feet wide and eight feet deep, just enough for him to stand comfortably upright in. He was pleasantly surprised by how warm it was inside. Rocks jutted from the floor at odd angles, but he found a flat stretch at its back. A scorpion scuttled away when he spread his sheet on the packed wet mud. His bed. His home. Max doused the burning stick and lay down on the sheet. He tried to meditate, but his weary eyes closed.

28.

In the days that followed, Max adapted slowly to the silent but inhospitable Himalayan terrain. Observing Baba Ramdas quietly from a distance, he learned to walk over the frozen stream without falling in by pausing every few meters and exhaling sharply the air that inevitably collected in his torso. On the opposite end, he would strip bark and needles from the pine tree and pull from the ground the mushroom-like root he'd seen on the first day. Back in his cave, he melted large quantities of fresh snow on his stove to collect just a small trickle of water, barely enough for cooking the roots and beans. Over time, he observed that the intricately shaped snowflakes trapped air in them, making snow a good insulator. Piling too much snow in the pan caused its bottom to burn without melting the snow, so he added just an inch at a time. He began to get more water sooner. Even so, it was usually midday by the time he ate his first meal.

In the afternoon, he would practice pranayama, now no longer a slow, meditative breathing exercise but a frenzied grab for the oxygen he had lost foraging and walking across the stream in the thin air. Evenings were spent in performing samyama on his navel to lower his metabolism so that his heart could supply blood to his body's extremities. Next, he focused on the Anahata chakra, the heart center, reducing his heart rate so it didn't pump irregularly in the low air pressure. Too depleted to perform samyama again, he dealt with the ever-increasing supply of spiders and scorpions by sweeping them out of the cave with a brush he'd carved from the pine tree. Once this was done, he would sit to meditate, but his body felt tough and rigid like steel from the day's exertions, and sleep overcame him immediately.

Two months passed, then three. He no longer had a watch or a calendar, but somewhere in the back of his mind he always knew exactly what day it was. The winter didn't ease. The lake remained frozen, the vegetation sparse. Max's heart was silent like the mountains around him. He went through the day, foraging food, making a fire, melting snow, collecting water, practicing pranayama, feeling a quiet detachment from his body and its needs, yet expending effort all day to keep it fit and functioning.

When it continued to snow in April, Max contemplated going back to the plains so he could spend more time in meditation. But Baba Ramdas's silent, majestic form held him back. What will, what concentration, he must have built in thriving alone on the mountain for twelve years. His face betrayed no strain of effort; his eyes never asked for companionship; he was alone, complete, in silent communion with the divine, the goal Max sought but which seemed to be slipping away from his grasp.

LATE ONE NIGHT in May, Max opened his eyes after his meditation to find the cave plunged in darkness. No moonlight danced on the entrance, no cliff shimmered in the distance. It must be later than he thought, way past midnight. His heart lifted. He had meditated through the night. Max hadn't experienced this complete suspension of time in a while. Elated, he had lain down to sleep when he smelled a strange odor—a mix of damp cloth and burning rubber. Max went to the front of the cave to investigate. His feet touched something soft, bristly, and wet. He tried to pick it up in his hands. A grunt broke the silence.

A bear.

Max froze.

The six-foot-tall bear hulked away from the front of the cave. Moonlight flooded in. It hadn't been as late as he thought. Max stepped back, his eyes fixed on the silhouette of the bear in the soft white light.

The bear looked around with its beady black eyes, shaking its head.

Max stood still.

The bear grunted again. Its eyes met Max's. It came closer, thrusting its black nose, its confused face forward. Foul breath washed over him.

Max inched back, maintaining eye contact. He slid his back against the cave wall, grasping for the magnesium stick. He couldn't find it.

The bear didn't seem interested in Max. Crouching down, it

was moving back slowly when its back hit the small cave entrance. Yelping, it charged forward.

"Stop," yelled Max, standing up and raising his hand.

The bear paused three inches away from Max. It shook its fur, spraying ice flakes on Max.

Max's heart thudded. He breathed slowly.

The bear moved back a little, lifting its front legs.

Max lowered himself slowly and thrashed around for the stick.

The bear raised itself higher.

Max's hands shook. He upturned the stones frantically.

The bear's head collided against the top of the cave. A roar shattered the night. It dropped to all four paws and charged at Max.

Max stopped looking for the stick. He closed his eyes and concentrated on the bear, the air between them, the consciousness connecting them both.

Tat Tvam Asi.

I am That. *One consciousness. One universal energy.*

A wisp of cool air enveloped him.

Shuffling steps. A shower of ice.

Max increased the intensity of his samyama, drowning out all sounds and sensations, just concentrating on an image of the furry face, wide eyes, and black nose in his mind.

I am He.

We are one.

An eternity passed. Or a minute. When he opened his eyes, the bear was at the mouth of the cave.

Max stood up, drowned in a wave of compassion for the scared, confused life in front of him. He picked up the magnesium stick lying below him and the knife beside it. He struck a flare and walked calmly to the front of the cave.

The bear turned around.

Max stepped outside with him.

The bear ran toward the stream.

The chiseled cliff face shimmered like a ring in the moonlight. The boulder sparkled, dripping with snow.

The bear disappeared into the night.

Max's eyes swept over the moonlike landscape, the ancient rocks eroded by centuries of glaciers, tall, still, yet breathing and alive. Not a whisper for miles. Max turned around and walked inside the cave. He didn't know if it was good karma or samyama that had made the bear leave. But he knew now why he had struggled with his meditation thus far. He had lost the life-and-death urgency that had brought him to the Himalayas. His hiking trip was over now. It was time to get back to work.

29.

From then on, Max focused less and less on the mundane business of living. When he couldn't collect pine needles and build a fire, he fasted. If he ran out of water, he ate snow directly without worrying if he was getting enough to be fully hydrated. Spiders and scorpions stopped bothering him when he left them in peace. If rainwater seeped into his cave and wet his bedsheet, he accepted it for what it was and didn't build a fire to dry it. He did pranayama only on alternate days and stopped his routine of washing clothes every three days. Instead, he spent more and more of his time immersed in meditation. Early in the morning, he sat outside the cave and performed samyama on the sun, flowing his entire living, breathing energy into it. His skin blazed and he became one with it and the stars, planets, and galaxies that surrounded it.

In the beginning, there was no space, no time—just a shimmering, vibrating energy, the sum of everything good and evil, beautiful and ugly, right and wrong, active and dormant, containing millions of possible universes within it. The energy fluctuated, helpless with its desire to experience itself, and out of the hundreds of possible outcomes, the universe we live in came to be. The energy now lived both within and without the universe. The elements in the manifested universe burst, exploded, contracted, evolved, forming combinations, then rejecting them, forming them again powered by the intelligence of this consciousness and governed by the singular law of cause and effect, action and reaction. Hot lava gushed within him, and the sun, the moon, the entire visible universe emerged from tiny, radiating elements. Billions of years later, life sprang out of molecular mass. From single cell to multicell organisms to animals and man himself, all were made of the same substratum, each linked by the same vibrating, intelligent energy, separated by their sense of I, governed by the same law. Every effect had a cause, every cause an effect.

Max studied man's cause and understood it was the same as that of all animate and inanimate cells—the original desire of consciousness to manifest itself. He saw the desire, a shimmering, vibrating burst of light, manufacturing a body to find an expression. The body with its five senses interacted with the world, creating more desire, and the desire individuated itself in another body when the old body was worn out. And so the cycle went. The human paradox was now clear to him. The nature of life was desire, and the nature of desire was its infiniteness and its inability to be satisfied. Earlier, it had been necessary to further evolution, to allow consciousness to express its full potential. Now when man had reached the peak of self-awareness, it was just an infinite circling loop. As long as it lasted, man would never be satisfied and would always be subject to the cycle of suffering. Again and again Max would be born; again and again he would live, want, suffer, and die.

Max arose from such samyamas shaking, his body ablaze with energy, too exhausted to even walk up to the stream to collect fresh snow. He would recover after a few days of rest and practice samyama on the people who had found their way out of the cycle: Jesus, the Buddha, Muhammad. And when he merged with them in meditation, the answers emerged—simple, logical, and decisive.

The way out of the cycle was to sublimate the I principle, relinquish all individual desire, to restrain the naturally outgoing mind fueled by the senses and turn it inward. Once it focused within, the mind saw its real nature of pure consciousness and rejected the individual desires and thoughts surrounding it. Jesus had sublimated his desire with helpless compassion for his fellow beings; the Buddha had silenced his craving with intense meditation and the practice of yoga; Muhammad had done it by forgetting himself in his complete devotion to his God. They had all become vessels of pure consciousness without any thought of their own individuality. Different paths, but they converged. All fingers pointing to the same moon.

Max walked out of his cave when such meditations ended, tired, dizzy, yet elated. The universe was revealing its most fundamental truths to him. The truth about suffering was clear. The way out of it was even clearer. He was walking on the path of the sages now, feeling lighter, bathed in bliss and certitude. One energy vibrated everywhere within and around him. With the arrival of spring, the trees sprouted leaves, the flowers bloomed, the snow melted. All this—the clear blue stream, the mountains in front of him, the pristine Ganges below him, the warmth of spring, the cold of winter, the bear that tried to maul him, the spiders and scorpions that slept in his cave, and he himself—beneath the surface distinctions of name and form, they were all made of the same substratum, the one eternal consciousness.

At times during his meditation, he would feel the consciousness rise up inside him with an overwhelming physical force and cry for a release. Without thought, he would pick up a stone and carve images on the walls of the cave, stopping only when his palms bled. Later he'd look at the pictures in the light of the fire. Trees enveloped in a calm, cooling wind, stick figures locked in an embrace, fantastical figures flying toward the sun, huge stormy waves in a sea, men and women in the throes of pain or in sexual ecstasy—he was drawing man and nature in all its glory and wretchedness. He had never been any kind of an artist before, yet an entire universe seemed to be alive and craving expression within him.

WITH SPRING came more animals—first the wolves, then the snow leopards. Max fetched water from the stream when the ice melted, sometimes careful to avoid dusk, when the animals congregated there, sometimes too ecstatic after his meditation to care. The leopards would stare at him, ears cocked, eyes ablaze, their thick, coarse fur standing erect on their backs. Max no longer practiced samyama on the single energy connecting them. Perhaps they sensed it in him, though, because they never approached him. Whenever he appeared, they would appraise him quickly, then return to drinking. Sometimes a young cub would nuzzle up to him, but the mother never objected when Max petted or played with him. He gave them names from his past. The leopard who drank alone was Ramakrishna; the serious, thoughtful cub was Andre; the melancholic leopardess older than her years was Sophia. But eventually his deepening meditation put an end to that practice as well. For the instinctual desire to separate and hold on to individual identities was the root of suffering.

Leopards gave way to occasional tourists in summers, coughing and sputtering as they hiked up from Gomukh, the source glacier of the Ganges. They stopped dead in their tracks when they saw him.

"Who are you?" they would ask. "A saint? Some god?"

Max obliged for photographs but never spoke. The world wanted identification, separation, and categorization, everything he was trying to eliminate. Despite having spent nine months in complete seclusion, he was still far from losing his sense of self, from slipping into blissful union with consciousness. During his meditation, he wasn't Max. He was the sum of all existence and knowledge, the singular energy he sought to become. However, this association ended when his meditation ended. When he arose, he was the same Max, though lighter, more at peace; yet his mind was still active, still *pursuing* the goal rather than having *become* the goal. Surely this couldn't be the final state. The union with consciousness couldn't be conditional on closing one's eyes and concentrating. It should exist in him naturally. He should feel its awareness in every moment, not a trancelike, self-induced state brought on by meditation.

Something was holding him back. Worse, this failure felt familiar. His bones were heavy with the knowledge of similar tantalizing glimpses in innumerable past lives, but he had never been able to pull the veil aside. Of what use were trivial accomplishments like walking on water and levitating? With the right discipline, anyone could concentrate on the udana, the upward-flowing prana, making the body so light that walking on air became easier than planting a firm foot in the snow. And the hundred-year-old yogis who looked twenty-five did nothing more than trap their prana with bandhas to make the body a closed system that never decayed or aged. All this was easy. Simple perambulations of the body. This wasn't his goal. Something had shifted inside him after the drought in the village. He didn't crave peace for himself anymore. He wanted to reach the other side so he could get back answers for all. This time he wouldn't let his body, his life, slip away until he reached his goal. Max cut down on food and pranayama and meditated with more concentration than ever before.

30.

Summer gave way to a cold, dry fall. Max had long ago run out of his meager rations. Now the shoots and roots he had been living on began to wither away as well. He ate less and less, but one day he knew he couldn't hold his body together without more food. Max forced himself to stop meditating and reluctantly make the hike down to Gangotri village, disappointed that the body's petty needs once again were interfering with his quest for transcendence.

After a few hours of scrambling down the sharp ice, he reached the established trail. He sensed human presence some miles away. Images of an Indian couple, a tall guide wearing a hat, and two young porters swinging ice axes flashed through his mind in quick succession.

The idea of meeting tourists with their questions and conversations overwhelmed him. He walked swiftly for the next hour in silence, encountering nobody. When the images started flashing quicker and became more sharply defined in his mind, Max slid off the narrow trail and down the steep precipice, forcing the prana into the bottom of his feet so the heat would make them stick to the ice. He squatted and crouched along the slanting mountain, moving slowly toward the frozen river a hundred vertical feet below.

"Look, a baba."

Above him, the group stood on the path. A couple, a tall guide, and two porters, exactly the images he had seen in his mind. They were more than fifty feet away, but their words rang in his ears as if they were standing next to him.

"Oh, God, how can anyone go down like that?"

"He is like Spider-Man."

They laughed, the harsh sounds assaulting Max's ears. Just like the laughter of the people who had gathered around the food cart in New York had jarred him years ago. Max recoiled at the sharpness of the memory. Was he any closer to answering the questions that had bothered him then? Max moved down faster.

"He looks a little mad."

"Isn't he a foreigner? Why do they come here? Craziness, man."

"Must have fallen into some guru's racket."

"These Americans, Europeans are lonely, man. Loneliness drives you mad. That's why I don't want to leave India."

"But just look at how fast he is going down."

"Spider-Man, Spider-Man, Spider-Man."

Max reached the river. He still heard their conversation from a hundred feet above over the noise of the river. He sprinted away, treading lightly on the thin ice. When the water appeared again, he walked over it without thinking. Suddenly aware the travelers could take pictures, he glided onto the rocky riverbank and ran over the sharp stones. Their voices finally stopped ringing in his ears more than a mile into his run. He slowed to a steady pace again, mentally preparing himself for the sights and sounds in the village by invoking the chatter of his previous life.

WHEN HE ARRIVED in Gangotri, Max walked to a small shop selling food and supplies. The shopkeeper shooed him away. When it happened again at the next shop, Max stole a glance at himself in the mirror outside an open-air restaurant. It had been almost a year since he'd seen how he appeared to others. He had dropped another twenty or thirty pounds and looked thin and wasted in his torn clothes. His dark hair was long, unruly, and matted, his arms and legs were caked in mud, and his fingernails were black from foraging. All across his hands and wrists, there were cuts and bruises, likely from the pine trees and the sharp edges of the rocks in the cave. They thought he was a beggar.

Max took damp money out of his pocket and walked back into the first shop. He opened his palm to show the shopkeeper the money.

"I want to buy food," said Max in Hindi, his voice sounding heavy and strange after months of silence.

The tall, lean shopkeeper, sitting on a chair in front of burlap sacks filled with grains, beans, and lentils, stared at him. He said something in the local mountain language.

Max concentrated on the man's heart and heard the thought originate before it became sound in the man's throat and words on his lips.

"You are young. Don't waste your time like this. Work hard. Work is God," the man was saying. "How much do you need?"

Max bought small bags of rice, kidney beans, and chickpeas, enough to last him several months. One day the shopkeeper would understand. They would all understand. Max wouldn't rest until he crossed over the boundary to the infinite.

MAX WALKED PAST the small hotels, restaurants, and sundry shops, pulled despite himself to the sounds of conversation and laughter. He entered the Gangotri temple and sat cross-legged on the concrete floor in the open courtyard. A bald orange-robed priest shaved the head of a small boy while his parents looked on indulgently. Men and women in colorful clothes prostrated themselves before a deity's statue. A smiling couple came up to Max and offered him an apple. Max refused with folded hands. He took out the paper bags with rice and kidney beans from his backpack and put them next to him on the floor so people would know he had food. But they wouldn't stop. Every few minutes, someone would stop by and offer him fruit or sweets or leftovers of a cooked meal. They were brimming with joy and wanted to share it with everyone, especially the lonely and destitute.

What happened 2 u ace?

Max pushed away the images of Andre and Sophia that were creeping into his mind on seeing the living, breathing people around him. He couldn't be distracted now. He had to work harder than ever before. He got up, packed up his supplies, and began his trip back up the mountain.

31.

Max plunged himself into samyama with even more fervor after his visit to Gangotri. But the harder he tried, the more the faint glimmer of consciousness dancing in the corners of his mind began to fade. Instead, phantoms from his past arose from the blackness within him.

In the darkness of the cave, he saw once again Andre's scared, confused eyes when he'd realized that his wheelchair wouldn't fit into the narrow bathroom door of their apartment in the projects. Deep, painful abscesses had formed in Andre's leg when he began crawling to the bathroom every day. Soon they became infected, and his left leg had to be amputated. Max's eyes welled up with tears at the memory of Andre sitting on his cracked wheelchair, one leg cut to its stump, another hanging useless. The images came in quick succession. His mother's shrunken, jaundiced face as the cancer ate into her liver. Pitbull's blood splashed over their building's metal door after a rival gang member slit open his throat. The memorial dolls with missing arms and legs on the tree in St. Ann's Park, swaying in the wind.

I'm merely seeing the painting of the moon, Max; you have a chance at seeing the moon.

Often he would stand at the cave entrance and stare at the half-moon above him, thinking of Anand's words from years ago. Why was the truth still eluding Max? He was no closer to experiencing the peace and stillness of pure consciousness than he'd been when he had first started his journey. He thought of karma and the laws of cause and effect. Were these memories of pain that never left his side just the effect of the pain he had caused himself?

I hear this after giving my life to you both.

His mother's shaking voice rang in his ears. Max had blamed her for their poverty, for getting pregnant with him at nineteen, for not planning her life better—all because he was angry at her after he abandoned Keisha. But it wasn't her fault. She hadn't even known Keisha was pregnant. Max had been afraid to tell her because she had always wanted him to leave the projects and never look back. The baby's cries resounded in the cave. Max put his hands over his ears. He had denied a life the chance to work out its karma. Could there be a worse crime? His mother had devoted her life to Sophia and him. Keisha had loved him. Sophia and Andre had cared for him. He had abandoned everyone. All he had given them in return was pain.

For so many lives, Max had hurt, damaged, destroyed. A

Scottish minister who had left his young wife to live alone in the mountains. The Israeli woman who could never really love her children and resented them for caging her. Max shuddered as the images from his innumerable past lives arose in his mind. Could there be an end to this endless cycle of causing and begetting suffering? He'd read of ascetics who inflicted pain upon themselves to speed up the universe's retribution for their misdeeds rather than allow nature to take its course. Could penance be his salvation?

LATE ONE WINTER AFTERNOON when the snow pounded the cave and the temperature dropped several degrees below zero, Max lifted his left arm up and decided not to put it down again until he achieved his goal. He relished the searing pain in his muscles and resisted the urge to tighten and untighten his fist. He wouldn't allow himself even the slightest relief. This time he wouldn't run away from his past the way he had at Ramakrishna's ashram. The effects of his past bad karma had to be burned away to dust. Only then could he be free from the bondage of cause and effect, destroy the individual and become the universal.

He kept his arm raised when he ate and performed his evening samyama. The stabbing pain went from his arm to his shoulder socket to his neck and skull when he lay down at night. Blood rushed to his forehead. His head pounded. Max looked up at the black stone roof of the cave and thanked the universe for his discomfort. He didn't put his arm down that night. Finally, some choice he had made was working.

The next morning, Max went out of the cave to relieve himself.

He struggled with unfastening and fastening his pants. When he came back in, he stripped off his clothes. He didn't need them here anyway. The discomfort of the cold was also good.

The sharp burning sensation in his muscles turned into a blazing fire the next morning. Tears streamed down his eyes. Max vomited and felt a little better. By afternoon, it felt as if someone was sawing off his arm with a sharp knife. Electric shock waves ripped through his body. The images from his past receded into the growing red blur in his forehead. Yes, his penance was working.

By the next morning, the pain was steady and constant. Max struggled to light a fire with one hand, eventually succeeding in finding a jagged edge of a rock to rub against the magnesium stick. He lit a small fire and slept again after eating a bit of chickpeas and rice.

When he awoke in the evening, he could feel the old farmer-driver from the village driving a large, red tractor over his arm again and again, wanting to cut off every nerve, every vein in it. Shakti's pealing laughter resounded in the cave. *You won't rest until you see him face-to-face, Max.*

He looked at his arm with detachment. This pain wasn't him. This body wasn't him. The mind that classified this numbing, grating sensation as agony wasn't him. He could overcome this. It was simple.

32.

Max didn't put his arm down through that month. His muscles withered. The pain refused to relent, but he didn't think much of it anymore. Melting snow and foraging for roots became more difficult with one hand, so Max just ate less. Hunger was good, necessary. He couldn't have left the cave, anyway. One storm crashed after another that winter. Max lit small fires to keep the snow from depositing on the entrance. The temperature dropped. One day he caught a cold. He was more surprised than discomfited by it. This wasn't supposed to happen. His body was immune to petty illnesses. Max did pranayama to expunge it, but he couldn't churn his abdomen at the same speed as before. His belly kept colliding against his spine, making him cry out in pain. The cold stayed. Another sign of purification. He lay down at the back of the cave waiting for it to pass.

A hazy fog filled the space between his eyes. He was slipping, falling into blackness, into infinity, progressing closer to his goal.

MAX WOKE UP after a day, maybe two, with his throat parched. He had eaten most of the snow on the cave floor, so he forced himself to get up. Dizzy, his head spinning, he crawled to the cave's mouth. Just a light snowfall. Max stumbled outside. He picked himself up, carefully keeping his left arm raised, and walked a little in the fresh snow. When he felt faint again, he knelt down on the ice. The afternoon sun cast a reddish-orange shadow on the sea of white around him. Max cupped his palm and collected a few snowflakes. His tongue stung. He forced himself to eat more.

Clouds covered the sun. The white mountains turned a glittery silver in the fading light. The stream shimmered in the still air. He looked around. No sign of Baba Ramdas, no sign of anyone, just silence, pure stillness. This world, it was so soft, so beautiful. Max began to cry.

Through his tears, he crawled back inside the cave. The feathery whiteness below him was colored with specks of red. He turned around. A trail of blood followed him inside. Max inspected his body dispassionately. Something had scraped his thigh. A steady stream of blood trickled from it. He should get the herb that grew right behind the cave and healed wounds. Maybe in the evening. All he wanted now was to lie down and fill his heart with the shining stream and silver cliffs. They were so symmetrical, so beautiful. Fresh tears came to his eyes.

A scorpion scuttled up his torso. Max didn't want to brush it off and hurt it. He let it inch up his ribs to his neck and dry lips. Everything was one consciousness. Beautiful. Max closed his eyes. The scorpion made its way farther up, opening its pincers wide. Max slept peacefully.

When he woke up, the cave was black. The scorpion had gone. He was alone, all alone. Just him and the infinite blackness. He should get the herb. He pushed himself up. His open wound stared at him. Deep, red, rich, alive, stunning. Max lay down again.

His body burned. He moved from his thin sheet. His naked body touched the cold, rocky floor. It felt so good, so comfortable. Finally he was at peace.

LOUD RUMBLING awoke Max. The cave shook and lifted slowly. He circled around in space, weightless, floating, slowly landing on the rocks below. It didn't hurt. Nothing hurt. The mountain roared again. The sound was within him. He moved and churned with the mountain. A chunk of cave broke open from the top. Bright, dazzling white light flashed across the black sky. Sheets of rain rippled from the blackness, washing over Max. Small bits of snow splattered through the hole. He didn't move. The light snow brushed against his face. So miraculous was this play of nature, this relative world, incomplete yet so magical. He didn't mind returning for another lifetime. Max closed his eyes.

BABA RAMDAS WAS shaking him. Max awoke and stared into his shining black eyes. Outside, it thundered, deep and powerful.

The cave shook again. In sign language, Baba Ramdas urged him to come outside. Max didn't want to leave. Baba Ramdas persisted. Max limped out slowly, careful to keep his arm raised, shivering. A mountain of snow had piled in front of the caves. Max looked up. The tall cliff was stripped bare. Three caves in the row of seven had collapsed. An avalanche. Baba Ramdas pointed to the black, starless sky, the air saturated with the smell of moisture. There will be more, his eyes said. Max nodded absently. He limped back into the cave and lay down again, staring at the sky through the hole.

White flashes. Another storm was coming. Maybe it would take this cave and Max along with it. This body would be shed away like a worn coat. He'd wear another coat. He was so tired already. Next time perhaps he'd be different, better—a good son, a kinder brother, a selfless father, someone capable of love. Max closed his eyes.

MORE THUNDER. FOOTSTEPS. Baba Ramdas came in with something in a leaf. Again he asked Max to come out with him. Max shook his head. There was nowhere to go, no one to see. He had abandoned everyone. Baba Ramdas lowered his black eyes, set the leaf plate down, and sat beside Max. He pressed his right palm against Max's open hand. Their eyes met. Baba Ramdas stood up and disappeared into the snow.

Max looked at the plate. Millet and eggplant. He smiled. The same meal he'd eaten every day for three years at the ashram. Such happy, simple times. He went back to sleep without eating.

• • •

WHEN HE AWOKE, the snowflakes spiraled slowly in the grayness above him, ice crystals shining in them. White light lit up the sky again and again. A glassy, fluid membrane shimmered over the flakes. He closed his eyes.

Sophia's snow globe. She would stare at it for hours. There it was, sitting atop the lone table in the room the three of them shared. There she was, the little girl smiling with her half-broken tooth. She never got gifts in real life, but the snow globe was always full of gifts.

Max opened his eyes. He stared through the fog in his forehead. The cave's mouth was half covered by snow. New flakes deposited on top. He would be buried in soon. Max closed his eyes again.

The snowflakes in the globe circled slowly. Sleigh bells sounded. Village children played with sticks at the mouth of the cave. A woman with a blackened, charred body stretched out a hand to him. His mother.

I chose her womb.

The snow globe sparkled above him.

His guilt, his loss, his sadness, every experience, every emotion from every life had led him to his mother's womb, to this cave, this bid for salvation. His past wasn't separate from him. He was meant to make his mistakes.

Trembling, Max sat up. He ate the millet and eggplant. Blood trickled up his veins. The cave's mouth was filling up. Max crawled to his T-shirt and pants and put them on, the cloth rubbing harshly against the cuts and bruises on his skin. Shivering, he walked over to his backpack and pulled out his jacket. Max put his good right arm in its sleeve. His left arm hung limp and lifeless by his side. He concentrated on his left hand's fingers, pushing them to move. Nothing. Max stumbled to the front of the cave, jacket flapping by his side. He pushed his body through the fresh deposit of snow and stepped out into the moonlit night. He had failed, he knew that now. But perhaps his body could still be of use to Sophia, to someone.

RAIN WASHED OVER HIM. Max walked over to the edge of the glimmering lake. He took a tentative step forward. No, he no longer had enough concentration. He turned around and walked along the stream, past the empty cave of Baba Ramdas, who had likely left for Gangotri, knowing that the snowstorms and avalanches weren't likely to relent that night. Max walked up a glacier cliff, circling around to the other side of the stream. The sky lit up around him, like fireworks on July Fourth. The patchy roof of their building. A jug of lemonade. *You never give up easy*, his mother had said when they both knew she was dying and yet he had suggested another surgery. The wind knocked Max down again and again. He got up, holding on to the cliff tighter each time to avoid being blown off. He reached the other side and made his way down the mountain, shaking his left arm, trying to get it to work again.

THE MOUNTAIN RUMBLED.

Max stopped.

A crash.

Max looked up. A giant wave of white swirled above him. It

rippled down slowly from the top of the cliff, blanketing trees in its path, hungry to envelop him, to take him along with it. Shards of ice rained on him.

A large black boot fell out of the ice.

Max broke out of his trance. He threw himself down and dug his fingernails into the snow, grabbing on to rocks, plants, grooves in the ice, anything. The avalanche swept over him. He slipped faster and faster.

A tree stump. Max rolled over it and held on to it with all his strength. His left hand, which had been so powerless, suddenly held. A giant slab of ice crashed a few yards in front of him. White powder. Blue ice stung his face. The mountain crumbled around him. Max burrowed a hole in the ice around the tree, forcing his left fingers to move faster, digging furiously, widening the hole until it formed a little pit. He entered it. For the rest of the night, he pummeled and pushed back the snow filling up the hole as blocks of ice crashed around him. When the mountain finally stopped shaking late in the night, he dug himself out of the pit.

He walked through the blizzard blindly, guided by a fading image somewhere in the shadows of his mind.

IN THE DISTANCE, Max saw a solitary light. As he walked closer to it, he knew it was the old Bhojbasa guesthouse. He had returned after all these years, the same wet, shivering, shaking, broken man. Max limped closer. He sat on the ice in front of the door, breathing slowing, moving his left wrist in circles, trying to shake off his dizziness and get a grip on himself.

After a while he stood up. As calmly as he could, he knocked on the front door.

The same old woman opened the door, her skin splotched with large patches of red. Without a word, she ushered him in.

Max stumbled inside.

She didn't seem to recognize Max, nor did Max feel the urge to jog her memory.

The room was still sparsely furnished, with just a thick rug and a chair next to the fireplace. Max sat on the rug.

"I get food," said the woman.

Max nodded, his eyes mellow with tears. The woman left. Max huddled inside the blankets she had handed him and warmed his blackened, bony hands above the fire. Some of his fingers had turned violet and felt as hard as wood. His left arm was now just bone with skin stretched tight on it. He shook it. The wooden door opened and shut again and again, letting in gusts of icy air. Max wrapped himself up tight in three layers of blankets and stared at the blinding flashes outside the windows.

He had failed.

EARLY THE NEXT MORNING Max awoke on the rug on the floor and drank the whole bottle of lukewarm water lying next to him. Exhausted by the effort, he slept again, waking only to go to the tin shack bathroom outside the guesthouse. The ice pierced his naked feet. He came back and huddled inside his blankets on the cold, wooden floor.

THE OLD WOMAN'S white sari brushed against his face.

"I heat food now," she said.

Max nodded gratefully. He stared up at the tin roof and listened to the rhythmic opening and closing of the front door, trying to stay awake.

THE OLD WOMAN was shaking him gently.

"You eat now. You not eat in two days," she said.

Max nodded again, trying to keep his eyes open.

The woman returned with a large plate.

Max sat up cross-legged. Bread, lentils, beans, yogurt—the food before him could last a month in the mountain. Max began to protest but stopped. He had failed. He had to enter the world of mortals again. He ate slowly, reacquainting himself with flavor and spices. Solid pieces went down his gullet, hitting the inside of his ribs. Blood crept up his veins slowly.

"I have money," said Max.

His lips hurt. The door thrust open. Max shivered in the icy gust, staring at the old woman's half Indian, half Oriental face. He wanted to say more.

"Not worry about money. Just eat. You are thin. Not healthy at all," said the woman.

Max folded his hands. He stared into her sunken yellow face and pale gray eyes. She was dying too. Sophia's heavy face appeared before him. Tears began to fall down his face. He wanted to get up and touch the old woman's feet to show his gratitude, but his eyes closed again.

The door banged shut.

33.

For days Max did little besides eat and sleep in front of the fire. Disconnected, dreamlike fragments slipped in and out of his mind. A girl, two children running, an iron slide, a man shivering, an army officer falling off a train, someone dying in a bed of snow, a slender woman with long, silky hair, an earthquake, a flood. His right hand's little finger and left hand's middle and index fingers blackened, shriveled, and went dead. Mechanically he applied the herb paste the old woman gave him at the base of his fingers. The paste helped his lifeless fingers fall off without pain.

Slowly the wounds in his hands and legs healed. His left arm began to move on command—painfully at first, but little by little with less discomfort. His body didn't burn with fever anymore.

He limped around the bare room, touching the wooden door that kept banging open and shut, adjusting the logs in the fireplace, running his hands over the crumbling timber walls, pressing his bare feet on the wooden floor, adapting to life again.

ONE DAY MAX awoke shivering from his afternoon slumber. The wooden door was wide open again. This time, Nani Maa, the old woman, was standing atop the chair driving a hammer through the bolt hinge on the wall. Her shriveled frame shook in the wind. The hammer kept missing its mark. Max limped up to the chair, standing a foot taller than her despite the chair.

The upper pin in the bolt's hinge was curved. Max took the hammer from her. It slipped from his hands, hitting the floor with a loud thud.

"I do it," she said.

Max shook his head. He didn't need his little finger to hold a hammer. He stretched his thumb farther away from his hand and held the hammer tight in the three fingers of his left hand. He pried out the pin, straightened it, and hammered it back in, a series of shocks coursing down his body and through his spine with each blow. Little by little, the bolt returned to its place and held tight.

Max pushed the door in. He bolted it. Again, the hinge loosened. The bolt slipped and the door flapped open in the frigid wind.

"Do you have a wrench?"

Nani Maa didn't understand.

Max closed his eyes and concentrated on the Ajna chakra in the center of his forehead. He looked for the Hindi word from the reservoir of memory of lifetimes past. The word wouldn't come to his lips. He concentrated harder, sweating despite the freezing wind. Nothing. He opened his eyes and stared into Nani Maa's wrinkled ash-gray face.

He drew a shape in the air.

Nani Maa nodded.

She shuffled to the cupboard in the corner of the room and rummaged through it. Max stepped outside into the ice, walked over the rocks, and broke a branch from one of the withered pine trees near the guesthouse. He cracked it into little pieces and returned with a twig.

Nani Maa handed him the wrench. Max held it with both hands and pulled out the bolt hinge. His muscles tensed. He rested for a few minutes, then put a sliver of wood below the hinge and started hammering the hinge in. His heart thudded. He missed a blow and hit his left thumbnail. He ignored the sharp pain and concentrated harder. He hammered again. One pin went in. He kept missing the second pin again and again. Sweating and shaking, he refused to give up. He kept hammering until finally the second pin went into its hole as well.

He stepped back and pushed the door. The bolt fit. The hinge held. The wind didn't blow the door open again.

"Good," said Nani Maa, her face impassive as usual.

Max straightened himself and walked erect, ignoring the pain in his knee. He was alive. He was fit. Even a corpse would start walking if it consumed the copious amount of food the old woman put in front of him every day. His eyes met Nani Maa's. He would take care of her in her last days before he left.

34.

Max helped Nani Maa more and more around the guesthouse. He still insisted on giving her money, but he knew the frail, weakening woman needed his physical presence more.

"Every day some change here. The place is not same on two days," she said.

Max saw what she meant. One day heavy snow warped the tin roof. Ice and water trickled in through the bullet-sized holes caused by the hail preceding the snowstorm. Max had barely repaired the tin panels by applying the roof filler lying in the bathroom when the bathroom's roof collapsed. He fixed an old tarp over the roof to get them through the winter rains. The tarp held, but water seeped in through the wooden floors of the hut. Next, ice blocked the crude pipe that drew water from the glacier stream a few feet below the hut. Every day there was something to repair. His mind remained numb, but his days were filled by the steady hum of activity needed to keep the small house functioning.

Nani Maa protested. It wasn't his work. She was still capable of doing things. Max stared at her proud, frail face. She was strong like his mother.

"It keeps me busy," he said.

"But you go back up?" she said.

Max wanted to caress Nani Maa's wrinkled, dry face. She had fed him, nursed him, brought him back to life twice. Now the light in her pale eyes was fading.

Max shook his head. "I won't go back to a cave," he said. "But I may leave for my home across the ocean after the winter."

Nani Maa's eyes lifted. A touch of color came to her yellow skin. He sensed her joy, but outwardly she shrugged.

"You stay as you like, go when you want," she said, adjusting her sari on her bald head. "I am used to being here alone. No one comes in winter."

She hummed while sweeping the room that evening but retired to her corner of the room without speaking as she usually did.

NANI MAA'S HEALTH worsened in February. Her belly swelled and her skin turned cold. The red splotches spread across her whole face. She slept more and more. Max took over the cooking from her, though she ate little of the rice and beans he made for her. Six years after his mother's death, he was seeing yet another body disintegrate in front of him. This time he didn't feel the same agitation build inside him. He had tried, he had tried so hard to penetrate the truth, but he hadn't been strong enough to find the answers. Now he had to accept pain, illness, death as the lot of everyone.

He asked Nani Maa if he could take her to a doctor in Gangotri or Uttarkashi.

She shrugged. "Time cooks everyone," she said. "What can doctor do?"

"Can I call your family?"

"I have no one in India," she said. "My sons in Nepal. Why they waste money to come here?" She paused and talked as if to herself. "My husband died. A widow has no status in society. I thought move change things."

Her sadness rose within him. Max would die alone too. He could go back home to New York, but he knew he had crossed a strange boundary. The world of people and their preoccupations seemed infantile in its innocence from where he stood. Yet there was a deep emptiness on this side of the boundary as well. He wished he could make Nani Maa more comfortable. Despite her protest, Max put her next to the warm fire and slept on the opposite side of the bare room.

LATER IN FEBRUARY, the blizzards stopped. The snow thawed a little and previously bare trees began to grow leaves again. The air remained frigid, but the sun shone for longer and longer every day. One afternoon, a short, squat saffron-clad yogi with a chubby face and pencil-thin legs stopped at the guesthouse. He wore torn ocher robes and his forehead was smeared with white paint.

"*Hari Om Tat Sat.*" He greeted Max with hands folded.

The yogi put his staff and small bundle of clothes down and prostrated before Nani Maa, who was sleeping next to the fire. He got up and circled around her weary, limp body, splashing water while muttering an incantation.

Max served him rice and lentils.

They sat down together to eat.

The yogi said something in Garhwali, the local language.

Max concentrated on his heart and was surprised to understand the words on the man's lips clearly. He focused on his Ajna chakra and was again startled to discover that he could converse with him in Garhwali easily. Nani Maa's care had done him good.

"By God's grace, she will get better," said the yogi, putting a large mouthful of rice in his mouth. "Where do you come from, bhai?"

"I've lived here for a month," said Max.

"You speak Garhwali well," he said. "Have you done any sadhana, deep meditation in Himalayas?"

Max hesitated. "I was in a cave before," he said.

The yogi nodded approvingly. "Which akhara do you belong to?"

Max didn't follow.

"There are three main communities for yogis: the Juna Akhara, the Mahanirvani Akhara, and the Niranjani Akhara," he said. He took his fingers out of the lentils and touched the three horizontal lines of white paint on his forehead. "See, I am in the Juna Akhara. This is our symbol. You have to choose one."

"Why?"

The yogi sighed and licked his fingers. "Community is necessary for a man of God. You will realize once you start wandering and need a home on the road," he said. "Have you traveled in India much?"

Max shook his head.

"You should start soon," he said. "I have been walking for twelve years. From Vivekananda's rock in Kanyakumari to the Amarnath shrine in Jammu and Kashmir, there is not a single pilgrimage these two feet have not done."

Max stared at the thin, callused feet of the man. He figured wandering was a way to reduce attachment to places and people, but didn't being a part of a community offset that?

The yogi pushed the leaf plate away. "Delicious, bhai, delicious. You cook very well. You are not from India. Where did you learn to cook?"

"Down in the South," said Max.

The yogi's eyes brightened. "You must have gone to the temple in Rameshwaram?" he said.

Max shook his head.

"Lord Rama prayed to Shiva there to absolve his sins after his war with the demon, Ravana," he said. "It's an essential Hindu pilgrimage, second in importance only to Kedarnath. Have you seen the buffalo shrine in Kedarnath?"

Again Max shook his head.

"Lord Shankara appeared in a buffalo's hind parts there," he said. "The shrine is very close from here. But first go to Amarnath in the Himalayas. They should be done in an order."

The yogi named more places he had visited in his twelve years of walking barefoot through India and asked Max if he had been to any of them.

Each time Max shook his head.

"You haven't been to any of Lord Shiva's pilgrimages," said the yogi. "You must be a Vaishnava, a follower of Lord Vishnu, then."

"No," said Max.

The yogi's eyes narrowed. "Who do you follow, then? Lord Shiva or Lord Vishnu? You have to choose."

What about the immortal soul within? Weren't these gods and goddesses and myths and legends just symbols of the infinite truth, representations of one attribute or the other of the one reality, the sum of all attributes?

"No one," said Max. "I follow no one."

"You are young," said the yogi. "There is much time to learn."

Perhaps it was wise to choose a form, even if a partial representation of the absolute, someone to love unconditionally. And maybe the forms even existed. Who was to say there was no Jesus in the sky or Lord Shankara in a buffalo's behind? Max knew nothing anymore.

"Choose Lord Shiva," said the yogi. "He is a powerful lord, a rebel, the original ascetic, the Mahadeva."

Nani Maa coughed.

Max excused himself and made Nani Maa a cup of lemon tea.

The yogi rested on Max's rug that afternoon as Max fixed the front door, which had unhinged again.

LATER THAT EVENING, an elderly yogi and a shy young man in his early or midtwenties came to the guesthouse. The old yogi was a startling sight—tall and muscular, his naked body covered in ash. A large, heavy rock was tied to his penis with a frayed white rope. The short, squat yogi from the morning bowed before the elderly yogi, who acknowledged the greeting by lowering his blazing eyes.

"He is Naga Baba, my guru bhai. I knew he was coming today, that's why I stayed over," said the squat yogi, introducing him with more than a hint of pride. "We are disciples of the same guru, the legendary Babaji. You must have heard of him. He could do anything, even walk on water."

Like Baba Ramdas, Naga Baba had taken a vow of silence. The heavy rock around his penis was a symbol of both his mastery over desire and his apparently superhuman strength. The unremarkable young man accompanying him was his disciple and would be initiated into the yogic life that night. Together they seemed an unlikely sight, the naked Naga Baba with his dreadlocked hip-length hair and his disciple wearing two thick sweaters and a jacket, smoothing his neatly parted, oily hair.

Outside, the sky darkened and a light rain began.

"You should start soon before it begins to snow," said the squat yogi from the morning.

Naga Baba nodded.

Max collected the supplies they wanted. Dry logs, eucalyptus bark, pine needles, a white cloth, a bucket of freezing cold water from the holy Ganges.

The four of them went outside. Naga Baba smiled, yellow teeth glinting in the full moon's light. He wiped his hand over his forehead, removing gray-black ash, and smeared it on the young man's forehead.

The young man took off his jacket, sweaters, shirt, and pants, shivering and shaking. His eyes were wet with tears.

Naga Baba ripped the man's thin undershirt. The young man stood naked in the snow, crying.

Max built a fire. Naga Baba cut the young man's thick head of hair with scissors and a knife. Next, he attacked his mustache. Red speckles appeared on the space between the man's lips and his nose.

Max put dry logs over the eucalyptus bark, threw in the pine needles, and started a fire. The man wept louder.

"His last tears," whispered the squat yogi to Max. "Now a new life begins. Open road, blue sky, the endless beyond, the eternal freedom of a yogi."

The young man seemed to be shedding tears more for his new life than his old one. He didn't look like he was enjoying the freedom of having the sharp, cold knife scrape the hair off his head in the subzero temperature. Someday he would do the same to another novice. Perhaps there was comfort in the ritual, some sense of belonging to a community with a shared belief, even if one's ultimate quest was solitary. Maybe Max could have benefited from that too.

Naga Baba finished shaving off the man's hair. He blew loudly from a conch shell, the sound reverberating in the silent night. The young man raised his confused, tear-stricken eyes. He began walking around the fire.

Naga Baba blew the conch louder.

The squat yogi chanted an incantation.

The young man circled the fire faster.

Naga Baba blew the conch with all his strength.

Louder, faster, the man spun, looking at the full moon above, sweating in the frigid wind, eyes rolling, mouth open.

At last Naga Baba stopped. He lifted the bucket of cold water high and splashed it over the young man's head. The man fell forward on the ice with the force of the water. His purification was now complete.

As the man lay on the ice, stunned by the cold, Naga Baba leaned down and whispered something in his shivering ears.

"His secret personal mantra," said the squat yogi. "These words will take him to Lord Shiva."

The man seemed to want to go inside the warm guesthouse more than up to Lord Shiva. Max helped him up. Naga Baba lifted him in his powerful arms, the boulder on his penis swinging as he took him inside the guesthouse.

Nani Maa had slept through the conch shells and chanting.

THE NEXT DAY Naga Baba and his shivering, newly initiated disciple left for a cave to stay in silence until the young man was fully indoctrinated in the Shaiva belief system. Later that evening, the squat yogi told Max that he could request that Naga Baba initiate Max too. Max was tempted. Beyond the comfort of shared belief, maybe he could learn some discipline from the fierce Naga Baba. But something held him back. He didn't understand what. Max thanked the squat yogi and told him he wasn't ready yet.

"You are young. The path is long and hard. Lord Shiva will wait for you," said the yogi and wandered off into the evening, likely to another pilgrimage point somewhere in the vast Himalayas.

MORE YOGIS CAME in March, all routinely disappointed by Max's inability to answer their basic questions. Whom did he believe in? Which sect did he belong to? Which holy shrines had he visited? More offered to initiate him, but Max still wasn't ready. He served them food, fetched water for their needs from the Ganges, gave them his blanket so they could rest comfortably in the cold nights, and wished them well for their journeys forward.

One day, a Khareshwari, a Standing Baba, from a nearby cave came to the guesthouse. He had been standing day and night for six years. Not once had he sat or lay down to sleep. His legs were thin as an electric wire, his toes withered to bone. Max marveled at the baba's discipline. He hadn't lasted a month with his arm raised.

"How do you overcome the pain?" said Max.

The Standing Baba shook his head vigorously. "Tapas is not pain, my son. Austerity is joy. The fire of mortification burns away the effects of past deeds from their seed," he said, standing in the doorway. "It hurt a little in the beginning. Now it's just bliss. Peace. Soon I will be liberated."

The baba's food had run out. Max gave him supplies for a month. The baba offered to take Max in as a disciple. His cave had enough standing room for two.

Max thanked him and promised he would consider the offer.

The Khareshwari too looked disappointed in him.

35.

As spring began to take hold, Nani Maa faded more quickly, sleeping more and eating less. Sometimes she would wake up in the afternoon and chant in Hindi from a small copy of the Bhagavad Gita. Max liked to hear her voice. It had remained steady despite the hacking cough she had developed.

"Do you believe in God?" she asked Max one day when he brought her tea.

She sat up on the rug, managing to prop herself against the wall. The splotches of red had spread from her face to her chest and arms. Her bald head had shriveled and shrunk. Max wanted to comfort her, to say something about a benevolent God who watches over his people. His lips quivered. He couldn't bring himself to lie.

"I believe in karma, in impersonal laws, in cause and effect," he said.

"All yogis who come here say this, but their faces not happy," said Nani Maa.

Max stared at her, struck by the sharpness of her diagnosis.

Nani Maa's hands shook, rattling the teacup. She looked up at him with her dying yellow eyes. "Must be something. Energy, something good somewhere," she said.

Her scared eyes grew bigger. She set the cup down and gripped Max's hands. "What happens to me after I die? What happens on the other side?" she said in Nepali.

Max held her hands tight. Without trying, he slipped into a state of deep concentration. He was a girl in the mountains, a young wife and mother in the plains, a woman alone once again. A middle-aged woman put a tin roof on an abandoned house in the mountains, lay the wooden floor, hauled food and supplies from the village, and ate one spare meal a day. Her skin was drying, hair falling. Redness entered her swollen eyes. She was older, tired, dying. Cold hands. Blackness. A flash of light. A Caucasian kid smiling, laughing, playing with toys under a Christmas tree in a brightly furnished living room.

Max shook out of his samyama. Her skin felt warm in his hands.

"You have lived a life of service," said Max slowly in Nepali. "You will be born again in a kind womb."

"Not always, not always," she replied in Nepali, tears in her eyes. "I was selfish. I left my old parents alone. That's why I am dying alone too. I am selfish now. You have been kind to me, yet I could not bring myself to help you."

"You saved my life, not once but twice," said Max. "You don't remember the first time I came here."

"I remember. I remember every day," she said. She lowered her eyes. "Years ago, you asked me about a man when you came. You weren't ready then. This time I wasn't ready," she said.

Surprised, Max recalled their conversation from years ago.

"The doctor from Brazil?" he said.

Nani Maa nodded. She slumped back from the wall to her mattress. "He used to stop here on his way up in the winters. Later, too many people came looking for him and he left the Garhwal Himalayas. Before he went, he told me to share with serious seekers who asked for him that he was going to live in a forest in Bhumthang in Bhutan. But you weren't ready for him when you came years ago."

"And I'm ready now?" said Max.

She nodded.

"I couldn't even walk when I came this time. And look at me now," he said, pointing to the missing fingers on his hands.

"I saw you then. I see you now. Your eyes were silent when you came this time. They remained calm through the pain. They are even calmer now," she said. "You should go to him. Bhutan is not far if you cut directly through the hills, maybe three or four weeks away."

Max took a deep breath. He pictured walking through the snowcapped mountains and entering yet another remote land where a man awaited him with a promise of deliverance. He felt a sliver of excitement. If he started walking now, he'd reach his destination in April. It would be sunny and warm then and he'd be able to renew his efforts afresh. Maybe then he could return with the answers he sought.

"I should have told you before," said Nani Maa.

Max saw the fear of death in her jaundiced eyes. She hadn't

wanted to die alone. Max pictured himself walking in the forest toward the man, toward his goal. His face melted and turned into the fierce Naga Baba's face, the squat yogi's, the shivering young man, the Standing Baba, Shakti, Hari, the kneeling Scottish Catholic priest, and other agitated, restless faces smeared with ash, silhouettes wearing orange robes and yellow garlands, rotating beads in their hands, wandering through buffalo shrines and ice formations in caves, throwing holy water on babies, praying to crucifixes, chanting, muttering, singing. They had all trusted in someone else, something beyond themselves, and the truth had eluded them. All of them clung to one belief or another with the same rigidity people of the world held on to their families and jobs. He had been no different. Why did he want to become one with the eternal consciousness? How did he know it even existed? Lifting your arm up to let go of your sense of self was no different than clinging to your child to further your sense of self. One ambition couldn't be replaced by another, an old attachment with a new belief. He had learned the simplicity of living, just being, when he was with Ramakrishna. He needed nothing more to go on. No new guru or belief would be his refuge. No longer would he be at war against human nature and be attached to the idea of detachment.

"Keep his secret safe. Perhaps it will be of use to someone else," said Max.

"You won't go?" she said. "He is a great man."

Max shook his head.

"I was scared," she said. Tears fell from her eyes. "My body was weak. If anything happened, if I broke my leg, I would die slowly in this snow. Then you came, and I just held on. So many times I was about to tell you, but I couldn't. I don't know what came over me."

Max held her bony hand. He touched her face. "I don't want to meet another great man," he said. "I want to be here with you."

36.

Nani Maa stopped eating completely in March. Her shriveled frame was racked by coughs. She moaned softly every time Max moved her to clean her waste, just wanting to be still. Max knew her body was shutting down, so he didn't force her to have food. All day and night she slept, sometimes peacefully, sometimes waking up, shaking with terror, shouting incoherently.

"Tell Daggu he has to take the last train out. They won't spare him. Please," she would shout and burst into tears.

Max would put his hand over her head and calm her down.

Nani Maa would sleep again and not wake up until the next nightmare a day or two later. Soon her pulse fell and her jaw slackened. The red splotches covered her whole body. She took long pauses between breaths. Max knew she would die any moment now. Sensing it could rain any day, he collected dry wood for her cremation.

LATE ONE NIGHT Nani Maa shook Max awake. She was sitting next to him in a bright red sari, a touch of color in her sunken face. Drops of water fell from her bald head. Her cold, wet fingers found Max's. She was shivering.

"The Ganges is so cold," she said.

Max lifted her wet, shivering frame and put her on the rug by the fire.

She stared at Max and opened her mouth. Her teeth chattered. "Will you stay here?" she said weakly. "This is all I have. Someone has to keep it, take care of the people . . ."

Max looked into her eyes. He saw his mother, whose attachment to her children and work had grown in the end. Even goodness shackled a person. Every concept bound. We all built houses on the sand, destined to fade away in dust. Max was gripped by the same melting, dissolving feeling he'd had years ago in the village near Pavur. He was breaking into pieces, falling, fluid, boundaryless, merging into Nani Maa, just one giant heart that felt her fear, her sadness, her goodness, her pride, her love, like his own. Tears stung his eyes, but it was her eyes that were red and watering. He was shivering from the bath she'd taken in the Ganges. His throat was tightening, she was dying.

Max coughed, trying to get a grip on himself.

He put his hand over Nani Maa's wet, cold head. Her eyes shut. Max covered her with a blanket. All night he sat by her side, holding her hand, listening to her labored sighs, a strange stillness growing within him.

. . .

NANI MAA DIED the next day. Max lifted her thin gray body from the rug, carried it outside, and put it over the dried wood. He piled more wood on top of her body and lit the pyre. When it was over, when her body had been consumed by the fire, he walked to the banks of the Ganges and immersed her ashes in the holy river. Once again he was alone.

37.

Max continued to take care of the guesthouse. New faces came in the summer. Yogis on a pilgrimage to Gomukh or Tapovan. Men and women seeking solitary spots for meditation. Stranded, lost hikers. Max gave them shelter for the night, fed them what he could, and showed them the routes to remote caves and mountain peaks, whatever they needed to reach their destinations.

They asked him questions. Who was his teacher? What did he believe in? Where was he going? All of their faces, like their questions, merged.

In response, Max smiled and words came out of his mouth: he had no guru, he believed in nothing, he just lived there. He talked to everyone, yet his heart remained silent. His dreams ceased and the images from the past, which had once haunted him, receded. For he understood now that the more he nurtured his guilt about Keisha, his concern for Sophia, his regret for his mother, the more these emotions would sprout, generating the seeds of more emotions, more discontentment. When the memories arose now, he observed them without reacting to them, without nurturing them, and they passed away, leaving him unaffected.

AS THE THUNDERSTORMS and blizzards resumed in the fall, the yogis began to make their way down from their caves. To prepare for them, Max built two additional rooms in the guesthouse and added new pipes to draw water from the Ganges. As his money dwindled, he planted and began harvesting crops from the small patch of flat land outside the guesthouse before the snow blanketed everything. Instinctively he sowed cabbages, cauliflower, turnips—all vegetables he knew would break through the cold, rocky earth. His hands, the plow, his body, the earth, his sickle, all seemed one, a living organism living in silent harmony with the peerless mountains, which turned from gold to orange, then orange to purple in the soft light of the fall sun. The crops grew flat, slanted, and twisted, yet they bore precious fruit that allowed him to serve more food to his guests.

EARLY IN WINTER, more yogis came down to ask him for help to meet their special needs before the winter snowstorms cut access to the guesthouse. The Dudhadhari Baba, who lived only on milk, wanted more cartons of milk. The Naga Babas, their long, matted dreadlocks indicating the length of their penance, sought wild herbs to strengthen their necks. Other yogis wanted more food, comfort, shelter. Max worked all day, giving everything he could, and was so absorbed in one activity or the other that he often forgot to sleep. When he did rest, it was never for more than an hour or two. He didn't seem to need sleep anymore. His body worked, but his mind was still, content, forming no new impressions, holding on to nothing. The void within him was growing. He fell more and more silent.

Late one winter day, the Standing Baba limped into the guesthouse. The wooden swing he rested his arms in while he was standing had rotted. He wanted to continue his austerity in the plains. Max held his hand and guided him down the steep, slippery mountain one step at a time. When the terrain turned particularly treacherous, he tied himself by a rope to the baba's frail frame, dragging him across the crevasses so he didn't have to balance on his weakened legs.

With moist eyes, the baba thanked him when they reached the village. "For many years, I have been afraid to make this walk down," he said. He touched Max's hands. "You have done much good here."

Max's heart leaped and expanded, occupying the space between them.

"You are not even from here," said the baba. "What is your name? Where do you come from?"

Max opened his mouth. For a moment he couldn't remember his name. He concentrated. "Max," he said weakly.

The baba's eyes softened. "Your palms are bloody from pulling the rope. Come with me. I'll apply some herbs to them," he said.

Max stared at the shimmering redness on his hands. He felt nothing.

"Please come," said the baba.

Max shook his head. "My wounds heal easily," he said.

The baba stared at him. "As you wish," he said. He raised his hand and put it on Max's head. "My blessings are all I have to give for your goodness."

Max folded his hands and floated down the bare path to Gangotri village, feeling the earth below his feet again. No, his actions were neither good nor bad. They were like those of the rhododendron and the pine trees on the mountains that were his home, which flowered without thinking, then withered away without clinging, helpless to act as they were.

IN THE VILLAGE, he walked into the small post office and wrote a letter to Sophia. "Dear Sophia. I hope you are well," he began.

Involuntarily, her image appeared before his eyes. She was heavier than before, but she was smiling, dimples forming at the corners of her lips.

"I'm happy here," he wrote, then stopped. What he felt wasn't happiness. It was something else. His old self that had sought happiness itself had dissolved, replaced by just a deep, expanding stillness that was completely empty yet strangely filled with life, energy, and bliss.

He put the nib of the pen to the paper. The words before him blurred and the paper appeared to float. Shimmering vibrations went up and down his spine.

"I send you love," he finished.

Max signed and posted the letter to his old address. Warm, fluid boundaryless love radiated from his heart, enveloping Sophia and every being in the world.

38.

The guesthouse emptied again late in the winter. Max felt no different in the lull than he had in the midst of activity. Once more, blizzards and avalanches struck. The guesthouse rattled and shook in the wind and the snow just as it had the previous year, the cyclical ebb and flow of nature. Max spent the days fixing roofs and unblocking pipes to keep the place ready for the next season.

EARLY ONE AFTERNOON amid a thick snowfall, a tall, lean man in a uniform entered the guesthouse. He folded his hands.

"I'm in the Indian army, sir," he said.

The sickle-shaped scar on his forehead glistened.

Max stared at him. "Viveka?" he asked.

The man raised his eyebrows.

"You look like someone I know," said Max. "Please sit."

The army officer sat on the chair next to the fireplace. Max served him tea and sat opposite him on the rug on the floor.

"A foreigner died in the mountains, sir," said the officer. "The American embassy contacted the Delhi government to find the body. I tell you, sir, our government has no money for the living, but these foreign embassies have dollars for dead people. Anyway, sir, if I can pinpoint a location, the Harsil army camp will send a helicopter to evacuate him. Can you help me look for him?"

Max nodded. "Which part of the mountain?"

"He told people he was going to Gomukh three weeks ago," he said. "With so many glaciers slipping, I don't think he would have made it that far."

"I will go," said Max.

"I can come with you," said the man.

"There is no need. The trail is dangerous from here up," said Max. "Was he hiking?"

"Hiking, meditating, racketeering, who knows, sir? These foreigners think the Himalayas are a joke, like the Alps or something. They don't realize that there aren't landmarks or signposts here. Every patch looks the same," he said. He coughed and lowered his eyes. "Not all of them, of course, sir. You yogis are different. Superhuman. Like God more than men, sir."

Like God more than men, sir.

The words came out of the man's mouth, but they were

Viveka's words. Max's eyes clouded. Something stirred deep within him. He was falling, slipping into a swirling mist.

"How old are you, sir?" asked the man. "I thought you would be sixty or seventy when the villagers told me you knew everything about the mountains. But you look very young."

Max's throat went dry. Past and present were jumbling, merging into one. One moment he was on a concrete street looking at a food cart's tin roof, another on a mountain in front of a wooden house with a tin roof, now floating in an infinite black timelessness. He held the corners of the rug.

"I'm not sure," he said.

"Your body has adapted to the mountains, sir," said the man.

The body adapts anywhere, sir.

Max looked closely at the man. Was he a ghost, an apparition? The man set his teacup on the floor. His hand, which had been holding the cup, exploded into tiny, radiating speckles of yellow light. The light spread to the cup, then to the wooden floor, turning the floor into a stream of glowing particles. Max gasped. He looked up. There was no one. Just one golden light. Everything had dissolved into it.

I have seen the unborn, un-aging, un-ailing, sorrowless, and deathless face-to-face.

Indeed, sir, indeed you have.

Max blinked. The man's face came into focus again, hazy and shimmering.

"I will find the hiker," said Max.

"Thank you, sir. I will come back again tomorrow," said the man. "Perhaps you will be kind enough to share some of your teachings with me also then, sir."

Millions of thoughts and ideas, a whole universe of voices, came alive within Max. Deep within him, a whisper arose. "I don't teach anything, Mahadeva," said Max. "I just live here. So you alone decide what you want and understand what you get. For me, yoga is both my path and my goal."

"Sorry, sir?"

These weren't his words, they were Ramakrishna's. But they had come from within him. They had existed in that moment. Max exhaled slowly.

"I will go now," said Max.

He left the guesthouse.

MAX CROSSED GLACIERS that had slipped on the path, treading lightly on their slanting slopes. He walked up the familiar trail, past the cliff that bent into the stream leading to his cave, farther up beyond the yellow-green shoots and the pine trees that had provided him food and fire. As he walked, his heart filled up with love, almost choking him. The emptiness expanded. A wave of warmth filled the void. Soon the warmth was a continuous column of bliss. His spine was fluid, vibrating. Tears fell involuntarily from his eyes.

Max reached Gomukh just after sunset. The air was alive with smells, the snow covered with faint footprints. Down a slope he slid, reaching a rock covering a small natural cave. Max stooped inside.

He stared at his own dead body in the moonlight.

Blue, crumpled, and curled up like a fetus.

Love, radiant and white, enveloped Max.

Friend, you didn't have to try so hard.

The supreme stillness was always within him. The ice was cold, the fire burned, the water quenched. He was That.

Max stared at himself.

A HAND MOVED.

A wave rippled within Max.

A head of brown hair lifted.

Max broke out of his trance.

A man lay on the wet floor pressing his hands between his armpits. His blue face was covered in a thin layer of ice. He breathed heavily in short, frosted puffs.

"My ears hurt," he said, blue-black lips moving slowly. He lifted his pale, white eyes. "My jeep is heated. Can you take me to my jeep?"

Max was breaking again, dissolving, merging into the man, into the gray stone wall of the cave behind him, the shaking icy, mud floor below them. Max. Max. He concentrated, holding on to himself.

The world assembled again.

Max lay down next to the man on the floor and enveloped the man's cold, wet body. He focused on his own navel and raised his body heat easily, transferring it to the man until he felt the man blazing. Higher and higher he went until the heat reached the fingers and toes of the man, warming them, thawing them, making them come alive once again. Max stood up, feeling just a faint sliver of pain in his belly.

"Come," he said.

Weightless and floating, he held the man by his hand and

stepped out of the cave. He stood behind the man, guiding him up the snow to the path leading down to Bhojbasa.

BACK AT THE GUESTHOUSE, Max wrapped the man in blankets and built a fire next to him. The man mumbled a weak thank-you. Max stood up and walked to the window. He traced a faint stream of white light from the moon to the tip of a mountain peak. The light radiated within him, cooling him, making him still, complete.

"WHO ARE YOU, BROTHER?"

The sun's rays streamed through the window. Max was bathed in its warm light. He turned around. The man was sitting up next to the fire, shivering, his hands tucked into his armpits.

"You've been standing by the window for hours. Your body shines. Who are you?"

The man's face blurred. His body became the orange glow of the fire.

"You built that fire without lighting a match. You brought me back to life. Are you God, a messiah? Does such a thing even exist?"

The fire shifted, shook, melted away. Everything moved within Max.

I am the seeker, the act of seeking, and the one who is sought.

"What's happening, brother? Your lips don't move, but I can hear your words."

I am the field and the knower of the field.

"Brother . . ."

A cry. A rustling river. An ocean of black. Bliss, pure bliss.

Suffering alone exists, none who suffer. The deed there is, but no doer thereof. The Path there is, but none who travel it.

There was just the One and no other.

HE HAD REACHED the end of his yoga.

Tadā draṣṭuḥ svarūpe vasthānam.

Then the seer dwells in His own true splendor.

ACKNOWLEDGMENTS

This isn't a book as much as a result of five years of my life trying to walk on the path of yoga. I stumbled and struggled often to reach the point where I became just a channel for this story to tell itself. Through all of this, my wife, Kerry, believed in me even when I lost faith in myself, and this book wouldn't exist without her exceptional creative and spiritual inputs. This book is as much hers as mine.

I owe a debt of gratitude to Mr. B. K. S. Iyengar, Swami Sivananda, and Mr. S. N. Goenka, spiritual icons I've never met but whose soul-stirring words have spoken to me as if they were living, breathing guides standing beside me.

My mother's lifelong interest in the *Bhagavad Gita* and my father's unwavering commitment to yoga had a profound impact on my decision to take a year off from work to deepen my meditation practice. Much of this novel was written in that year.

Kerry and I met many wonderful people on the road, a lot of whose journeys merged into Max's journey. My special thanks to Dhanakosa Buddhist Retreat Center in Scotland; Dhamma Atala and Dhammalaya Vipassana centers in Italy and Kohlapur, respectively; the Sivananda Yoga Vedanta ashram in Madurai; Aranya and its patron Varun Sood in Goa; Obras and its patrons, Caroline, and Ludger in Portugal; Monal Guest House and its patrons, Deepinder, and Poonam in Uttarkashi; and Spiros and Ursula in Greece for their generosity in hosting us.

My in-laws, Joan and Michael Monaghan, made our year away from home easier by giving their bighearted, unconditional support, as they always do.

My colleagues Lisa Mann, Sanjay Khosla, Gina Schenk, Julie Donahue, Deanie Elsner, Doug Weekes, Bharat Puri, and Xavier Boza will always be special to me for making exception after exception to allow me to bring my full self into corporate America. Such big people, all of them!

If the characters and settings in the book feel authentic, I give much credit to Jonathan Kozol's compassionate, deeply observed books on the Bronx projects, Jeff Hobbs's *The Short and Tragic Life of Robert Peace*, and Alex Kotlowitz's *There Are No Children Here*. I can also not overstate the deep effect of the Buddha's quest as captured in Herman Hesse's *Siddhartha*, Karen Armstrong's *Buddha*, and Arundhati Subramaniam's *The Book of Buddha* on my writing—and my life.

The book wouldn't have been published without my agent, Mollie Glick. She's the rare deal, a mainstream agent supporting off-the-beaten-path voices.

Jake Morrissey, my incredibly competent editor at Riverhead, gave me an equivalent of a two-year MFA with his unrelenting but compassionate edits through the course of the book. I'll always be grateful to him for treating this book as if it were his own and helping me get to the real heart of the story I wanted to tell.

Chiki Sarkar's warm, exuberant support lifted me up during the lowest points of writing this book, something I'll always treasure. The book is so much stronger for her thoughtful edits.

Sarah Cypher, Marlene Adelstein, Shatarupa Ghoshal, Anshuman Acharya, Hriday Sarat, Trupti Rustagi, Saurabh Nanda, Rachael Belfon, Anna Ghosh, and close friends and family, thank you for your thoughtful input at various stages of the book to give it the shape it has taken today.

Ayush Pant—what a powerhouse presence to enter this book at a late stage! I'll be watching from the sidelines as you go from strength to strength with Aurelius marketing and give wings to many authors' efforts. Thank you for believing in the book as you did.

My appreciation also for Chetan Syal, John and Masako Mamus, Melissa Chang, and Mike Ricca—such a responsive team that sets the bar for creative excellence and passionate execution.

And a final word for my small family—Kerry, Leela, and Coconut—for filling my heart with joy and sharing with me a love that knows no bondage or attachment, the love of a yogi.